GB MA JL
LH

MA

Copy 2

D0881649

SNAKE DANCER

Vicki Blair

authorHOUSE®

AuthorHouse™
1663 Liberty Drive
Bloomington, IN 47403
www.authorhouse.com
Phone: 1 (800) 839-8640

© 2019 Vicki Blair. All rights reserved.

No part of this book may be reproduced, stored in a retrieval system, or transmitted by any means without the written permission of the author.

Published by AuthorHouse 03/22/2019

ISBN: 978-1-7283-0069-6 (sc)
ISBN: 978-1-7283-0067-2 (hc)
ISBN: 978-1-7283-0068-9 (e)

Library of Congress Control Number: 2019901852

Print information available on the last page.

This novel is a work of fiction. Names, descriptions, places, and incidents are products of the author's imagination. Any resemblance, to actual persons, places or events are entirely coincidental.

Any people depicted in stock imagery provided by Getty Images are models, and such images are being used for illustrative purposes only. Certain stock imagery © Getty Images.

This book is printed on acid-free paper.

Because of the dynamic nature of the Internet, any web addresses or links contained in this book may have changed since publication and may no longer be valid. The views expressed in this work are solely those of the author and do not necessarily reflect the views of the publisher, and the publisher hereby disclaims any responsibility for them.

Dedicated To:

Alex Morgan

My Katila O'waci

ACKNOWLEDGMENTS

My intent for *Snake Dancer* was not to discredit or belittle the cultures or the religions of the Lakota Sioux or the Appalachian churches that take up serpents; instead it was to pay homage to the faith of both cultures. Although I don't completely understand the faith of either group, I know we each have to walk in the light that God leads us. I just know I have some very dear friends from both of these cultures who have made a positive impact on those around them.

A great big shout out goes to Timothy Dale Strongbear, my Oglala Lakota Sioux connection, for his help with better understanding "The Way of the Pipe." I have a strong respect for Tim and for his heritage and could not have written this book without him.

Without the support and encouragement of my family, friends, and beta readers, this book would never have come to fruition. My family and friends are my greatest cheerleaders and my lifeline. The feedback I received from each reader was invaluable.

Special thanks also go to Mrs. Judith Brown and Lauren Hopkins for providing the editing and clean-up for this book.

PROLOGUE

As soon as I saw the pond in the distance, my heart began to race, and I could hear Red Ruby's tail shaking against her specially-made box. The other snakes I was carrying in the bag began to squirm around as if on cue. Since snakes have an uncanny way of sensing fear and apprehension in others, I knew they were only reacting to my anxiety. Coming back to this Kentucky version of Eden was causing my mind to conjure up four years' worth of pent-up emotions—the most dominant being regret.

Since my dad wasn't able to free the snakes—the tools of his Holiness ministry—it was only fitting that I was the one now releasing these members of our household into the forest. Red Ruby had been in our home for as long as I can remember. Her big red rattler was famous in our church circuit. Red Ruby was not only an anomaly—she was also a celebrity. When Ruby visited a church house, the crowd spilled over into the vestibule because most knew they would see either a miracle or a death.

Before I set my captives free, I rested at the water's edge. I looked at my reflection, trying to catch a glimpse of that naive thirteen-year-old girl of four years ago. I couldn't; she was gone. I truly thought that by keeping my sin to myself, I was doing everyone a favor. Wrong. A secret sin can lie dormant for a while, but mark my words: eventually someone has to pay for it—even if that someone is completely innocent. I learned that lesson the hard way.

Life lessons are one of my dad's favorite topics—especially for me. The oldest of four girls, I was taught how to catch and care for the church's menagerie of snakes. The first lesson I learned was to have a healthy respect for the serpents. Even though I was freeing them today, I still had to be cautious. Snakes have no loyalty; they will gladly bite the hand that feeds them. Carefully, I stepped backward as I thrust the snakes in the bag forward. Some slithered out of sight quickly, while others took their time as though they were relishing the feel of freedom. Out of respect for Red Ruby, I waited for the horde of serpents to vacate the mossy knoll before I let her loose. She was special. In some ways I hated her, yet in other ways I loved her.

I raised the box high enough so I knew she could hear me. As if I were speaking to a good friend, I said, "Ruby, I've got to leave now and take care of my family. I can't vindicate all the wrong that's been done to us, but maybe you can." The vibration of her rattle was her only reply. I carefully opened the box and let her come out in her own sweet time. Knowing our lives would never be the same, I watched from a distance as she meandered her way to freedom.

CHAPTER 1

Most weekdays, we all piled into the church van and rode to school with Momma, but today I drove so I could leave directly after school to pick up Dad's supplies. My dad was not only the pastor of Middle Fork Church of God, but he was also one of the best tile layers in Kentucky. On the weekends and after school, I helped him. My specialty was mosaics. Perry, my ten-year-old sister, mosaic protégé, and partner in crime, was waiting in Dad's old work truck this morning with a mug full of hot coffee she'd made for me. When Dad bought his new truck, I claimed the twenty-year-old, rusted-out Chevy as my own. It wasn't pretty, but it got me where I needed to go.

Perry, like my dad and I, was an early bird. She preferred going to school early, which almost never happened when she rode with Momma. My mom preferred the pressure of being right on time or a minute or two late rather than being too early and having to wait. Laurel and Whitley, my middle sisters, were both okay with Momma's aversion to "earliness" because it gave them more time to work on their hair. They took the Bible literally about their hair being their glory. It took them a good hour to get ready each morning. Not Perry and me—ponytails and braids were very efficient.

"Come on, slowpoke!" my little sister hollered. The freckles on her nose only made her cuter.

"What's your hurry, girl?" I asked.

"Are you kidding?" She blew out a breath of exasperation. "I just need some peace and quiet from those curling iron queens. Les, I'm sure glad you aren't one of those kinds of girls."

"But I used to know my way around a curling iron," I told her. I could see with my peripheral vision her reach up and touch her braid. We are such similar creatures even though we don't look a thing alike.

Perry gave us time to get earshot away from the house before she looked over at me with her most mischievous grin and said, "Are you ready?" I knew I was being a bad influence, but I felt it was one of the more harmless of my vices. I nodded and gave her a thumbs-up sign. She tuned the radio station to country music and turned the volume as loud as the old truck's AM/FM radio would go. Country music was as taboo in our household as watching television. The only time we were able to watch TV was when we stayed at a friend's house, which wasn't often.

When Blake Shelton's big voice came bellowing over the speakers, Perry actually squealed with reckless abandon. She leaned back and placed both feet upon the dashboard. I smiled when I noticed what looked like a pair of jeans sticking out from underneath her long skirt tail. For the next twenty minutes, life was as good as it got. We drove with both windows down, singing country music at the top of our lungs. When we saw the tip of the school's chimney stack peek through the treetops, we were both disappointed. It had been such a nice ride. No longer were we the daughters of the Holiness pastor but instead just two normal girls riding down the road together.

When Perry opened the truck door to leave, I softly punched her shoulder and said, "Later."

"Later," she said, using her cool voice.

I rolled up my window and waited until I was out of the school's pickup line before I turned the radio volume back up. Becoming engrossed in my thoughts, my mind went to the subject at hand—my future. In less than three months, I would turn eighteen and be a high school graduate. I had no clue what would happen after that. Momma kept trying to press me to make a decision. She wanted me to follow her path and go to her alma mater in Missouri. Dad was fine with me going to the community college and continuing to work with him during my spare time. My sisters' reactions to my dilemma varied. Whitley didn't care where I went as long as she could come visit me. Laurel just wanted my room. And Perry wouldn't even talk about the possibility of me leaving her.

When I tried to picture the twenty-one-year old version of Leslie Lewis, I couldn't conjure her up. I knew I was smart enough to go to college, and based on all my college acceptance letters, they thought so too. While a change of scenery would be nice, I wasn't naive enough to think I'd get the same acceptance other places as I'd found in my hometown. I could envision being the college pariah sitting alone in a dorm room once my new friends found out about our snakes.

When I saw the flashing light announcing I was nearing the school, I realized I couldn't remember anything about my drive after dropping Perry off. Shaking my head from side to side, I tried to push all these thoughts down a rung or two so I could enter school in the right frame of mind. My mind required protection at every level. Since Jeb Seeley's death, I'd become a prisoner in my self-made box, which required me to set some hard rules to follow. My acts of defiance were restricted to wearing jeans, country music, *Grey's Anatomy*, sarcasm, and extremely limited church attendance—all of which the majority of the Holiness church considered damning enough to send me to an eternity of hellfire. My parents had changed a lot over the last four years. Once they would've been the very ones pointing their fingers at me. I guess now they were just hoping I'd get it together before it was everlastingly too late.

I intentionally passed up the student parking and instead pulled the Chevy into the lot reserved for the staff. Since the old Chevy technically belonged to my mom too, I felt justified parking in the faculty lot—a much shorter walk to the high school building. This wasn't an act of defiance as much as a perk of having a parent on the school's staff. My mom taught music at Appalachian Christian Institute—or as we all called it, ACI. It was a private school for local kids as well as kids who lived in the dormitory. Its remote location at the edge of Leslie County, Kentucky, isolated it from the rest of the world and made it a good place to send unruly students. I'd encountered my fair share of the new punk kids, both boys and girls, trying to earn a spot on the school's rebel list. Whether it was the snakes or my reputation on the basketball court, these new students usually didn't come around, which was okay with me. I was fine hanging out with my two best friends, Beth and Kelsey.

The three of us are the most unlikely of friends, totally different in almost every aspect. In spite of our differences, our friendship works. As soon as I entered the school building, Kelsey was waiting for me. Kelsey Van Hook lives in the dormitory and only sees her mother during holidays. Her dad completely out of the picture, she's more of a thrown-away kid than a troubled one. She doesn't lack for any material thing; her closet is full of the latest styles of hipster clothing and shoes. Her wardrobe isn't what initially drew me to her—she thought it was cool that our family lived with snakes. Starved for a family, she would gladly adopt mine—snakes and all. That sealed the deal for me.

Kelsey was all smiles this morning—too big of a smile to suit me. Something was definitely up. Sporting a three-quarter-length jersey, jeans, and Chuck Taylors, she was dressed casually—a bit too casually. For a girl who liked to stand out, today she looked like any other student. I wasn't sure if I should slow down or speed up. Too late. Her hands were trembling like she'd seen a ghost. "What's wrong? Why are you dressed like that and why are you shaking?"

"Nothing's wrong. On the contrary, everything's right. The stars aligned and everything is perfect at ACI. You're not going to believe it but I just saw the best looking guy I've ever seen in my entire life. I think I'm in love."

I rolled my eyes. "Kels, just last week you said the new boy from Illinois was hot, and he had bad hair and crooked teeth."

"Hey! What's wrong with a Mohawk? Plus, not everyone can afford orthodontia," she defended her opinion. "But I'm telling you, this guy is the *real* deal. He's model gorgeous not quirky gorgeous.

He's just plain and simple beautiful. You just wait and see. You have gym first period, don't you?"

"Yeah. Why?"

"Cause I think he's the new basketball coach and gym teacher."

"A good looking gym teacher, that's all ACI needs." I didn't squelch any of my disdain as I said it either.

I watched my friend's face fall in disappointment at my lack of enthusiasm so I tried to appease her a little. "Sorry. I promise to check him out and give you my full review at lunch if that'll make you happy." The corners of her mouth turned up slightly.

We both stopped talking and turned to see who belonged to the footsteps we heard running in our direction. It was Beth. Beth Rudder is a cheerleader and a bona fide beauty queen since she won the title of Miss Leslie County last summer. Although her parents go to the Baptist church, her grandparents are Holiness like my family. She understands me better than most. She's actually one of the few students allowed to come home with me.

"Wait up!" she yelled. Beth was just so darn cute. Her short haircut was bouncing with each step, and her teeth were bright from a distance. "Wait! I've got to show y'all something! Look what I found this weekend." She practically bubbled over with excitement. Taking a deep breath in an effort to contain her effervescence, she proclaimed, "Les. I found the perfect prom dress for you." She started dragging me to one of the benches in the hallway.

Breathe in, one, two, three. I tried to compose myself before speaking. "I told you I'm not going to prom."

Beth cut me off. "It's our senior year, and you *are* going to prom whether you want to or not. Right, Kels?"

Kelsey looked at me before she answered. The look of death I was giving her wasn't lost on her. "Don't look at me." In surrender, she threw both hands in the air. "I don't want to have ole *sourpuss* on my bad side and find a snake under my pillow. You're on your own."

Before I could say another word, Beth shoved a folded page she'd torn from a magazine into my hand. It's not that I didn't want to go to prom. It was that I knew how my church felt about prom dresses and dancing in general. Dad already took enough flack because of me, and I didn't want to give him any more headaches. Besides, Brother Seeley, the head elder of the church, would love nothing more than to find a way to discredit him so he could be replaced with a pastor he could control. It also didn't help that he had a vendetta against me—he blamed me for Jeb's death and brought up my wicked ways to the church elders every time he could. So far, the other elders hadn't taken Brother Seeley's bait, but I didn't want to add any more wickedness to my already long list of sins, for my dad's sake.

"Go on, look at it!" Beth demanded.

Not wanting her to throw one of her "only child" tantrums in the middle of the hallway, I slowly unfolded the slick piece of paper and in front of me was the most beautiful gown I'd ever seen. It was floor length with long sleeves—all prerequisites for the Holiness book of fashion. It wasn't a vanity-seeking pastel, but rather a modest yet elegant black. Best yet, it wasn't body hugging but rather loose and flowing. It would even pass Perry's twirl test. She would try on a dress and spin just to see if the dress would twirl just the right way.

Beth knew me like a book. "I knew it. I knew you'd like it."

"Yeah, it's pretty, and my dad would probably be okay with it, but …"

Beth cut me off. "It's a done deal. I already have it ordered."

"Well, you can just call and cancel it, can't you?" Even to my own ears, my protest sounded weak.

"No cancellation policy."

"You did what? Have you lost your ever-loving mind?"

Kelsey, like part of a wolf pack sensing that the prey was weakening, joined in with Beth, by saying, "It's perfect for you. Your mom and dad will be fine with it."

Part of me wanted nothing more than to get all dolled up and go to prom. Only I knew nothing good could come of me wearing that dress. For the last four years, I'd worn jeans, baggy tops, and a ponytail so as not to draw attention to myself.

"Please, Les. I couldn't bear to go to our senior prom without you." Beth's bottom lip stuck out in a pout.

"It's against my better judgment, but since the dress is nonrefundable, I'll talk to my parents tonight. Happy?"

Beth wasn't expecting me to give in so soon. She still had that pouty look on her face until my words sunk in. When it did, she let out a victory war whoop. Then the first bell—a warning bell—rang.

"Oh no, the bell! I haven't even been to my locker yet." I took off sprinting toward the gym with my book bag in tow. Sixty whole seconds to spare before I'd be considered late. I could see the gym door. I was home free. I pulled down on the long bar planning to push my way into my first period class but was stopped in my tracks. The door wouldn't budge. I tried again. Still nothing. Then I began to beat on the door trying to get someone's attention. The second bell sounded its shrill ring. *Uh oh. I'm officially late.*

Still pounding on the door as hard and fierce as I could, I finally heard someone on the other side. Righteous indignation rose up in me. *Why would someone lock that door after the first bell!* I was really angry because it wasn't my fault I was late. I had a good ten or more seconds to spare. As soon as I heard the pop of the lock, I came through the door protesting, "I wasn't late. The door was locked and …" I ran smack dab into a wide and muscular chest that didn't move at all when I hit it. It was like a hitting a rock wall. The wall sure smelled nice though–all spicy and clean. I was five foot eight, and I still had to look up a good foot to see the man's face. That's when my world changed.

CHAPTER 2

I'd never been speechless in my entire life. In those few seconds, my tongue grew so fat it wouldn't flap. I tried to look away, but I couldn't. Kelsey was right. I was looking into the dark eyes of the most beautiful guy I'd ever seen. His short, thick hair was dark and his skin was smooth and tanned. He looked like an Indian warrior without the feathers and face paint. I couldn't see any flaws no matter how hard I tried, and trust me I was close enough to get a very good look.

His voice caused me to quit assessing him. "You're late," the new teacher stated, his tone dry and stern. However, he never attempted to get out of my way. He just stood there with his chest pressed into mine, looking at me as if I had a third eye right in the middle of my forehead.

I managed to step back a couple of steps to have some breathing room. When my senses and my voice returned, I challenged him, "Actually, I wouldn't have been late if the door wasn't locked early." I didn't need any write-ups this close to my graduation, and I was danged if I was going to let this new teacher cost me demerits no matter how good he smelled or looked.

Furthering the distance between us, he moved back a step and said, "From now on, Miss ..." He looked at me to provide a name.

"Lewis. Les Lewis," I told him as I stood to my full height. I didn't want to let him think I was affected by him in any way even though my insides were shaking. Now I understood why Kelsey was shaking earlier.

"From now on, Ms. Lewis, I expect you to be here before the first bell and be dressed by the second bell. Got it?" His voice was stern, but his eyes told a different story—there was a twinkle hidden right beneath the surface.

"Yes. Mister ... "

"I'm Coach Zuzeca."

"Zoo-zetcha?" I pronounced it slowly to make sure I heard him correctly.

"Just call me, Coach Z. It's easier." Now he was all smiles—voice, face and eyes—and he even put his hand out for me to shake.

I reluctantly put my hand into his, fearing he would feel my trembles. The warmth of his naked skin touching mine felt nice too nice. I quickly pulled my hand back to my side and headed toward the dressing room with my eyes looking downward so no one could see the redness of my cheeks.

I walked around in a fog for the rest of the day. All I could think about were those penetrating eyes. School couldn't let out soon enough. Finally, being safe in my truck and alone with my thoughts, I felt like banging my head against the glass window. The facade I'd created could've all come crumbling down today. My mind betrayed me just like every other body part. Even now, I had to wrangle it back to safe thoughts, it was too full of prom dresses and good-looking teachers.

I refused to turn into a lovesick schoolgirl and wasn't foolish enough to think dating a teacher was even possible. That kind of relationship was strictly taboo at ACI. Plus, I had no intention of getting entangled with any boy. Guys just complicate things and won't stay neatly in any box.

When I was younger, I had a new crush every day, kind of like my middle sisters, Laurel and Whitley. They are both boy crazy.

Although she wouldn't admit it, even little Perry loved the attention of the older boys at church. Jeb Seeley was my last crush. He was the oldest of Brother Seeley's four sons. It used to be a standing joke that there was a Lewis girl for each Seeley boy. Not only did we go to church together—we were neighbors.

By road the Seeley's lived over five miles from us, but through the woods, they were less than a mile away. The back of our farm joined theirs next to the coal banks. Even though Jeb was five years older, he always paid me a lot of attention, even as a little girl. He was tall and athletic, and all the boys gravitated to him, the girls too.

Now, Jeb was gone, and his parents blamed me. I didn't even like to look at Brother and Sister Seeley. At least Brother Seeley's animosity toward me was better than Sister Seeley's defeated and lifeless stares.

When I started breaking out in a cold sweat, I realized I was way too close to the edge of my box. I tried to redirect my thoughts. *Maybe prom dresses and gym teachers were better to think about than conjuring up my past.*

It might've been my imagination but in gym class today I could feel Coach Z looking at me. I found myself playing especially hard when our class played a pickup basketball game on the half-court. I'm not sure what I was trying to prove. Maybe subconsciously my intent was to make sure he saw me in the same light as all the other guys at school—the tomboy. Mainly, I needed to halt those piercing, soul-searching brown eyes of his from viewing my tarnished soul.

I felt a burst of relief bubble up from inside when I turned onto the long, gravel approach of our farm. It would be easy to push these thoughts aside within the security of my home.

Wrong. As soon as I got out of the truck, Laurel and Whitley bombarded me. "Did you see our new basketball coach?" Laurel, my hormonal fifteen-year-old sister, could hardly contain her excitement.

Following her lead, Whitley said, "Oh-em-gee. Me and my friends all made excuses so we could just walk by the lunchroom when he was in there eating. I just about fainted when he caught me looking at him."

I had to work hard not to laugh just imagining Whitley and her gang of awkward thirteen year olds sneaking around to get a look at the new teacher. They wanted to look at him while I wanted to hide from him.

Oblivious to all the hoopla surrounding the arrival of the new teacher, Perry bounded out the front door and yelled. "Les, something's wrong with the big copperhead we just caught last week!"

"What? Please tell me you weren't in the basement alone!" I yelled at my little sister. I ran past her with Laurel and Whitley following close behind to see what was going on in the snake room and to make sure she hadn't let any escape. Only Momma, Dad, or

I could be downstairs alone and that was only when we wouldn't be getting into the cages. Normally, we worked with the snakes in pairs. Although the snakes were used as instruments of faith in the church house, we didn't play any faith games at home but acted solely as the snake's caregivers.

Even though I'm no longer a churchgoer, I'm very much a believer in the snake handling practice. People can say what they will about snake handling in church, but there's something about it—something pure and true. I've been lulled into a complete trance as I listened to the rhythm of the stomping and watched the spirit-filled folks swaying and dancing while holding these venomous creatures. Some of the more faithful even wrapped the snakes around their shoulders, letting the heads and tails dangle on both sides like wearing serpentine scarves.

Once we made it in the house, Perry was still trying to justify her actions. "I just had a feeling something wasn't right. Sure enough, something was wrong. I may have the gift of prophecy like you do," she said referring to the feelings I got from time to time. Dad called these feelings my gifting. I just called it weird feelings.

I remember Daddy mentioning that he thought the copperhead was a fat one when we found it sunning on the road last week. As I walked down the stairs, I was trying to remember if we put it in one of the cages with the big air vents on top. If we did and it was pregnant, then those babies could possibly get out through the air holes—that could be a disaster. Baby snakebites were toxic too.

I knew my suspicion was correct when I saw the slime-covered outline of one of the babies wriggling in the straw. Copperheads are different from other snakes; their babies are born live covered with a thin, slimy substance. Looking at the air holes, I felt it was best to go ahead and move them to a safer container. "Go get Mom," I ordered Perry.

"Can't I watch the rest of them be born?" Perry whined.

"You heard me. Go get her."

While I waited for Momma to help me move the snakes to the safer cage, I completed inventory to make sure all the other snakes were accounted for. Each cage and each box were labeled with the kind of snake as well as where it came from—some we found, others we bought. We recorded each time the snake was fed and the times it was taken to church for the Lord's work. Some preachers actually wanted their snakes to be sickly; it made handling them less dangerous. Not Daddy. He wanted to treat each of God's creatures with care, and he wanted the Spirit to move without any aid from him.

As soon as I heard the creaks of the stairs, I began to explain the situation, "Momma, I need your help in moving the new copperhead and her babies to the big glass cage with the extra small vent holes."

"Can we not wait till Clay gets home? I need to finish supper."

"I'm just afraid those little ones could get out through the air holes."

I could tell she was preoccupied and wasn't in the mood to fool with the snakes, but she knew I was right. She grabbed the long-handled snake tongs.

"Momma, did you get to meet the new basketball coach today?" Whitley asked while she watched us transfer the snakes, one by one, to the other cage. The babies were still coated with the slimy sacs.

"Yes, Coach Zuzeca seems like a sweet boy," she said clearly oblivious to his looks.

Laurel asked, "Is he really an Indian?"

"Yes, he is. He's a member of the Lakota Sioux Indian tribe." Then she spoke to me. "Les, after we get them all in the big cage don't forget to make new cards for the babies so Dad won't have to tonight."

I nodded my head that I would.

Laurel refocused Momma back to the topic of Coach Z. "Mom, where's he from?"

I was having a hard time concentrating on my task because I was just as interested in hearing what she had to say about the new coach as my sisters.

"Coach Zuzeca? Oh, he's from South Dakota."

Perry said, "We just studied Native Americans. The Sioux Tribe is classified as one of the prairie tribes."

"Very good, Perry." Momma never missed an educational opportunity. "Tell me what else you learned about the Sioux."

I tried to see this conversation through someone else's eyes. They would think it was very wrong for a mother to be offering a history lesson to her four daughters all while transferring venomous snakes from one cage to another. A call to social services or child protective services would be in order. Other parents cautioned their kids about topics like drugs and sex, but our number one talk always revolved around social services and foster care.

Perry explained. "Sitting Bull was from the Sioux tribe and ..."

Clearly not enjoying the history lesson, Laurel interrupted. "Do you know if he's married, and why did he come to ACI?"

Ignoring Laurel, Momma said, "Very good, Perry. Tonight you get an extra thirty minutes on the computer." Then Mom turned back to Laurel. "Why do you care if he's married or not? He's a teacher and much too old for you."

Laurel said, "Someone said he was only twenty-three years old. If that's true, he's eight years older than me and only six years older than Les. After all, Dad's seven years older than you are, Mom."

"Actually, Les turns eighteen in May, which makes him only five years older than she is," Whitley corrected Laurel.

"Whoa. Don't bring me into this equation," I protested.

Whitley was a hopeless romantic and turned the conversation around to Momma's favorite story. "Momma, tell us again how you and Dad met."

As she casually transferred the snakes, she said, "Whitley, you've heard the story a hundred times. You know I was engaged to another guy until your daddy, Brother Clay Lewis, preached at a revival near the college. I knew then he was the one for me ..."

Perry interrupted. "Momma, did Daddy bring any snakes with him when he preached?"

"I guess not. All I can remember was the way he looked at me with those big brown eyes. It was like he saw my soul."

My palms became sweaty as she spoke because I understood what it was like to have dark eyes prying in your soul. That was almost how it felt when Coach Z was staring at me in the gym. I dropped the tongs. The sound the metal made against the concrete floor caused everyone to jump. The rattlers' tails were singing frantically in warning. "Sorry," I said as I picked them up.

Whitley didn't seem phased by the commotion my clumsiness caused. She asked, "What ever happened to the other guy?"

"He married my roommate, and they live in Arkansas on a rice farm."

Laurel had a slight smile on her face before she asked, "So if you were twenty and Daddy was twenty-seven when you met, why aren't

21

we allowed to date someone older. What if Coach Zuzeca is the one God has for me?"

"When you're twenty, we'll talk about it. Plus your dad wasn't a teacher."

Whitley was undeterred by his age or his teaching status. "Well, if he's not married then I may have a chance to marry him when I grow up. Whitley *Zoozetchah* has a nice ring to it, doesn't it?"

Perry had her hand on her hip and was full of sass when she reminded her sister about the rules of marriage in our family. She was a walking, talking rule book for the Holiness church. "Whitley, before you think about marrying him, you better find out if he's a Christian or not. Dad says we need to make sure we're not unequally yoked with heathens. You also better make sure he's not afraid of tongue-talking people." She paused and said as an afterthought. "Probably need to find out if he's afraid of snakes too."

"Momma, is he married, or does he have a girlfriend?" Whitley would rather talk about weddings than any other topic. She'd been planning hers since she turned five.

"I think someone said he had a picture of a pretty dark-haired girl on his desk."

"That could be his sister or aunt or someone like that," Laurel rationalized.

When I accidently dropped the cards I was writing on, Perry helped me pick them up. "What's wrong with you, Les? You got a bad case of the dropsy or something?" Perry was studying me trying to understand why, all of a sudden, I couldn't hold on to anything.

"I think my hands are a little stiff."

"By the way, what are you girls doing in the basement at this time of the day?" Mom asked.

Perry's eyes got as big as saucers as she silently pled for me not to rat her out.

"Just a hunch," I said rather nonchalantly.

"Oh yeah," Momma said, "Beth told me to be sure and ask you about a prom dress. I thought you said you weren't going to prom?"

Laurel and Whitley were halfway up the stairs but came back down when they heard the words *prom dress.*

"Prom dress. What in the world?" Perry looked at me rather confused. "Surely you're not going to prom and get all fancied up, are you, Les?" She liked the fact I wasn't a girly girl. Like me, she was planning on giving up dress wearing all together when she turned thirteen too.

To make sure everyone understood my level of annoyance, I blew out a stream of air and rolled my eyes before I spoke. "Beth took it upon herself to order me a prom dress. I really don't want to go, but my evil friends are really putting a guilt trip on me."

"Momma, if Joseph Seeley asked me to his prom, could I go since you're letting Les?" Laurel's question was an easy one since chances of Joseph asking Laurel to his prom were slim to none. For years, he acted as though Laurel didn't even exist.

"Hold on a minute. No one is going anywhere until your dad and I discuss this." As Momma headed up the stairs, she said, "Les, be sure all the latches are closed before you come up." After she took a step or two, she turned as an afterthought and said, "Bring me the picture of the dress so I can see it before Clay gets home."

CHAPTER 3

All week, my dad kept me busy after school helping him with the business—mostly running errands instead of laying tile. Since I drove to school all week long, Perry was in seventh heaven. I didn't realize anyone else could tell I was acting weird, but before she got out of the truck one morning, Perry let me know she'd be glad to listen if I needed to talk about anything that was bothering me. I assured her I was fine.

Since the anniversary of Jeb's death was quickly approaching, Perry probably thought that was the reason I was acting a little strangely. My family and friends felt the need to tiptoe around me during this time each year. I'm sure they were afraid I would fall into that same deep chasm I fell into after he died. I stayed in bed for weeks unable to function. Thankfully, I dug myself out of that hole, inch by inch, and had no plans of ever returning. I tried to focus on one day at a time.

Maybe it was my imagination but Coach Z seemed especially attentive to me this past week. I noticed he hunted me out during class to talk while ignoring the attention other girls gave him, especially a new girl in class named Sadie. The girls in our school were so brazen. I tried hard not to be one of those girls even though I was pretty certain the tingly feelings I had when I talked to him meant I was no different than they were. I just tried not to be so obvious. No one, not even Beth or Kelsey, had any idea I officially had a crush on my gym teacher.

Today, Perry and I left extra early and stopped at Dairy Queen. She insisted on having her juice poured into one of the to-go coffee cups so she could carry it into school like it was Starbucks. I'm not sure how she heard of Starbucks since the closest store to us was an hour drive, and we had no television, but she was as happy as a pig in mud when she bounced out of the truck that morning with her Dairy Queen cup. I arrived at ACI and parked in the faculty lot. I hadn't taken ten steps before I heard someone calling my name. A whiff of Irish Spring soap assaulted my senses. I knew it was Coach Z even before I turned around.

"Hey, Lewis, wait up."

I waited on him even though everything in me told me to run. His hair was still damp from his morning shower. He was dressed in a hooded-college sweatshirt and gym shorts. He must not have read the handbook since shorts were strictly prohibited at ACI—even if he was a gym teacher. Though, I wasn't going to be the one to point this rule out to him.

"Since when did you become faculty?" He pointed to my truck that had been carefully backed between two other parked vehicles.

"My mom works here." I tried to remain emotionless and just answer his question. Even though I looked straight ahead as I walked, I could feel the heat of his eyes on my face. *Quit looking at me!*

"I didn't know your mom worked here. Who is she?"

"Sister Ruth Lewis. She's the music teacher."

"Oh yeah, I've met her. She's really nice. I just didn't put two and two together."

"Most say I look more like my dad since we both have dark hair, and my sisters all have some shade of my mom's red hair." *Why am I telling him all this?*

"How many sisters do you have?" he asked.

"Three younger sisters."

"Well. We have something in common. I had three younger sisters too."

Had? Did he just say he had three sisters? Does that mean he doesn't have three sisters anymore? I was afraid to ask so instead I said, "So, you must understand my pain."

"Yes, I do."

"Do you miss 'em?" I immediately wished I could take the words back.

He didn't say anything for a few paces. "I really miss them." Then doing a complete one eighty on me, I wasn't prepared when he asked, "So, why don't you play on the basketball team anymore?"

"It's a long story. You probably wouldn't understand," I answered. I then picked up my pace when I spotted Kelsey in her usual place in the foyer. "See you before the *first* bell." I smiled at him as I made my way to my safety net waiting for me only yards away.

"Good. Ms. Lewis, you know what happens when you're late to my class." He never missed a beat as he continued to walk past me toward the gymnasium.

Kelsey made her eyes bug out before asking, "What am I missing? You just walked into school with Coach Z like you two were an item or something. Everyone's been talking about how stuck up he is, but he didn't act stuck up with you at all. In fact, he seemed *very* friendly."

I waved my hand in dismissal. "You're crazy. He just parked near—," I stopped talking when I saw Beth walking up the steps with Anthony Adams, the basketball center. "Look over there. What's Beth doing with Anthony?"

"What's in the air today? First you come sauntering in with Coach Gorgeous and now Beth's with ACI's version of LeBron James. What am I missing? Is it man crush Monday or what?"

We all but pressed our faces against the glass as we peered through it trying to decipher what they were talking about. I said, "I bet he's asking her to prom."

"I bet you're right. Watch 'em. They're laughing. I think she just said yes. Uh oh, she's heading this way. Quick! Act like we're talking about something else." We scurried back to our seats on the bench in the front foyer and turned to each other in mock conversation.

Beth's grin was ear to ear. She waited until she was close to us before she half spoke and half sang—it was her special language of sing-song, "Guess who has a date to prom?"

"Who? You?" Kelsey was carrying it a bit far.

"I do. I'm going with Anthony Adams. Do you think we'll look weird with him being so tall and me so short?" Beth asked. She was more worried about the height difference than the color difference.

"You can always wear really high heels." Kelsey showed why she was valedictorian material.

"I thought you still had a thing for that new guy from Jersey," I mentioned. It was hard to keep up with Beth's love life. Her average relationship lasted a week. Two weeks would be considered a serious relationship. This stemmed from the fact she was in love with a guy she met three years ago while in physical therapy. All other guys fell flat in comparison with the Greek God. Henry Noble was Clarksdell Greyhound's double-threat legend—star quarterback and homerun hitting shortstop—at a sport's powerhouse school in a neighboring town. I have to admit his golden curls and chiseled abs did have that Adonis effect. I know this because for the past few years, Beth made me go with her as we stalked him by going to Clarksdell ballgames. The fact he had a girlfriend and was unobtainable made him all the more desirable in Beth's eyes.

"No, he was too clingy," Beth explained about the guy from New Jersey. She always had one character flaw or excuse after another. Truth was that no one could measure up to Henry Noble in her eyes.

"Have you considered asking the Greek God to prom?" I asked.

"I wish, but he's still with that *ugly* girl."

I mocked her, "Really, really ugly." In fact, there was nothing ugly about his girlfriend. If he was Adonis, then she was Aphrodite. Actually those were our code names for them.

Kelsey turned to me and asked, "What about you? You're not gonna back out, are ya?"

Ever since my parents gave me their approval for prom, I'd been looking for ways to get out of it. "I'm going, but I'm going alone. I don't want to go with a date. Understand?"

"I'll be your date," Kelsey volunteered. "We can have a girl's night."

"No. I promise I'll be fine. You need to find a date and have the time of your life. I just don't want to be saddled with some guy all night. I want to go and eat that filet mignon, go *ooh* and *aah* over everyone, and then get in the truck and drive myself home when I've had enough."

Beth wasn't having any of it. "Why do you always have to be like that? You used to be normal. Now you're a complete weirdo. It all happened after ..." She stopped talking when a light bulb went off in her head. "That's it. Why don't you ask one of the Seeley brothers? Last time I saw Joseph Seeley, he had potential."

"Don't even go there. Laurel would never speak to me again. She's been in love with him for as long as I can remember," I explained. That wasn't the only reason—I couldn't be in the same room with a Seeley more than a few minutes before wanting to curl up in a fetal position.

Kelsey asked, "Can teachers go to prom with students?" I gave her my meanest stink eye hoping to silence her. No luck.

"Beth, you should've been here earlier. Here, Leslie and Coach McDreamy came walking into school like they were an item. They looked good together too."

"Shut up. Are you kidding me? Coach Z and our girl, Les, were chatting it up?" Beth asked.

Kelsey responded, "Yep, just like best friends."

"Hmm. This is very interesting."

I didn't give them the satisfaction of a reaction. Instead, I turned and walked toward my first period class.

CHAPTER 4

In preparation for the marathon Sunday church service, weekends are always particularly hectic at our house. The meal after church is almost as important as the preaching. Not only does Momma play the piano and lead the choir, but the potluck meal also falls under her bailiwick. That means she spends all Saturday night cooking, and she's the last person to leave on Sundays once the church's kitchen is put back in order.

Whitley and Laurel usually help Momma with the cooking duties, while I help Dad with the weekend farm duties. Perry just flits between both groups. Once Dad figures out which snakes to take to church, I help him transfer them to small carry boxes. Some of the boxes are hand-hewn heirlooms going back as many as four generations of Lewis preachers. A few of the special boxes are very ornate like Red Ruby's box. It has a Plexiglas top, and the wood on the sides is outlined with red jewels. Dad doesn't normally take Ruby to regular church services—he saves her for revivals and special movements of the Lord.

Most people didn't understand this clandestine Appalachian-based type of Christian worship. Early on, my sisters and I learned the importance of keeping our church life secret. It was virtually impossible to explain snake handling without experiencing it. Since I've attended hundreds of services in my life, I've seen the mist and the miracles. I've also seen death as well. Before I quit the church, I personally witnessed several people bitten by snakes. My most vivid snakebite memory was when my grandpa was bitten on his cheek by an eastern diamondback rattler. After surviving over fifty-two different bites during his lifetime as a minister, we were all shocked when Grandpa died within fifteen minutes of this snakebite. Being only six years old, my momma tried to protect me from seeing him, but when she wasn't looking, I sneaked on the platform. Grandpa's face was swollen the size of a basketball and was red and purple, but that wasn't what I remembered the most—it was his smile.

The only thing my dad had in common with my grandpa was that they were both snake handling preachers. If he were alive today, he'd be the first person pointing fingers at me and telling me I was on the road leading to hell. When my dad was a young boy, he was bitten by a cottonmouth. My grandfather wouldn't take him to the hospital—even when my dad's whole arm swelled up ready to burst Grandpa just kept praying and anointing him with oil. Finally, Uncle Gabriel, my dad's older brother, snuck and took Dad to the hospital after Grandpa fell asleep. The doctors saved my dad's life, and Grandpa never forgave either one of his sons for their act of betrayal and lack of faith—especially Uncle Gabe. Grandpa would've rather my dad died than been seen by a doctor. My uncle Gabe left the church shortly after that, but my dad only clung tighter to his faith hoping to one day receive his dad's forgiveness.

While my dad starts the Sunday loading ritual, I study him trying to find flaws. I'm sure he has some, but to me, he's close to perfect. After all the covered dishes, snake boxes, and the family are nicely packed into the van, I stand on the end of the sidewalk and watch as my family drives off. Then comes my time. I have up to six hours, sometimes more depending on what happens at church, to do whatever I want to do. When I first stopped going to church with my family, I used to cry the entire time they were gone. Not now. I've learned to enjoy the solitude. On the snowy or rainy days, I work on creating a mosaic using leftover and broken tile pieces. When it's pretty outside, I hike, ride the four-wheeler or something outdoors. My favorite thing to do on nice days is to fish. Since Jeb was the one who taught me to fish, it was hard at first to even think about fishing after he died. As long as I don't fish at the coal banks then I'm fine.

Middle Fork River is not too far from the house, and I've found the perfect fishing spot on the riverbank. It's where I have church. It makes me think of what my Uncle Gabe told my dad when Dad was trying to talk him into coming back to church. Uncle Gabe said, "Clay, would you rather me be at church thinking about fishing, or would you rather me be fishing thinking about God?"

I've never felt the need to buy a graphite rod or expensive spinning reel—my fishing isn't fancy. My dad's old Zebco fishing pole, complete with bobber, hook, and sinker, is my fishing weaponry of choice. I mostly dig my own worms and every once in a while, I'll buy crickets. Bluegills love crickets. Today, I took a book to read while I waited on the bluegill, catfish, or the occasional largemouth to take my bait. Sometimes I keep them, but most of the time I release them back into the river.

Since today was a pleasant seventy-degree March day, I rolled up my pants to let my pale legs see a little sunlight. The sun felt nice on my tender skin. The fish hit in spurts. Before long, I had a pretty big fish on my line that was putting up a nice fight. It escaped from my hook right when I had it to the bank. I was so preoccupied with landing the fish that it took me a few minutes before I realized I was no longer by myself. My back was to the intruder, but I felt his presence. In case it was a bear or a dangerous animal, I froze in my tracks. When my visitor cleared *his* voice, I nearly jumped out of my skin. A man could be the most dangerous predator of all.

The sun was directly behind the man who was twenty yards away, so I had no idea the identity of the intruder interrupting my perfect day. I wasn't sure if he was a mass murderer or a rapist. I commanded my body to quit shaking as I looked around for a rock or a stick to use to defend myself if need be.

His hands up in surrender, he said, "Don't shoot. I'm unarmed."

The wind brought his scent to me. I immediately knew who he was. "Coach Z, is that you?" My legs were wobbly underneath me. A bear would've been less intimidating.

"Yes, it's me. I thought I recognized your truck parked on the side of the road. I was worried something was wrong and followed the path looking for you," he said as he came closer. "Catching anything?" He motioned with his head toward the water.

I was having a hard time speaking without my voice sounding all choppy with nerves. Standing in a defensive posture, I mustered up, "Mostly bluegills so far. I just lost a big bass at the bank." I started to ask what would have brought him out this way, but I dismissed the thought as unimportant.

"Mind if I use your other pole?" he asked as he pointed to Perry's pink pole lying on the ground next to me. Sometimes, Perry joined me on days church didn't last too long.

"Sure, if you don't mind that it's pink." Offering him my pole would've been the Christian thing to do, but it didn't even register as an option at that time. As he was fooling with the pole, I tried to assess his fishing skills.

He cast the little pole, but it only sailed ten or so feet before it landed with a wobbly thud. He reeled it back in and this time his cast flew twenty feet. *Definitely a novice.*

The almost smug look on his face told me that he was proud of his weak cast. "The river current seems slow today, or is it my imagination?" he asked after I didn't offer up more conversation.

I decided that conversation had to be better than the awkward silence so I answered. "I think because this is one of the widest and deepest parts of the river, the appearance of the current is a little deceiving. About a mile downwind, the current runs almost at rapid level—especially after a big rain."

"I find out something new about you every day. You are occasionally late, you're very good at basketball—better than most of the guys at school I've seen play—yet you don't play on the high school team. Now, I find you on a Sunday on a riverbank fishing *alone.*"

"Yep, sounds like you know all about me," I softly replied.

"Far from it. I haven't figured you out at all."

"Figured me out? I'm not trying to be illusive or obscure. I like to fish and play basketball. Is that a problem?"

His laugh caused his whole face to light up. "*Illusive* and *obscure?* Where did those words come from? Isn't this Kentucky?"

"Hey, watch it, Mr. South Dakota," I warned him. He had my dander up, and I felt the need to defend my state. "Don't ever underestimate a Kentuckian just because we talk with an accent. My momma's been feeding us vocabulary words just like she feeds us supper. Our education is one of her top priorities." I stopped talking while I watched his bobber go all the way under.

His eyes followed the direction I was looking. "Whoa," he said as he set his hook and began to crank the reel like a real amateur.

From the bow of the pole, I could tell it was a big fish. He pulled the pole to give it slack as he wrestled the largemouth to the bank.

"I can't believe this. You talk about beginner's luck. I've been coming to this same spot forever, and I've never caught a trophy mount like that one."

"It must be this pink pole. It's lucky."

"It's lucky all right—lucky it didn't break from the weight of that fish. I can't wait to tell Perry."

His eyebrows lifted in question. "Perry. Who's Perry—your boyfriend?"

"No. I don't have a boyfriend. Perry's my ten-year-old sister." Before it became awkward that I just admitted I was *boyfriend-less,* I changed the subject. "So what kind of Indian doesn't know how to fish?"

His laugh was big like I just said the funniest thing in the world. "What are you talking about? I just caught this whopper of a fish. Don't you know that I'm a *hokuwa* king. Fly fishing for trout on the Cheyenne River is more my style though. Nothing better than smoked trout for breakfast." He paused, and his mood became serious when he said, "Let me ask you something." He waited until I was looking at him, and he was sure he had my full attention. "Do I look different to you?"

"What do ya mean?"

"I mean, has this pink pole taken away my *manliness*?" When I didn't answer, he further explained, "You know, my man card."

I tried really hard to keep a straight face, but he was acting silly as he first used the pole as a wand then twirled it like a baton. I couldn't help but smile. "You're crazy. You better watch that hook or you'll think man card."

"Uh oh. There it is. Leslie Lewis does have a smile, and I saw it. It's a nice smile too. Why are you always so serious?"

My smile vanished and an angry glare replaced it. "What's with you? You interrupted the only peaceful time I have all week. You catch a monster bass, and as if that's not enough, now you're trying to psychoanalyze me." I could tell he wasn't expecting this kind of reaction from me. I softened a little when I said, "If you want to fish, then fish. Just no more personal questions or trying to figure me out. Okay?"

"Okay, okay, I'm sorry. You've fascinated me since that first day in class. I've never met anyone like you."

"Okay, I get it. I'm different. Now, will you please just shut up and fish?"

And fish we did.

Did he just say that I fascinated him?

CHAPTER 5

At first, I was relieved when my family didn't make it home from church at their normal time. One look from my dad and he would know something was up with me. I really needed the extra time to get my head back on straight. When my family wasn't home by dark, I began to worry a little. I kept checking the phone to make sure I could hear the dial tone. It was working. They should've been home at least a couple of hours ago. I told myself there could be several different explanations for them being so late, but I knew deep down the only explanation was that someone must've gotten bitten at the service—I could feel it. Finally, I heard the crush of the gravels come down the driveway. I ran outside and began to count the outlines of bodies I could see in the van to make sure everyone was accounted for. *Dad, Mom, Laurel, Whitley, and Perry—whew, they were all there.* I stood at the end of the sidewalk waiting for them. Perry was the first one out of the van, and she made a beeline straight to me.

"Les, it was awful. You should be glad you quit the church." Her eyes were big.

I looked to the other family members hoping they'd offer up an explanation of just what had been so awful. No one seemed eager to talk about whatever tragedy had occurred today. Even in the dim light, I could tell Mom's whole body was drooping, and Dad's dark complexion was ghostly white. I just stood there blocking the sidewalk until someone told me something.

Laurel walked on by me carrying one of mom's stainless bean kettles. "It was horrible," she said. "Poor Joseph and the other boys."

Whitley patted me while shaking her head as she followed her sister. She was carrying a couple of empty casserole dishes.

Perry finally blurted out, "Sister Seeley died at the church."

My heart dropped. I started imagining what could have caused Sister Seeley's demise. I had never seen her take up serpents. Surely, she wouldn't have started today. If she died because of a snakebite, then that would mean my dad and our church could be in a heap of trouble.

"What happened to her? Was it one of the rattlers?" I braced myself for the answer.

"No. She drank the strychnine and died," Perry emotionlessly explained as if this were a common event.

"Do what?" That wasn't any better than being snake bitten.

Dad had yet to say a word while he unloaded the van. This unnerved me the most. I left my post on the sidewalk and helped Dad unload the boxes. I picked up a couple and followed behind him to the basement. It was odd, but even the rattlers were being unusually quiet. Perry lugged one of the smaller boxes down the stairs. "Dad, I just don't understand," she said as she was trying to make sense of everything.

Join the club.

Dad let down the boxes right on the steps and kneeled in front of Perry. "Honey, I wish I could help you make sense of things, but I don't have all the answers. Only the Lord knows why things happen the way they do."

"Does that mean Sister Seeley didn't have enough faith when she drank that poison or that she had sin in her life?" Perry asked.

"That's between her and her maker. It's not for us to judge." Dad gave her his pat answer.

"Why did the police want to take *you* to jail?"

"Baby girl, not everyone believes the same as we do. Some people believe that Jesus's mother is the one to pray to. Others don't even believe in God at all …"

Perry interrupted. "How can anyone look up in the sky and not know there's a God?"

"I don't know, honey," he answered.

"Are you going to have to go to jail?" she asked.

"It's up to the good Lord. You know that Paul in the Bible went to jail. Sometimes that's in his plan. I don't know yet." His voice changed from sympathetic teacher to the authoritative preacher. "Now go on up, and get ready for bed."

We all knew better than to argue or protest when he spoke in his preacher voice at home. His mind was made up. Perry knew this too. As she was going up the stairs, I called out, "You're not going to believe the big ole bass your pink pole caught today." I conveniently left out anything about who was using her pink pole.

"How big was it?"

"It was a good five pounder—maybe more."

I thought it would make her happy, but instead she stomped her foot. "Ah man. Did you bring it home?"

"No. I didn't want to lug it back to the truck."

"I wish you could've at least taken a picture. Daddy, she really needs a cell phone," she said as she made sure her frustration was heard with each stomp.

On the narrow stairway, Perry met Momma coming down as she was going up. "Honey, quit that stomping, or you'll disturb the

45

snakes. Make sure you wash your face real good before you go to bed. You're about the age to start getting pimples."

I held back my smile when I heard Perry protesting under her breath. Mom joined us as we transferred the snakes from the boxes to their cages and recorded today's activity. We did so in silence until Momma broke it by saying, "Clay, if I didn't know better, I would think Sister Seeley drank that poison hoping she would die."

"Honey, why would you say such a thing?" Dad asked.

I just kept my mouth shut and listened to the two of them. I tried to make myself invisible so they would forget I was around. They were hesitant to talk church business in front of me or any of us girls.

"I know. I know. It's just that the anniversary of Jeb's death is this week. You know as well as I do that she hasn't been right since he died. She's not handled snakes or drank the poison years before that. Why did she do it today?" She seemed to ponder on that for a minute. "I watched her come up to the altar while I was playing the piano. I remember thinking something wasn't right. She didn't just take a drink. She chugged it."

CHAPTER 6

Normally, I'm a fairly light sleeper. Tonight was no different. I heard the hateful ring of the telephone and could hear my dad's footsteps as he raced to answer it. Checking the time, I saw it was two in the morning—no good calls ever come at this time. Dad answered by saying in his preaching voice, "Hello, this is Brother Clay."

I slightly cracked opened my door and positioned myself so I could better hear the conversation. I knew who it was, and I knew what it was about before the phone was even answered. I'm not sure if it was my prophetic gifting or just common sense.

Dad said, "I see." (Pause.) "When did he leave?" (Pause.) "Thanks for the warning, Joseph. I'll make sure he gets back safely."

"Clay, what was that all about?" Momma asked.

"It was Joseph Seeley. He said his dad was on his way over here to talk to Les. He wanted some answers about Jeb's death."

I could hear Mom's gasp all the way to my room. "Clay, what are you gonna do? He can't talk to Les."

"I know. Let's just pray until he gets here."

I started to shut my door, but I saw a shadow heading my way. It was Perry. She was a light sleeper too. "What's going on?" She asked in a loud whisper.

"It's Brother Seeley. He's on his way here and wants to talk to me. He wants answers about …"

She finished my sentence, " …the day Jeb died."

"Yep."

"Are you gonna talk to him?"

"Nope."

"Why don't you just tell him what happened?"

"I can't." I expected her to argue with me, but she didn't.

We heard the loud sound of his truck's engine and the sound of the gravels spraying as he slid to a stop. Changing our position from the doorway to the window, we slightly lifted the lower pane just enough to hear what was being said.

Brother Seeley was wobbling as he walked, and his voice was loud and crass. "Brother Clay, I'm here to get some answers. Go get that girl of yours."

Perry whispered, "I think he's drunk as a skunk." She was standing on the bed so she could see out the window.

"I think you're right," I whispered. "Hey, what do you know about being drunk anyway."

She just shrugged her shoulders. "Just cause I'm ten doesn't mean I'm ignorant."

Dad's voice was kind and caring when he said, "Brother Seeley, come on up here and sit on the porch with me while Ruth brews us up a pot of hot coffee."

Brother Seeley stood at the bottom step of the front porch. "I ain't interested in any of your woman's coffee. I'm here to get some answers. I want to know what happened to my boy that day at the coal banks."

"I've told you over and over what happened. The police even told you what happened. He slipped on the wet ground and hit his head on a rock."

"My boy was a running back. He was good on his feet. He rushed for twelve hundred yards the year before he died. He wouldn't have slipped. I've seen him stay on his feet in two inches of mud. He was gonna go somewhere if he just didn't go fishing with your little ole Jezebel girl."

"She was just thirteen years old—practically a baby," Dad defended me.

"Why I married my woman when she just turned fourteen. Don't you know the younger ones are …" He stopped when he heard the squeak of the door. Momma had a tray in her hands. The smell of coffee floated up through the window. Her voice was like a minty balm as she spoke, "Brother Seeley, come on up to the porch and have a cup of my good coffee. You've always bragged on what a good coffeemaker I am."

It was working. He started up one step as he answered, "I did say you made good coffee, didn't I?"

I cringed when I saw him look my momma over like he was eyeing a big piece of chocolate cake. "Clay, you are one lucky son of a gun."

"Eww," Perry whispered.

"The coffee's getting cold. Brother Seeley, come on up and tell me about what kind of team Leslie County's going to have next year."

Evidently that struck a chord with him. "Well, I guess I can drink one cup as long as it's good and strong."

"Yes, sir. I made it just like you like it," Momma answered as she put the tray on the table and went back inside.

Brother Seeley and Dad sat on the porch for what seemed like hours and talked football. I heard every play Jeb and Joseph ever ran. I found it odd that other than talking about Sister Seeley's age when they married, he didn't mention anything more about her. Perry fell asleep on my bed, but I was too afraid to close my eyes.

At the first hint of daybreak, I heard him say, "I didn't mean to keep you good folks up all night." He was very apologetic and seemed a little embarrassed. Dad told him not to worry about it and promised not to tell anyone. As he was leaving, Momma came out on the porch and invited him and his boys to supper on Saturday night.

Noooo!

CHAPTER 7

The school's staff referred to this week as deadline week since it was the last chance for seniors to sign up for the senior trip, order caps and gowns, and buy tickets to prom. Even the slacker teachers were all buzzing around trying to make sure their paperwork was ready for the end of the grading period. On the home front, the week crawled by. My family and the church were being heavily scrutinized over Sister Seeley's death. My parents hired an attorney. I was still a little on edge by Brother Seeley's late night visit. But it possibly did some good because he'd been especially nice to Dad ever since that night. He probably didn't want the rest of the congregation to know about his drunken escapade. Who knows, maybe something good could come out of Sister Seeley's death after all.

I didn't drive to school all week. I rode to school with Momma and my sisters because our momma hen wanted her baby chicks close to her now that our church was at front and center of this controversy. For those who didn't know that our church played these deadly faith games, they did now. I noticed funny looks by some of the students, but I didn't get harassed like my younger sisters did, especially Perry. Dad even let her miss school and go to work with him one day because some of the kids were picking on her.

My best friends asked a few questions about what happened with Sister Seeley, but they didn't make a big deal about it. They were more interested in talking about prom, our dresses, and the senior trip. Our class had been fundraising for this trip for the last three years. We're going to Nashville, Tennessee and staying in the Opryland Hotel. We even have tickets to the Grand Ole Opry. I'll get to hear country music at its finest.

Since I was riding with Momma today, arriving at school early was out of the question. I was barely able to make it to gym class before the first bell rang and that was with me sprinting. Coach Z had been pretty standoffish all week, which was probably a good thing. Though I suspected he now knew all about my family and about our church. Right before Friday's gym class was over; he came over to where I was standing and gave me a printout of Sunday's weather forecast. His weather report wasn't lost on me. I asked, "Do I need to bring your special pole?" He just smiled.

I was surprised to see Beth's lime green Volkswagen in front of my house after we arrived home from school on Thursday. Even more surprising was the fact Kelsey was with her. Usually, the dormitory kids didn't leave campus without an act of congress. "Sister Ruth, we're here to kidnap Les. She's had a tough week, and the Root Beer City Drive-In over in Clarksdell would be just what the doctor ordered. Did you know they make their own root beer there, and it's delicious?"

Perry squealed, "I love root beer. Can I go, please, please?"

Momma said, "Perry, honey, I need you to stay here tonight. I thought you wanted to download that game on the computer."

I could see my little sister wavering. She looked at me then at Momma. "Can we download it now?"

"We'll see," Momma answered. We all knew when she said, *"We'll see"* that it was the same as her saying yes.

I was in a state of bewilderment. I couldn't believe that not only was my momma going to let me go all the way to Clarksdell on a school night with my friends, but she even bribed my little sister so she wouldn't be upset. I just looked at her waiting for her common sense to kick in and for her to explain just why it wasn't a good idea for me to go on a school night. This so didn't make a lick of sense. Something was wrong with the universe.

"Les can go as long as you have her home by dark," she spoke directly to Beth.

By dark? We could barely get there and back before dark. Oh well, at least I knew I still lived in the same strict universe.

"Piece of cake," Beth answered.

I knew Beth must really need my support for her to agree to those terms.

Kelsey got out of the front passenger seat and let me ride shotgun so I could be the chief navigator. Plus, I had to keep Beth focused. Her driving scared both Kelsey and me. "So where are we really going?" I asked once we were in the car. "And does this have anything to do with Henry 'Adonis' Noble?"

"Funny you mention his name. A little birdie told me Clarksdell plays at home tonight and guess what?" Beth answered.

Both Kelsey and I answered in unison, "What?"

"Root Beer City Drive-In is right in front of Clarksdell's baseball field."

"Imagine that," I replied.

I only had to tell Beth to look at the road three times on the forty minute drive. I felt like I definitely earned my hotdog and root beer. After we finished our hotdogs, we entered the stadium. It was the top of the third inning and so far it was a scoreless game. It was like everyone there knew we were interlopers. All eyes seemed to follow us as we went to the top row and sat down under the canopy. I watched Beth search the stands looking for Henry's girlfriend, Aphrodite. If she was there, she wasn't seated with the other Clarksdell girls sitting to the right of us.

Kelsey spotted her. "Six o'clock," she said and nodded her head below us. "Looks like Aphrodite is sitting with Adonis's parents."

Beth said to Kelsey, "I didn't know you knew what his parents looked like."

"I don't, but their shirts say *Noble's Mom* and *Noble's Dad* on their backs," Kelsey explained.

Aphrodite's long straight blond hair looked like she stepped out of a magazine. Her sunglasses were perched on the top of her head. The back of her shirt had Henry's number ten in jersey-sized numbers at the center. *Noble's Girlfriend* was written overtop the number. Her shirt matched his parent's shirts. They looked like one happy family.

For the most part, we behaved ourselves until Henry was on deck to bat. Beth stood up and waved to make sure he saw her. I could tell the minute he spotted her. He smiled and waved back to her. His attention to Beth was short-lived. He stopped mid-wave when he saw his girlfriend turn around to look at us. She must not have noticed when we arrived. Aphrodite was clearly not amused to see the three of us waving to her guy.

When Henry hit a long double, we cheered loudly (probably a bit too loudly). We must've created quite a spectacle because it seemed like everyone in the stands had turned around and were glaring up at us. I began to feel a little uneasy when I noticed a few of the girls to the right whispering and pointing, they were plotting. *Not good.* Also, the sun didn't have a whole lot of sky left to travel in the west. Missing Sister Ruth's curfew wasn't an option. I nudged Beth. "It's time to go."

She reluctantly agreed.

Again all eyes were back on us even though we tried to make our departure as inconspicuous as possible as we paraded down the metal stairs sounding like a herd of cattle. When we were within yards of Beth's car, I smelled perfume and heard a horde of petite clicks on the asphalt.

"Don't turn around. Keep going. Aphrodite is following us," Kelsey announced.

Even though I knew all about the story of the pillar of salt, I turned around anyway and looked. Behind Aphrodite were four other pretty girls—all goddesses in their own rights.

Beth said, "Keep on going. Don't look back."

I knew we weren't going to get out of here without a scene. "Might as well hear what she has to say," I rationalized to them and stopped. Beth stopped too. Kelsey walked a few paces on but quickly turned and came back to support us.

We were outnumbered. The strong mixture of perfume and hair products was nauseating.

Henry's girlfriend spoke up. "I'm not sure what you ACI girls think you're doing in greyhound territory, but you aren't welcome here. Go back to Leslie County."

If Beth was scared, I couldn't tell it when she said, "We just spent fifteen bucks to get into the ballgame. As long as this is still a public facility, I'm not sure how you plan to keep us away. Besides, we just *love* Clarksdell baseball."

Then Aphrodite said something that made Beth's night. "Beth Rudder, I have your number. You stay away from Henry. For your information, we've been going out for *three* years. We're *crazy* about each other. Do you understand me?"

Beth smiled before she asked, "If he's as crazy about you as you say he is, then why do you care if I'm here or not?"

Bam! My little cunning friend just silenced the goddess. Her mouth was opened as she tried to formulate an answer. She looked to the other goddesses for help, but they offered none.

Finally one of the girls spoke out. "You're not welcome here. Go back to the sticks where you belong. You are way out of your league here."

"Is that right? Well, ladies, it's been lovely chatting with you," Beth said before she slowly and confidently turned and headed toward the car. Kelsey and I fell in a couple of steps behind her, guarding her back like the loyal friends we were.

Standing there they resembled a confused pack of dogs rather than deity. Unsure whether to follow or not, the Clarksdell girls never moved from the middle of the parking lot. As we pulled out of the parking lot leaving their turf, I knew they wouldn't lose any time remarking their territory like the dogs they so closely resembled.

As soon as we were a safe distance away, we all busted out laughing. Beth gushed, "What about her knowing my name? Especially since I don't know hers. I wished I would've asked her that."

Kelsey added, "What about them knowing we're from ACI?"

I said, "It's not like we were *that* obvious when we went to watch his football games."

Beth was all dreamy eyed when she asked, "Did you see his smile when he looked up and saw me? Only way she would know my name is because Henry told her."

I could tell the wheels in her mind were turning. She wasn't wearing the official girlfriend jersey and sitting in the middle of his parents, but I wouldn't count her out just yet.

CHAPTER 8

My parents hired a smart attorney. All of the legal matters looming over my dad and the church disappeared like they were swept under a giant rug. His attorney, who respects my dad's passion for protecting his religious beliefs, advised him to lie low for a while—meaning no more snakes or poison at the church. She explained a second incident would not be a good thing. My dad, true to form and his convictions, explained to her he couldn't make any promises since his allegiance was to God first even if it meant jail time. Sometimes I almost think he secretly wants to go to jail like his apostle heroes.

Our church, Middle Fork Church of God, is small and consists mainly of twelve or so families. (Even though I attend only on special occasions, I still consider it my church.) Unfortunately, you can't tell if a church practices snake handling as according to Mark 16:18 by the church's name or denomination. You also can't Google "snake handling church" and find one either. Word of mouth is the only way you'll be able to find a church that uses snakes in their worship services.

Since what we practice is illegal in Kentucky, we have to be very careful who we invite. We have sister churches in all the surrounding states, and once a year we congregate in West Virginia for a large snake-handling Holy Ghost revival. (This year's revival is scheduled the weekend before prom in Jolo, West Virginia.) Our kind all stick together in times of trouble too. Our phone seemed to ring off the hook after word got out about our predicament as the various pastors and our friends from all over called to offer their support.

Sister Seeley's funeral turned into a circus when some of the congregation felt led to bring out the snakes. The funeral director actually stopped the service until the snakes were put away. I didn't attend the funeral especially since it was held on the four-year anniversary of Jeb's death.

I tried every way imaginable to get out of Saturday night's supper with the Seeleys, but when Momma puts her foot down, there's no changing her mind. She was hoping it would be a good thing for all of us, but I wasn't as optimistic. I tried to tell her what a mistake it was, but she just quoted scripture to me and said miracles could happen. I could tell Dad wasn't crazy about the idea either, but the invitation was already made. We couldn't un-invite them now.

Laurel, Whitley, and Perry were excited about the three Seeley boys being at our home. Joseph Seeley was a few months younger than me and was a junior at Leslie County High School. The other two younger boys, James and Jacob, were born a couple of years apart in stair step order. The Seeley boys went to the county school instead of ACI so they could play football. I'm not sure where they got their size, but all three of them looked like poster boys for the local fire department calendar. Laurel thought Joseph was the most handsome boy alive. I personally didn't see any beauty in him—inside or out. His head was as oversized and misshapen as his body. Mainly, I didn't like how he treated my little sister. He acted as repulsed by her as I was by him. The more he didn't like Laurel, the more she liked him. *Go figure.*

Whitley just wanted to marry one of the Seeley boys. She didn't care which one. Perry reminded me so much of myself at that age. She flitted back and forth seeking any attention she could get. She wasn't content playing dolls with the other girls her age; she preferred to be right in the middle of the older kids passing football or playing basketball. She was pretty good at sports even while wearing a dress.

As a consolation for having to dine with the Seeleys, Momma fixed all of my favorite foods including chicken and dumplings and her homemade peach cobbler. That kind of made the whole Seeley thing at least palatable. I pulled out the longest, unattractive skirt I could find from the back of my closet. I didn't want to give Brother Seeley any more reasons to be critical of my dad. When looking from their perspective, I knew it was difficult for the church people to understand why my dad gave me so much freedom—especially since he wouldn't give them any reasons behind my transformation. He'd just say, "She'll figure things out for herself someday."

From the minute the Seeleys arrived at the farm, I thought things were very weird. I knew they were guys, but I expected them to be at least a little downtrodden over the loss of their wife and mother. Instead it was like a big party with them eating second and third helpings of the food. Even Brother Seeley, who was ordinarily a sullen man, seemed to be almost jovial. He actually tried to engage me in conversations a couple of times. I answered politely with short answers.

After the meal, the Seeleys didn't immediately go home as I'd hoped. Whitley and Perry took the younger boys to the barn to show them our horses. Laurel and Joseph sat on the front porch drinking lemonade. He actually acted half-way civil to her. Daddy took Brother Seeley downstairs to see his setup for the snakes. Although Dad and I caught most of the snakes, according to Brother Seeley they still belonged to the church. When the church got low on funds, he'd always suggest selling Red Ruby as an option since we'd had many offers to buy her over the years. Dad would never consent to it.

I helped Momma with the dishes afterwards. When we were just about done, I heard Perry yelling for me. On edge anyway, I dropped everything and ran to see what was wrong. I stuck my head out the door, and Perry called out, "Come play basketball with us!" Even Laurel, who hated anything involving a ball, was on our makeshift dirt court ready to play.

Relieved nothing was wrong, I declined. "I'd make the numbers uneven. You've got six already." With Jeb gone—so went the theory of a Seeley boy for each Lewis girl. I was now the odd man out.

Perry was serious when she said, "Whitley and Laurel only count for half a player since they're no good at basketball."

Slightly embarrassed, Laurel threw the ball hard at Perry and said, "Speak for yourself, you little minion."

The Seeley boys laughed, which caused Perry to lash out more at Laurel. She threw the ball at Laurel's head. Fortunately Laurel's reflexes were good, and she was able to duck. I was the only thing between the ball and the picture window in the living room. The ball felt at home in my hands.

Joseph said, "Come on, Les."

We played until it was too dark to see. Brother Seeley and my parents sat on the porch and watched. Even in skirts, the Lewis girls rose to the occasion and won two out of the four games.

CHAPTER 9

Although Saturday night with the Seeleys turned out to be rather uneventful, I was sure glad it was over. Only problem was … Momma invited them back next Saturday night. At least the Seeley's helped to occupy my thoughts. Thoughts of Sunday and fishing with Coach Z were looming close to the surface of my mind. I can't outright say I'm in love with Coach Z or even express in words how I feel about him. To be perfectly honest, I'm just not experienced enough to know if what I'm feeling is love, heartburn, or the excitement of finding a new fishing buddy. Plus, I'm not naïve enough to think he wants anything but friendship from me either. I decided not to read more into his attention and our fishing trips than what was there. I just wish I would quit thinking about him all the time.

Even though he was a teacher at a Christian school, I still kept my guard up around him when we were alone. As far as I know, he could be a predator looking for gullible girls to victimize. Problem with that theory: I'm no longer gullible, and I refuse to be a victim.

If Sunday morning was any indication of how the rest of the day would turn out, then it was going to be a good one. I was between sleep and awake when I realized both my mom and dad were standing next to my bed. I rubbed my eyes to be sure they weren't deceiving me. After the fog in my head cleared, I groggily asked, "Is everything okay?"

"We have a little surprise for you," Momma said as she handed me a wrapped box.

"What? It's not my birthday yet?"

"No, it's not. But we decided to go ahead and give you an early graduation present." Then she added with a twinkle in her eye, "Plus, it will be helpful when you go away to college in a few months."

I quickly removed the wrapping paper—no going slow and saving bows for me. "It's a cell phone," I said in a whisper.

Daddy said, "Now, there will be a few rules, and I'll take your monthly bill from your paycheck each month. You have limited internet usage, so you'll have to use it sparingly. Is that agreeable?"

"That's fine." I would've bought one for myself a long time ago if they would've agreed to sign the cell phone contract. I couldn't sign until I turned eighteen.

When Dad tilted his head and raised his eyebrows, I knew a more serious talk was on the way. "I don't want you to turn into one of those teenagers who never look or listen to anything because they're always pranking with their phone."

By this time, I was sitting straight up in the bed. "No problem." I knew I would never become one of them. When Beth's parents grounded her from her cell phone a few months back, she actually went through withdrawal.

Perry came bounding in my room. "What's going on? Is Les in trouble or something?"

I showed her my phone.

"Sweet! Now we can take pictures and play games. Oh, Les, *we're* gonna love it!"

Laurel and Whitley's reactions weren't as positive as Perry's. In their eyes, I guess it was just another special concession that was made for me. Dad did tell Laurel that when she was graduating she would get one too.

As soon as the excitement was over, it was a typical Sunday morning as the entire Lewis family, sans me, was getting ready for church. The morning couldn't get over soon enough to suit me. Short of pushing them out the door, I did everything I could to help them be on their way. Perry was the only one that even noticed I'd been extra helpful today.

She said, "You must be really itching to go catch another monster bass today. Save some for me, will you? We should just eat and come on back as long as no one dies or anything."

They were ready to head out the door. *Finally.* Even though my momma kept reminding my dad about the lawyer's advice as well as about a bunch of thrill seekers possibly being at church today, he was antsy about not having any snakes available. At the last minute, he asked me to fetch one of the copperheads. "Just in case," he said. He promised Momma he'd leave it in the van, but at least it would be nearby if they got caught up in the Spirit and needed it.

At my normal Sunday spot on the last square of the sidewalk, I watched until my family was out of sight before I hopped in the truck. I wore my regular fishing attire, but did take some extra pains with my hair. Instead of my normal ponytail, I changed things up a bit by wearing my hair in a long Sacajawea-looking braid. I dabbed my Christmas perfume on my neck and on both wrists. Coach Z always smelled so nice; I, at least, didn't want to smell like fish bait.

After a couple of hours of fishing, I began to think Coach Z wasn't going to make it. I tried not to let myself be disappointed. Thankfully, I didn't have to spend much time sulking because just when I had given up on him coming, there he was. Again, I didn't hear him until he was right on top of me. He was definitely light on his feet. "*Hau,*" he said in what I assumed to be a Lakota greeting.

"Good morning," I answered. It would officially be morning for another hour. The earliest Perry would be arriving would be around three. I mentally calculated how much time we had left before I needed to head home. Normally, I could trust Perry with secrets, but the fact I was fishing with my good-looking teacher would prove to be too much for her little mind to handle.

"I brought you something," he said as he handed me a cup of coffee from Dairy Queen.

"Thanks."

"What's that face about? You don't like coffee?"

"I love coffee. I was just checking to make sure it wasn't apple juice. I hate apple juice." I sipped conservatively in case he had laced it with something. I knew I was playing with fire.

"Are you sure you're American? Americans are supposed to like baseball, hotdogs, and apple juice. It's a prerequisite."

Even though I knew he was baiting me, I corrected him, "It's baseball, hotdogs, and apple pie. Not apple juice."

He laughed. "What? Ms. Obscure wasn't impressed with my use of 'prerequisite.'"

"Actually, I was a little surprised. My momma would've definitely appreciated your ten dollar word."

"How would she appreciate this?" He stood up to his full height and in an accent that sounded like a mixture of Mr. Darcy meets

Tonto, he said, "In preparation for our outdoor aquatic adventure, I brought us a succulent sustenance."

In between laughter, I said, "Please don't ever talk like that again. Please."

"So you're not interested in my picnic?"

I was no longer laughing. "Picnic. You brought a picnic?" I tried to keep the concern from my voice.

He took a Dairy Queen bag out of his backpack and threw it at me. "Take your pick. Burger or chicken."

Relief ran all through my body. Picnics were a thing of my past. A Dairy Queen sandwich didn't count as a picnic. "Thanks," I said. "Chicken works for me."

While unwrapping his sandwich, he asked, "Did you bring my lucky pole?"

"Sure did." I handed him Perry's pole. "Today you have a choice of worms or crickets. Bluegills love crickets."

"I didn't think you were supposed to kill crickets? It's bad luck." His forehead crinkled, and he lowered his brows.

"I think that only applies to killing crickets in a house."

He looked at me suspiciously before saying, "Just in case, maybe I better stick with the worms. I don't need any bad luck. Me and ole pinky here aim to catch us another whopper today." He used the pole as a sword as he jabbed in the air with it.

I think I smiled more in that last half hour than I had in a few years.

For a while we both sat on the same large rock as we intently watched our bobbers for movement. The current was swifter today and was pulling our lines downstream. I had to work hard to keep my line from colliding with his. We fished in silence for several minutes. He was probably afraid I would throw another fit on him if he talked too much.

I decided to break the ice in a big way. "I guess you heard about all the trouble at our church? Heard it even made the Mountain News."

"You *heard* it made the news. You didn't watch it?"

"I probably would have if we had cable."

"Is that part of your religion?" He reeled in his line to check and see if he still had bait. He did. He threw his line back out.

"Partly. We do have a television and occasionally watch some DVDs. We really don't have much time to watch even the movies. We stay busy on the farm and with our tile business. It used to really bother me that I couldn't watch UK basketball games. Now, I don't care. I'll go to my friend's house and watch the big games with her family. Beth also records *Grey's Anatomy* for me, and we have marathon TV watching sessions from time to time."

"Is Beth the blond with the short hair I see you with sometimes?"

"That's her. We've been friends for years. My other friend, Kelsey Van Hook, has blond hair too, but it's longer." *So far he seemed more interested in television and my friends than my religion. This was good.*

"*Grey's Anatomy.* Hmmm. That shows okay, but *The Walking Dead* is better." Then out of the blue, he changed the subject on me. "I met two of your sisters with your mom the other day. They do look more like your *ina* than you do. They also dress more like her. Is the dress thing part of a church ritual or something?"

"Yeah, something like that. I guess *ina* means mother."

"Yep. Stick around me awhile, and I'll have you speaking Lakota like a natural."

"Stick with me awhile, and I'll teach you how to fish."

I could tell he wasn't amused. He just grunted a little before saying, "Since you fish on Sundays, does that mean you don't go to church?"

Before I spoke, I looked at him suspiciously, trying to determine if his motive for knowing was to try to save my jeans-wearing soul or trying to psychoanalyze me again.

I started to protest only to remember I was the one who invited him into my personal life when I brought up the Sister Seeley incident. "It's a long story. I wear dresses when I go to church, but I only go a few times each year."

"Your parents okay with that?"

"Kinda."

His line reeled in, he said, "Let me try one of those crickets."

"You may have bad luck. You sure you want to take that chance," I said as I pulled in my third bluegill since we'd been sitting on the rock. He'd yet to have a nibble.

"Just give me the can, already," he ordered.

After he changed his bait, it was no time before he started catching fish.

"Okay, here's the deal," he said. "Let's play a little game."

My heart fell in my chest. This was beginning to feel all too familiar. "What kind of game?"

"The question game. When I catch a fish, I get to ask you a question. When you catch one, you get to ask me a question. Interested?"

I liked the part about asking him questions; it was the part about him asking *me* questions I didn't like. Only I knew I had an advantage—I was clearly better at fishing than he was. "Okay. I'll play your game. I predict I'll know all of your dark secrets before we leave here today."

"Don't be so sure. I brought a little Sioux magic." He pulled out a snuff can, but it didn't contain tobacco. It was gray and looked slimy. He rolled his bait in the substance before he threw it back out into the water.

Coach Z had his Indian magic, but I'd take cattails any day of the week. I threw my line in the midst of the cattails near the river's edge. They didn't let me down, either. I tried to think of my first question as I reeled the small bluegill to the bank. "What made you come all the way from South Dakota to teach at ACI?"

He laughed a little when he said, "It sure as heck wasn't for the money."

"My mom says that teaching at ACI is a ministry and shouldn't be done for the money. I could make more money helping my dad lay tiles than my college-educated momma does working full-time at school." I don't know what made me become Chatty Cathy, so I stopped blabbing and asked again, "So, why did you really come?"

He laughed before he said, "I came to find you, *o'waci.*"

"*Oh-what-chee?*" I repeated. "Can you just talk in English so I can understand you? So go ahead and answer the question. After all, *you* were the one who wanted to play this game."

"Besides finding you, I mainly wanted to get out of South Dakota and see this part of the country. Kentucky is a basketball coach's dream place, right?"

His expression and his answer didn't go together. Before I could help myself, I asked, "Be serious. Is that the reason?"

He smiled as he set his hook. "*That* can only be answered by catching another fish," he said as he began cranking the little reel as fast as he could. He did a little victory dance after releasing his nice-sized bluegill. "Now it's my turn to ask the *obscure* and *illusive* Leslie Lewis a personal question." I could tell he was enjoying my agony.

"All right, already. Go ahead, ask it."

"What's the real reason you didn't play basketball for the school? Everyone said you were one of the best girl players they'd ever seen." His voice actually seemed soft and caring.

That was a fairly easy question. "It's easy to be a star in middle school. I wish I had a reason that would satisfy this fixation you have on me playing ball, but truthfully it just wasn't a priority for me." *Now it all made sense. He was only interested in me because of my basketball skills. Actually that didn't make sense because I couldn't play on his next year's team.*

After some thought, he said, "I don't buy that. That's not a good enough answer. Besides, my fish was bigger than yours so you need a better answer. If basketball isn't important to you, then what is?"

I started to pull the "need to catch another fish" card, but instead I caught myself wanting to tell him. "My little sister, Perry," I said right off the bat. Then I added, "Laurel, Whitley, my parents, our farm, our business, Beth, Kelsey, our church, and my faith." I couldn't believe I vomited all those words out without stopping.

"I thought you didn't go to church?"

"Want another question answered, catch another fish."

I was really hoping to catch another one myself. I was starting to get into this question game. I didn't buy his answer before, either. A sane person wouldn't one day just decide to pack up and move to a strange place to teach for practically no salary. There was a story there.

"Yes!" I exclaimed as I set the hook on my next fish. Confident in my ability to land it, I started asking as I reeled, "So you used the word *mainly* in your last answer: What other reason made you decide to come to ACI?"

"You're liking my little game, aren't you?" He paused before he asked, "Are you sure you can handle my answer."

"I guess so."

"Are you sure you won't laugh at me?"

"I'll try not to."

He was having a hard time going from kidding to serious as he answered. "Something happened to Mahala, one of my little sisters. After she joined our people in the sky, I saw her in a dream, and she told me to come here."

I wasn't sure if he was messing with me or not. When he didn't crack a smile, I figured he was being serious. "Oh," I said. "I'm sorry." I wasn't sure what to do or how to react. Part of me wanted to know what happened to Mahala, but the part of me that didn't want to know won out.

He didn't say much after that. I caught him looking pensively toward the river. I almost wanted him to catch another fish even though it meant I would have to divulge something else about me. But when I caught the next one—a catfish, my competitive side overruled my sympathetic one.

"Why did I even suggest this game?" He protested but was smiling as he said it.

I decided to let him off easy on this one. "What's your full name?"

"Timothy Dale Zuzeca." He said it fast.

I repeated, "Timothy Dale Zoozetchah?" For some reason, probably my Kentucky accent, his last name gave me trouble. It didn't sound natural coming from my lips.

His bobber went clean out of sight. Excited, he said, "It's a big one. I hope it doesn't break this little pole." It didn't. It was another catfish.

"Be careful taking the fish off your hook. Don't let it stick you with its fin. It's sharp as a needle and actually has venom in it."

"Really? I didn't know that. I guess you would know a lot about venom." This was the first time he'd mentioned anything referring to the snake situation since I'd mentioned it earlier.

77

"No, no. no. You can't trick me into answering a question unless that is your official question," I wasn't going to make things too easy for him.

"Okay. Let me think a minute."

Remembering my new phone, I said, "Here, while you're thinking let me take a picture of you with your fish. I just got it this morning."

I examined him closely through the phone screen. He smiled a big cheesy grin. If someone could have a perfect smile then it was him. His teeth were white, and his entire face lit up. He had a ball cap covering his dark hair. His jeans weren't tight, but the fit only emphasized his long, muscular legs. Just looking at him caused goose bumps to run up and down my arms.

"Take it already before this fish pokes me with its venom."

I was trying to gain composure. "I'm trying. This is my first picture with my phone."

"Was your phone a present?"

"Is that your question?"

He made some kind of guttural sound that was supposed to show his level of frustration. "Can we just stop the game and talk like normal people?"

"You say that because you know I'm much better at fishing then you."

He smiled. I couldn't resist it. He was just so cute that I answered him. "My parents just gave it to me this morning as an early graduation present. Besides my sisters, I think I'm the only student at ACI who doesn't have a phone. Plus, I think Mom's trying to use whatever carrot she can to entice me to go to college in Missouri."

"Missouri. That's a nice state. Are you planning to go there?"

"I'm not sure what I'm gonna do yet."

"Surely with test scores like yours, you're planning to go on to college." He knew he'd made a mistake as soon as he said it.

"What? You looked at my test scores?" I wasn't sure what to think. My mind was trying to come up with a good reason for a gym teacher to be checking my school record.

He tried to make light of it. "Yes. I'm very selective who I fish with so I wanted to make sure you measured up. I'd say a thirty on your ACT score makes you worthy."

I shot him a look to make sure he understood I wasn't amused.

"Lighten up. I reviewed all my students' files. I think it's important for teachers to know their students. But *you* really need to go to college."

"I'd like to go to school but not sure if I want to go that far away from my family. Missouri is a long way from home."

"You just need to go somewhere. You're too smart not to go, Ms. *Obscure* and *Illusive*." He changed the subject. "So back to an earlier question. I'm a little confused. Earlier you mentioned your church and your faith were important to you, but I thought you didn't go to church."

"Even though I don't go to church a lot, my church and my faith are still important to me. They are part of me even if they're a confusing and complicated part of me." That was the best I could do. Then I turned the question on him. "What about you? I thought you had to be a Christian to be a teacher at ACI, but I was reading on the internet about the Sioux and ..."

He stopped me before I could finish my question. "I knew it. You were checking me out online, huh?"

I could feel my face getting hot. Since I had absolutely zero experience in flirting, I wasn't sure how to be playful back. Part of me wanted to take his bait and run with it just to see where it went, but the rational side of me knew better. Using my best voice of sarcasm, I said, "Oh yeah, you big Indian stud. I was checking you out '*fo sho.*'" I watched his expression change. I almost saw disappointment in it. "Actually, I started out looking up fly fishing and then one thing led to another. Now I'm an expert on your people."

"Good luck with that. I've been an Indian all my life, and I'm still not an expert."

"Stop trying to confuse the point. If you don't want to answer then just tell me it's none of my business."

"Hey, it's you who doesn't want to talk about herself. I'm an open book. Go ahead ask away."

"Everything I read about the Sioux showed that that their religion was 'poly-thee-istic' or something like that. It talked about Mother Earth, Father Sky, and The Great Spirit." I stopped when I realized I'd probably just really messed up.

"Ah, *o'waci*, you are very bright."

"What do you keep calling me?" I asked.

"Calm down, it's just a Lakota term of endearment. It means *dancer.*"

"What? I've never danced in my life. Do I really look like a dancer to you?"

"Oh, there's a dance in you. You just have to find it."

I was getting a little tired of all his mysticism, so I asked one more time. "So are you gonna tell me if you're a Christian or not, or do you just want me to drop it?"

"After my *tunkasila* or my grandfather died or as we say, joined his people at the great council fire, my *unchi* remarried a Christian missionary. I'm not sure if you read this in your research or not, but for many years it was illegal for the Sioux to practice our religion. For years after the government stole our land, they attempted to breed our religion out of us. The problem with that is that the Sioux's religion is our way of life." He paused there. I could identify with what he was

...

telling me even though no one had tried to breed the snake handling out of us just yet.

He then explained, "My *unchi* drank the Kool-Aid of Christianity, so to speak. My sisters and I lived with her for a while and had to drink the Kool-Aid too. There are some similarities to the true Christian faith and the Sioux's Way of the Pipe. Only the spirituality of the Sioux is not a religion that we can fit in a nice box."

I couldn't help but say, "Our snakes fit nicely into boxes."

"I bet they do. So to answer your question, I'm as Christian as a Sioux Indian can be. How's that for an answer?"

"I guess it's okay as long as it's okay with the school."

"I understand the teachings of the Bible and of Jesus Christ, and I was even baptized into the church when I was a kid. Somewhere along the way, my beliefs kind of blended. But a few years back, my ancestors called to me wanting me to return to my people's way of the sacred pipe."

I really couldn't comprehend what he was telling me. I couldn't understand anyone ever wanting to turn from Jesus.

"Okay." He can be whatever he wants to be. After all, we're just fishing partners and don't have to be yoked in any way.

"Is everything okay with your mom and dad?"

"Everything seems to be fine since their attorney got the charges dismissed."

Without hesitation, he asked, "Did you quit the church because of some of these deadly practices?"

"Absolutely not," I answered as I gently set the hook. "There is nothing better than to be in one of our services when the Holy Spirit moves and everyone is dancing, singing, and even shouting."

He said, "Sounds like you all smoke the pipe too."

CHAPTER 10

All through high school, Beth, Kelsey, and I sat at the same table for lunch. This year we didn't have many classes together, but luckily it worked out that we could eat lunch with each other. Today something looked awry with my universe when three people, not two, were sitting at our table. And the third person was sitting in *my* seat! The skinny girl with the long, curly hair turned around so I could get a good look at her. I disliked her instantly. I'm certain I've seen her around school, but I didn't know her name. I pulled the extra chair out from the table hard to make sure everyone knew I wasn't happy to be sitting in this seat.

"Les, meet Paige Benton." Beth seemed so happy I was afraid she would bubble over any minute. Evidently, this wasn't a charity case. Beth sometimes got caught up in her do-gooder ways, and Kelsey and I had to pay the price for her generosity.

"Hello." My voice was frigid.

Kelsey said, "Paige is a junior and is in my third period class. She's only been at ACI for a few weeks."

My eyes narrowed slightly when I realized Kelsey was involved in this lunchroom betrayal too—it was a conspiracy.

Paige didn't speak but kept right on eating. She did raise her hand in a slight wave in greeting to me. I knew instantly the reason she was at ACI; she'd been banished to the farm as punishment. More than likely, she'd already been assigned to one of the harder farm projects since tired students don't have a lot of time to be unruly.

Kelsey piped up. "Guess where Paige went to school before coming here."

I narrowed my eyes as I tried to read her mind. "Have no idea."

"Clarksdell High School," Beth said almost reverently.

Then it all began to make sense to me. Paige continued to eat her lunch in silence while my friends filled me in on the significance for her being at our table; she was a Clarksdell source for them.

"Aphrodite's name is Misty Shane and Paige hates her too," Beth explained.

Paige nodded in agreement. She was still eating like it was the best food she'd tasted. I almost expected her to lick her plate. *Yep, with that kind of appetite, she's definitely working on the farm. She's a bad girl.*

Beth pulled out her phone and swiped it a few times with her thumb. "Look, here. I found Misty on Facebook."

At the mention of Facebook, I remembered my new phone. "Oh yeah, look what Mom and Dad got me as an early graduation present."

"Shut up! Leslie Lewis is armed and dangerous with a cell phone. You have officially just raised about three notches on the cool kid list," Kelsey said when she took it from my hand. They all began to program my phone numbers into theirs. Even Paige did. I wasn't sure how I felt about this strange girl having my phone number.

Luckily, neither Kelsey nor Beth perused my new phone's photos. I sure didn't want to explain why a picture of Coach Z with a fish was on my phone. I knew I needed to delete it, but I wasn't ready to just yet. Actually, I'm not sure if I even knew how to delete it.

Paige finally stopped eating and said, "Oh yeah, Misty's going out of town this weekend. She's in some pageant."

Anthony Adams, Beth's prom date passed by our table. He stopped and motioned for Beth to follow him. She did. They spoke for a few minutes then she returned to her seat.

Kelsey said, "Please tell me he didn't want to back out of prom."

Beth was a little more confident in her charm and beauty than to worry about that. As she spoke her head moved from side to side, her eyebrows were raised, and one side of her lip looked like Elvis.

"Are you kidding? He'd be crazy to dump the only bona fide beauty queen in this school."

With not one little crumb left on her plate, Paige inserted herself into our conversation. "You're going to prom with him? He's black."

Beth said, "So?"

"Are your mom and dad okay with it?"

"Yeah. They like Anthony."

Paige said, "Well, in Clarksdell, you could expect to wake up to a burning cross in your front yard." She was referring to the fact that Clarksdell was pretty much an all-white town.

Rather rudely, I said, "Thank goodness we're not in Clarksdell then." After completely dismissing Paige, I asked Beth. "So what did Anthony want?"

"He wanted to know if one of you." She pointed at Kelsey and then at me before saying, "would like to go to prom with his buddy, Scout Weston. You know the point guard."

She first looked at me. "Don't look at me. I told you I'm not going to prom with anyone."

Then she looked to Kelsey. I could tell that Kelsey was pleased, but she didn't want to appear too eager. "Well, I'll have to think about it."

Beth said, "Please go with him, Kels. We can double date. It'll be fun."

Kelsey looked at me. I guess she wanted my approval. "Absolutely. Scout's a nice *white* guy," I said for Paige's benefit. "I promise you I don't want a date. There's not one guy at ACI that I want to have to deal with for three or four hours. I know me. All I would be thinking was how soon I could ditch him, go home, and put on jeans."

Kelsey said, "I bet I know one guy at the school you would go with."

Beth joined her. "Yeah, I bet I know one too."

I telepathically screamed to my friends in my head. *Please don't say it out loud! Please don't say it out loud!* I didn't trust this strange girl sitting in *my* seat. The last thing I wanted was for a troublemaker to know anything about my personal life.

"Coach McDreamy would be a great date," Kelsey said. Evidently, her *ESP* must not have been working on the same channel that I was signaling.

Beth chimed in. "You know, he's been asking some folks about you."

I wanted to die. No, I changed my mind. I didn't want to die—I wanted to hurt my so-called friends. I couldn't believe they were talking about Coach Z in front of *her*. Paige's "troublemaker" meter must've been going off. She was sitting straight up and taking mental notes. I had to say something. "He thinks I'm a good basketball player. His only interest in me is concerning basketball. End of story."

Paige said. "I sure wish Coach McDreamy was interested in me even if it were basketball. Maybe I'll join the team."

Needing to change the subject (and fast) I asked, "So we know for sure that Aphrodite or Misty Shane will be out of the picture this weekend. Does Clarksdell play close by?"

That did it. The conversation went back to a safe topic. My life was complicated enough living with one secret. My new secret fishing partner only complicated matters even more. Maybe it was a good complication. The jury was still out on that.

CHAPTER 11

Commencement services would be held on Saturday, May 16. Prom was on Derby weekend, and the senior trip was two weeks away. Momma was putting pressure on me to make a decision about college. She'd submitted my applications to Ozark Christian College, Lee University in Cleveland, Tennessee, and the University of the Cumberlands in nearby Williamsburg since that was where both Beth and Kelsey planned to attend. I'd been accepted into all three schools.

For some reason, I couldn't let myself plan on anything after graduation. My guidance counselor said it's common. She said that graduating from high school is a big step, and deciding what to do afterwards, is one of the biggest decisions I will ever make. So, for now, I've decided to finish high school before I make plans about my future. At this very moment, I'm satisfied with the way things are going.

The other day at school, Coach Z actually came and sat down with me on the bleachers while I was changing shoes. I noticed several of my classmates watching us. I'm sure most of the girls probably hated my guts.

Our conversations always started in code about the weather. "Rain in the morning, but should clear up by eleven or so," he informed me.

"Rain's not always a bad thing," I told him. "Sometimes rain brings the fish to the surface."

"But, sometimes it drives them deeper," he said. I was sure there was hidden meaning in what he was saying, but it was lost on me.

"Hey, I've got an idea. Do you have any hiking boots?" I asked.

"Didn't you know hiking boots are a *prerequisite* for being part of the tribe?"

"So, they took the place of moccasins?"

"They're deer skinned and double for both."

It was a very lame attempt at humor, and I made sure the look on my face told him my feelings. "By the way, you need to move on and find a new word. I'm already over *prerequisite*."

He rolled his eyes before he said, "I'll have to get the dictionary back out."

I said, "Forget the dictionary. If you want to fish with me, then park behind the red barn you pass right before the usual parking place. I'll pick you up there."

"You think I'm riding with you in that old truck of yours?"

"If you want to catch some monsters, you will."

He gave me a sheepish grin. "What time?"

"Nine thirty." I added, "Don't be late."

"The bells don't ring on weekends, you know." Then that was it. He was back to being my teacher. He blew his whistle, and we all lined up to start calisthenics. As we ran around the gym, Sadie, one of the most brazen of the girls in my class, sidled up to me and said, "How do you do it?"

"Do what?"

"How do you get Coach Z to talk to you like that?"

I feigned ignorance. "What are you talking about?"

"I've tried and tried every topic known to man to get him to talk to me. He won't give me the time of day," she explained.

"Maybe you should consider trying out for the school's basketball team."

Our words were both beginning to slow down as we rounded the last lap. "I don't think it's all about basketball as you say. Did you know he looks at you when he thinks you're not looking?" she asked. "Actually, you are kind of pretty in a weird, exotic kind of way."

I wasn't sure if she paid me a compliment or an insult. It didn't matter. I just kept thinking about her saying that he looked at me when I wasn't looking. I already knew it because I'd felt his eyes on me, but it was nice to know I wasn't imagining it. It made me happy clear down to my toes. On the other hand, it scared me a tad too.

The next day, I was relieved when I saw only Beth and Kelsey at our table. Then I saw Paige in line with her overloaded tray. I gave her a break yesterday but not today. I rushed to the table before she was seated and explained, "Sorry, Paige, but can you sit over there." I motioned to the seat on the other side of the table. "I've eaten at this same seat for three years. I feel weird sitting anywhere else."

Defiance was written all over her face. She started to ignore my request, but I guess after she thought it over, she had a change of heart. I was pretty sure I'd made an enemy. I had a bad feeling about her. She was trouble; of that I was certain.

Paige played her trump card when she turned to Beth and said, "I found out Clarksdell plays in Laurel County on Saturday at five."

Beth said, "Perfect. Thanks, Paige."

Ordinarily we would've made our plans to go to the game while sitting at the table, but today we didn't. Beth was probably afraid I'd make a scene or something.

Paige again spoke up, but this time she addressed me. "You know everyone is talking about how Coach Z has a thing for you, don't you?"

"Why would anyone say that?" I tried to sound very irritated.

"Someone said he's always talking to you and looking at you in gym class."

Beth added, "I told you he's been asking people questions about you."

"Good grief." I tried my best to blow it off. "That's ridiculous. He's my teacher. I talk to all my teachers. Besides, I think he has a girlfriend."

Girlfriend. Why did the very thoughts of this cause me to become nauseous?

CHAPTER 12

Perry went with Dad and me on Saturday morning to finish a job.
The client wanted a mosaic using very small tiles in varying shapes
and colors. She wanted a large sunflower design in the center of the
floor. The rest of the floor would be larger slabs of black porcelain.

While lying on our bellies, Perry and I worked the tiles just like
we were piecing together a jigsaw puzzle. It took us five hours, but it
turned out beautifully. The client was thrilled. Dad would finish up
the rest of the floor on Monday. Perry entertained us all day long by
telling crazy stories.

I was allowed to skip supper tonight with the Seeleys and instead
go with Beth to the ballgame. Kelsey's mother was coming to visit
so she couldn't go with us. She only came a couple of times each
semester. Kelsey was excited to see her mom but usually wasn't sorry
to see her leave.

Dad was cautiously optimistic about supper with the Seeleys tonight. He hoped to finally be able to call a truce and form some kind of alliance with Brother Seeley instead of having him as an adversary. I still didn't trust the man and didn't want to be around him. My sisters were ecstatic, and Momma didn't mind the extra work since she always prepared a large meal on Saturday nights anyway. If it helped improve the relationship between Dad and Brother Seeley, then she would cook all night. Even though she didn't say it, I think Laurel was secretly happy I would be out of the picture tonight. She didn't want to compete with me for Joseph's attention even if it was on the basketball court.

Beth picked me up at four. It was rather chilly so I dressed for the occasion. Plus, I brought a big blanket. Beth had taken a lot of pains with her appearance. Even though she was dressed warmly, she was cute as a button in her fleece pullover. We sat with the North Laurel fans directly behind the plate. We were in luck. It looked like the Clarksdell goddesses were supporting Aphrodite at the pageant and weren't at the game.

I could tell when Henry spotted Beth. His eyes lit up, and he waved like he was happy to see her while warming up in the batter's box. She hollered, "Hit me a homerun!" A few of the home team fans didn't like that we were cheering against them. The ones directly behind us gave us an ultimatum to either go to the visitor's side or to sit there quietly. We felt the second option was the best one.

When Henry actually pulled a ball toward left field, we both watched in anticipation as it sailed over the fence. As he headed toward home plate, he saw no one but Beth Rudder. I saw him mouth to her, "That was for you." The fans on the visitors side couldn't see his face so they had no idea that anything of significance just took place—but it did.

After the game, I knew she wanted to stick around to get a chance to talk with him, but she didn't. "That would look too desperate," she said as we headed to her car. We heard the clicking sound that cleats make when they meet the blacktop coming up fast from behind.

"Wait!" Henry cried out.

We both froze in place at the sound of Henry's voice. I could definitely understand why Beth was so infatuated with him. He was really tall, and he filled out his baseball uniform nicely. His face was flawless, and his smile was sincere. His hat covered up most of the curls, but the escaping blond tendrils curled around the rim of the hat. This was the first time I'd ever seen him close up so I paid attention to every detail. Taking mental notes, I would be prepared for Beth's questions as we analyzed this meeting on the way home.

"Hey, I wanted to say thanks for coming to my game." I knew he was saying this to Beth, but he made me feel like he was just as grateful for me being there.

"Thanks for the homerun," she calmly stated. Her tone wasn't flirty or flippant; it was confident and almost seductive.

"Don't thank me. You were the one who inspired it." His tone matched hers.

"Henry, meet my best friend …"

When I realized she'd possibly forgotten my name, I stepped in. "Hi, Henry, I'm Les."

His big hand swallowed mine. "Nice to meet you, Les. Thanks for coming with Beth to my game."

"My pleasure."

"We better get going," Beth explained. "I don't want to get you in trouble with your *girlfriend*."

He lowered his head in embarrassment and kicked at a rock on the asphalt. "I'm sorry about the way she treated you. I heard she wasn't nice to you the other night. She's a little on the jealous side."

"No problem. I'd probably feel the same way she did. I just enjoy watching you play ball. As you know, I'm a *big* fan of yours." As she started to walk away, she said, "I hope to see you hit more homeruns soon, but I really have to go."

Beth turned around to walk on to her car. After she walked a few steps, he said, "Could we meet up somewhere in a couple of hours?" I could hear the desperation in his voice.

Beth took a piece of paper out of her purse and wrote her phone number on it. She placed the paper in his hand and actually let her hand linger there for several seconds. "Henry, give me a call when you and your girlfriend break-up. Until then, I'm not interested." The smile never left her face. She wasn't angry. She only stated facts.

Who is this girl? I could tell she made an impact on the Greek God. He was spellbound and speechless.

I'm not sure if it was my prophetic gifting or not, but I knew right then and there Beth hadn't seen the last of her Adonis.

We stopped and got a milkshake from Steak 'n Shake before we headed toward home. I was in luck. I had barely missed the Seeleys. Perry met me at the door and began to give me a play by play of all that happened tonight. Laurel walked past me without saying a word—which was odd for her. I assumed it was because her head was so far up in the clouds because of Joseph's attention that she didn't even notice me.

Before now, I'd never really worried about Joseph and Laurel because he seemed so indifferent to her. This change in events had me concerned. Laurel was so vulnerable. Part of me wanted to demand that my parents put a stop to these Saturday dinners. I was sorry that Sister Seeley was dead, but the Seeleys could learn to cook for themselves. Nothing good could come of this relationship. Of that I was certain.

CHAPTER 13

When I saw the red barn up ahead, I looked to see if I could see any signs of Coach Z's truck from the road. I couldn't. That didn't mean he hadn't arrived yet because the barn was big enough to hide twenty or more trucks behind it. That's the reason I suggested it—though more for his protection than for mine. Although our Sunday morning fishing outings had been completely aboveboard and innocent, it would be hard to prove. Travel on this back road was limited mainly to the mailman and the other residents living along the way. I realized the risk of someone recognizing his truck and becoming suspicious was pretty farfetched, but I still thought it best to err on the prudent side. *I wonder what made Coach Z drive out this way in the first place. I need to remember to ask him that.*

As I drove around the barn, I prepared myself for the possibility of him not showing up. My worry was short-lived. He was there waiting for me. His black truck looked as though it had been freshly washed; the rain had a way of making everything look better.

The rain stopped an hour ago, which was earlier than Coach Z's original forecast. It made for a muddy hike, but hopefully the path up to the waterfall wouldn't be too slippery. I watched him as he removed his large body from the cab of his truck. He was just over six foot tall and lean in an athletic kind of way, but I wouldn't necessarily consider him chiseled. He was dressed in one of his many sweat suits (his gym teacher's uniform). He wore a black rain jacket overtop his sweats. As usual, his hair and face looked freshly scrubbed.

I couldn't help but compare him to Henry Noble. Granted, Henry was a good-looking guy, but to me, Coach Z was even better looking than the chiseled football god. Or maybe he was just more my type, if I actually had a type. "Hello," I called out my window. "Glad you didn't miss the bell."

"Haven't you heard, my little *o'waci* that Indians are always on time," he answered as he opened the passenger side door and slid in. "Take me to meet these monster fish you told me about."

I drove up the road a piece until I came to the fork then followed the road to the left. After I drove another mile, I found a parking spot on the widest part of the roadside. "Here we are." I used my phone to check the time. "It'll take us a good thirty minutes to make it to the falls."

We both wore backpacks. My fishing pole was attached to the side of mine using built-in Velcro straps. Coach Z carried the pink pole. The trail leading to the falls was wide and well-traveled. The air was fresh and fragrant and had brought a renewing to the greenery on both sides of the path. It enhanced the smell of springtime— a combination of freshly-bloomed honeysuckles, mountain laurel, and wild rhododendrons. It was Kentucky at its finest.

We walked along the dense trail in silence. Finally, Coach Z, in an almost reverent whisper, said, "This is what Daniel Boone must've felt like."

For some reason, this struck me funny, and I began to laugh. Not just a little laugh, but a body-shaking-let-everything-go kind of cleansing laugh. It was contagious.

After we walked a few more steps, he said, "Leslie Lewis, every time I think I have you half-way figured out then you do something completely out of character. Your laugh is adorable."

Feeling a little brazen, I said, "Coach Timothy Dale Zuzeca, you can know me a hundred years and never have me figured out."

"Is that so? Are you telling me you are some kind of mythical creature or something?"

"Au contraire. I'm freakishly ordinary. Just think of me as Leslie Lewis, one of your gym students who likes to fish and just happens to be the daughter of a snake-handling, Holiness preacher."

He stopped walking and turned so he was directly facing me. He put his large, warm hands on the sides of my face so that I was looking directly into his eyes. I swallowed hard and fought back the fluttering deep inside as I waited to see what was about to happen. He said, "Les, I want you to remember something. What your parents do or don't do, *does not* define who *you* are. Do you understand me?"

At this point, no sound would come out of my mouth. I only nodded in understanding. I never wanted him to let go. But he did. Just as though nothing had happened, he resumed walking. Only something did happen. Something magical. Something touched me all the way to my soul. I knew I'd never be the same. Yet as he walked ahead, he seemed oblivious to what he'd unleashed within me.

"Come on, pokey," he hollered. "I can hear the fish calling for us."

I tried my best to get a handle on myself and the situation, but the change in me was drastic, like receiving sight after being blind. Even the green of the foliage was a deeper, vibrant, more-exaggerated color than only minutes before. I shook my head trying to get ahold of myself. These feelings were unnerving.

For the rest of the walk, our conversation consisted of idle chitchat until we saw the waterfall. Actually, we heard it before we saw it. The water was forcefully tumbling off the twenty foot falls into the green pool below. Other than the churning of the falls, the rest of the picture could be described as serene. We were surrounded by a semicircle of foliage-lined cliffs opening up to the secret waterhole. Regardless of how many times I'd been to the Little Mallard Falls, I was still in awe of its beauty.

"Daniel Boone, Crazy Horse, and Geronimo!" he yelled.

It was enough to pull me out of my lovesick trance and cause me to laugh once again.

He pulled a couple of bottled waters and some deer jerky out of his backpack. "They were out of apple juice so I had to get water," he joked. "Here try this," he said as he handed me some of the jerky. "I made it myself."

I smelled it before I guardedly put some in my mouth. "Not bad," I mumbled.

Now that several questions were out of the way, we both seemed more at ease around each other. We were able to fish in comfortable silence. He and Perry's pink pole got the first bite. It was a nice largemouth—probably weighed a couple of pounds.

Today, he seemed ready to talk more about his sisters. Their names were Stephanie, Mahala, and Mackenzie. He didn't give me the details, but Mahala took her own life only months before he came to Kentucky. She was fifteen.

He talked a lot about his mother and grandmother, but I gathered his dad was either dead or absent from his life. He loved living on the reservation or the *rez* as he called it. At the same time, he hated it too. He said it was a hard life.

It turned out to be a lovely afternoon. We caught a total of twenty-some fish. Then we heard them. Intruders. We looked at each other to determine if we should take the chance of being seen together. I knew what he was thinking without him speaking. We both started reeling in our lines without any discussion. We quietly gathered up our belongings, and thanks to the wet forest floor, our getaway was a quiet one. Our homeward descent was quicker, but navigation around the steep places was a little trickier.

I smelled it before I saw it stretched out along the rocks. Snakes have their own odor. The black king snake was not interested in moving to allow us to pass. We would have to either go around or go over it. He flicked his tongue at us almost in challenge. Out of instinct, I started to pick it up but was afraid it would freak Coach Z out.

While I was contemplating what to do, Coach Z gently reached down and picked up the snake. He held it gently yet securely while he examined it. "He's a beauty, isn't he? See the glossy shine?" he asked.

I came near him and let him transfer the snake over to my hands. I answered him. "The glossy shine is what distinguishes the black king snake from the rat snake. Right?" This snake seemed comfortable and not at all tense or anxious. I then gently released it back to its original resting place.

The look on his face was a mixture of satisfaction and intrigue. "I guess you really are the snake handler's daughter, aren't you?"

"What happened to your speech about being my own person and all? Cause that's just how it is; I will always be his daughter."

"What would you've done if the snake were poisonous?"

"You really want to know?" I asked.

He nodded his head. "Yes."

"I would've put it in my backpack and taken it home with me."

He threw his head back and laughed deep and loud. "Little *o'waci*, you are one of a kind."

When we reached my vehicle, I said, "Coach Z."

He stopped me. "Just call me Z. By the way, do you know what Zuzeca means in Lakota?"

"No." It hadn't even dawned on me that his name had a meaning.

"Snake," he said. "Zuzeca means snake in the Lakota language."

"This is weird. Your name means snake and my family handles snakes. I guess that's the reason I can so easily manhandle you when we fish," I teased. The significance of what he just said wasn't lost on me but kidding was easier.

"That's gotta be it."

As he was heading toward his truck, he called out, "I won't be in town next Sunday. You'll be on your own."

I already missed him.

CHAPTER 14

On the ride to school in the church van on Monday, Laurel and I said very little during the twenty-minute ride. Even Momma asked me a couple of times if something was wrong. If I didn't have to turn in my permission slip for the senior trip, I would've stayed home today. I just knew everyone was going to take one look at me and know something was different. I was no longer capable of camouflaging my soul with britches and a ponytail.

My phone vibrated. I almost jumped out of my skin. After I realized where the vibration was coming from, I looked at the screen on my phone. Beth's text said. *Come to the restroom.* When I saw Paige seated in the foyer alone, I knew the reason they were hiding out in the bathroom.

"Hey!" Paige called out like we were best friends.

I said, "Hello," but kept on walking. I didn't want to give her any encouragement to follow me.

Kelsey and Beth were sitting on the bench in the ladies room when I arrived. As soon as I walked through the door, Beth ordered, "Tell her about Henry." I'm sure she wanted me to tell it so she could relive it.

I placed my arm around Beth. "Our friend here is quite the player. She was so smooth. Kelsey, you would've been so proud of her. She had Adonis eating out of her hand."

Kelsey looked up at me like she was seeing me for the first time. "Do you have makeup on?" she asked.

I actually laughed before I answered, "Are you out of your mind? I've never worn makeup in my life. Why in the world would I start now?"

Kelsey shrugged her shoulders. "I don't know. You just look a little different."

I knew it! Evidently, I am an open book. Just one look and even Kelsey knew something was different about me. She just didn't realize it was because I was unofficially in love or lust or something with Z.

Beth didn't look up. She was so engrossed in the conversation about Henry Noble, she probably wouldn't have noticed if a tornado touched down. "Les, tell her what I said when he asked if we could meet up."

I acted it out as I spoke. "She walked right up to Henry and gave him a piece of paper with her phone number on it and said …" I used my best exaggerated impression of Beth. "Call me if you break up with your girlfriend."

Kelsey put her hand over her mouth. "Oh, wow! What did he have to say to that?"

"What could he say? I give him three weeks before he calls her."

The door opened and there stood Paige. She was mad, but she tried hard not to let it show. "Are you guys having a private meeting?" she asked. "Or can anyone join?"

As sweetly as I could speak, I said, "The meeting is over. Come on in. You can have *my* seat. I'm just leaving."

I had ten minutes before the first bell. I wanted to see Z, but it was getting harder and harder for me to conceal the way I felt. I knew he was my teacher and a good six years older than me or actually five years and six months. My parents would never agree for me to date someone who was a heathen, even if he had been baptized when he was young. When I was in the sixth grade, he was graduating from high school. Plus he may have or may not have a girlfriend. We've yet to broach that topic. Not to mention that he is probably just interested in having a fishing buddy.

When I entered the gymnasium, there were a few guys shooting balls on the far end of the court. Z was standing near the dressing room entrance. It was unavoidable; I had to walk right past him. I lightly punched him in the upper arm when I passed by.

"Hey, snake handler," he greeted me in a low voice.

"What happened to me being the dancer? Oh-watch-ee or whatever you keep calling me is actually growing on me." I really wanted to ask why he couldn't fish next Sunday, but part of me didn't want to know. Since spring break would begin next weekend then it was possible he was traveling back home.

When Sadie or Ms. Weird and Exotic as I had started referring to her in my mind, tried to get next to me, I tried to move inconspicuously so I didn't have to talk to her. It worked until we had to run around the gym.

"Guess what I heard," she said to me as she struggled to keep at my fast pace.

"I'm not a mind reader, Sadie," I told her. "If you've got something to say, then just spit it out."

"Word is that Coach Z has a girlfriend. He even has a picture of her in his room. He told Mr. Williams that he would be seeing her over spring break. Mr. Williams told his wife, who told my cousin, who told me."

I tried to put on my bravest face on even though my heart officially broke in two.

CHAPTER 15

Beth came over to my house to help me pack for the trip to the country music capitol, insisting I had to up my game. My wardrobe consisted mainly of non-hipster style work jeans and outdated Pentecostal ware. She enlisted my sisters and Kelsey (via Facetime) on her mission. I would try on clothes, and they would give it a thumbs up or a thumbs down. Mostly thumbs down. I'd been trying on clothes for what seemed like hours and packed only one pair of pants and a shirt in my suitcase.

Finally an exasperated Beth said, "Enough. Cough up about two hundred dollars, and I'm going to go buy you some new clothes."

I really did start coughing. "Two hundred dollars. No way. My clothes are just fine. Right, Perry?" I asked her since I knew she would agree with me.

"Les, you just need to do what she says. Even your jeans are starting to look a little ratty." The little traitor.

Laurel agreed. "You're gonna need new clothes for graduation and for college anyway."

"Yeah, Les. Quit being so weird," Whitley chimed in.

Beth could be a tyrant; all five foot nothing of her. "Just go out in the yard, Les, and dig up one of your hundreds of coffee cans and get me some money." Her hand was on her cocked hip. I knew I was outnumbered.

I didn't bury my money like Beth accused me, but I did have stashes. I pulled out my sock drawer and had over a hundred and fifty dollars there. I had fifty dollars in my pocket. I handed the money over like a whipped pup.

"Thank you," she chirped victoriously.

"Now Beth, you know me. Don't go buy anything all flashy. No flowers or ruffles. Got it?"

She answered, "You can always go with me so you can try things on."

"I'll go too," Laurel volunteered.

Whitley said, "Me too."

Perry watched me to see how I would respond before she volunteered to go or not.

I contemplated going, but it was only a short few seconds before my good sense kicked in. After all, Beth couldn't do too much damage with only two hundred dollars. "Nah. Dad needs me to work on the fence. I trust you. Just no frilly stuff. Got it?"

"Got it. You can wear your jeans on the ride down on Wednesday and back on Saturday. You'll need to be comfortable. So that just leaves Thursday and Friday. Oh. Let me see your shoes."

Laurel said, "She wears the same size as me, so she's welcome to wear any of mine."

"Laurel, let's check out your closet." Beth looked at me with a mischievous grin hoping to irritate me before saying, "You have much better taste than your sister." Whitley and Laurel followed Beth like she was the pied piper while Perry and I just hung out in my room.

"You aren't mad at me, are you?" Perry sheepishly asked.

"Why? Just because you turned traitor on me."

Shrugging her shoulders, she answered, "I don't know. You've just been different lately."

I pulled her close and gave her a quick hug. "Next to Jesus, you're my very best friend," I said to her before I began tickling her unmercifully.

"I love you so much, Les," she said when she was finally able to talk.

"Love you too."

CHAPTER 16

All in all, the week had been uneventful. Everyone was busy preparing for spring break and the senior trip. I have to admit, the arrival of my prom dress eclipsed the excitement of everything else. It was every bit as lovely and elegant in real life as it was in the magazine picture—maybe even prettier. The sheer sleeves on the dress provided just a hint of skin. The V-shaped neckline didn't plunge but revealed a modest amount of my "décolletage" (as my momma calls it). The bodice material included elastic and would provide just the right amount of structure and support. Yards of pleated black, shiny fabric completed the full skirt. It hung on the door of my closet where I would look at it often too often. I was in love with the dress. Only there was a problem; I couldn't bring myself to try it on.

It wasn't because I was being stubborn; it ran much deeper than that. Maybe it made me remember the Leslie Lewis of old—the naïve girl before my secret sin made me into the weird person I am today. I just knew I wasn't ready to see myself in it. Not yet, anyway. When I try it on, I need the conditions to be just right. I want to look my very best. I want to attempt to be the Leslie of old—the Leslie who used to like purple, picnics, and glitter.

I had no qualms about modeling the two new outfits Beth picked out for me for the trip. I probably would've never chosen them for myself, but they were tolerable. I did draw the line about wearing the bright red scarf she bought. Much too showy for me. I ended up giving it to Whitley. She was thrilled.

Paige Benton joined us for lunch on Monday, Tuesday and Wednesday. After she was through with devouring the food on her tray, she seemed to devour every word we said. I tried to ignore her as much as possible. I think Kelsey felt the same way I did even though she wasn't vocal about it. Since Kelsey lived in the school's dormitory, she'd learned the importance of being able to judge character. The troubled kids who came were often expert manipulators and con artists. All it took was a couple of bad experiences for her to be wary of newcomers in general. She only trusted Beth and me. Beth, on the other hand, wasn't ready to cut the ties with Paige completely since she was her only inroad to Clarksdell and Henry Noble. However, she wasn't ready to welcome her into her bosom of trust either.

It took a few days, but Paige finally got the hint and moved on. On Thursday, she began sitting with my gym classmate, Sadie, who in my opinion was a little too interested in Coach Z. I wasn't interested in having Paige and Sadie as my friends, but I didn't want them as enemies either. Somehow, I think it was too late.

I noticed out of the corner of my eye that Sadie and Paige kept looking over at our table. It was obvious that we were the topic of their conversation. After that, Sadie watched me like a hawk during the entire gym class. Like vultures, they kept circling knowing sooner or later someone was going to slip up; when that happened, they planned on being there.

I caught myself being distracted a lot during my classes. All it took was seeing the letter "Z," and I was a goner. The letter now had a new meaning for me. At school, I called him Coach Z, but I liked that he told me to call him Z. It differentiated me from the other students. Not calling him coach put us on a level playing field. On Sundays, we were equals.

Something was definitely up with Z. He seemed to be pushing me away. Ordinarily, we talked very little during the school week, but this week it was even less. I knew it was for the best. Being secret fishing buddies would have to be enough. I was sad on Friday that he didn't offer up forecast information or a Lakota endearment. Nothing. I was just another one of his gym students.

I moped around a little over the weekend, when Monday rolled around I was starting to look forward to our trip to Nashville. With the uncertainty of our futures, it would be a good opportunity to make memories with my best friends.

The three of us would be sharing a room. Most of the other rooms had four in it. Having my mother as a member of the faculty had its advantages. She was able to pull a few strings so that it would be just the three of us rooming together.

On Sunday, I received an anonymous text. *Catch a big one for me.* I didn't respond. I didn't recognize the phone number, but I felt fairly certain it was from Z. None of my other friends would've given a hoot whether I caught a big one or not. I only had one problem; I couldn't remember giving him my phone number. I couldn't bring myself to go fishing alone on Sunday; instead, Perry and I fished at the river on Monday, the beginning of our spring break.

Perry alternated from being talkative to being absorbed in her thoughts. At one point, she said, "Les, are you really going to go away to college?"

"I'm not sure," I answered truthfully. "I'm not going to make a decision until after I graduate."

"I really don't want you to go. I don't know what I'll do without you. Is it wrong that I prayed that God wouldn't let you go away?" Her voice quivered a little.

I wasn't sure how to respond so I summoned up past father-daughter talks. I tried to think of how Dad would explain it. "It's okay to talk to God about anything. He cares about your feelings and concerns no matter how big or small. But remember that Dad always says to be careful what you pray for … because you just may get it."

"What does that mean?"

"What if God answers your prayers through making me too sick to go away to school? I don't want to be sick."

Her eyes big and her voice loud, she said, "Les, I don't want you to be sick either. I just can't stand the thought of you not being here. When you're gone, I don't have anyone to talk to or fish with or anything."

"Sure you do. You've always got Whitley and Laurel. Plus you'll be busy helping dad with the snakes and the farm work."

"All the curling iron queens want to talk about is hair care, skin products, and the Seeley boys. I'd rather just as soon talk to the cows and horses than have to listen to all their nonsense." She paused while her little brain was turning. "Do you really think Daddy will let me do all the things he lets you do with the snakes?"

"He will probably do you just like he did me. He will start training you. Just remember, taking care of the snakes is not a game. One mistake could cost you your hand or even your life," I cautioned her.

"Don't worry about me. I'm planning on staying pure at heart. Even if one bit me, no harm would come to me. I'd be just like Sister Sizemore at church. When that big old cottonmouth bit her in the face, she didn't even quit praising and singing. Her face didn't even swell ..." she stopped midsentence when her bobber went under. "It's a big one, Les! Help me!"

Her pink pole was bent almost double. I thought it would break. She worked nearly ten minutes just to get the fish to the bank. I stood at the edge of the water so I could help pull it out.

"Can you see it? It feels like it weighs a ton!" Perry yelled to me even though I was only a few feet away.

I was amazed that the line didn't snap. She insisted I take a picture of her with the catfish that was nearly as big as she was.

"Let me see the picture!"

My heart leapt in my chest when I realized I still had never deleted Z's photo. Thankfully, she was content with letting me hold the phone while she looked at it. "I still can't believe it. I bet that fish is a state record."

After the excitement of the big fish wore off, she was hungry and ready to go to the house. "I bet since Momma's not working today, she'll have a big dinner waiting on us."

When we left to go fishing, Momma had papers strewn all over the kitchen table. She was trying to get income taxes ready to file.

She was so caught up in the numbers earlier that I doubt she even heard us when we left. "If not, I'll fix us something." I told her as I gathered up our belongings.

On the drive home, Perry turned to me and asked, "Would it be wrong if I asked God to make you just sick enough so you couldn't go away to school, something like chicken pox or a stomach bug?"

CHAPTER 17

It took me a whopping fifteen minutes to pack Tuesday evening. Every time I spoke to Beth this week, she was either packing or making lists about packing. She'd created a list which included everything I needed to bring right down to my underwear and deodorant. Since she'd shopped for me, she felt like she was my self-appointed stylist. One time she called just to make sure I packed the right shoes. "Don't forget to bring Laurel's black wedges so you can wear them with the black pants and the red sweater Friday night to the Grand Ole Opry. I think you'll need the extra height, or the pants will be too long." After her fifth wardrobe-related call, I quit answering.

Since I had to be at school so early on Wednesday morning to catch the bus for our trip, Dad volunteered to drive me. I loved spending time with my dad. On the drive over, we talked about the trip. He told me about preaching a revival close to Nashville, and how a woman who never played the piano in her life got filled with the spirit and could play like she was Jerry Lee Lewis (whoever he was.)

"Dad?"

"Yes, baby girl."

"Can we quit having the Seeleys over to our house?"

He didn't immediately answer. I could tell he was mulling it over in his head. "Has something happened?"

I shook my head while saying, "No. I just don't have a good feeling about it."

He turned to look at me. I think he needed to see my face in order to determine if there was something I was leaving out. After he looked back to the road, he said, "I don't think we can get out of it this week, but I'll talk to Ruth about it. You know those girls will have them a fit."

The silence in the truck for the rest of the ride was too quiet. Instead of wasting any more time on the Seeleys, I started going through a checklist in my mind to determine if I'd forgotten anything Beth had on my list.

Dad carried the family suitcase over to the bus and set it down. It was one of those without wheels or the popup handle. My dad hugged me tightly. Both of us wiped our eyes after the embrace. Dad was so tenderhearted. This was the first time I'd spent more than a couple of nights away from my family.

"Here," he said as he handed me a wad of cash.

I didn't know if this was a trick or what. In our family, money was never given but was earned. "I've got enough," I told him.

"Take it," he ordered. "It's not a lot, but I want you to have it in case you have an emergency. Remember, you can always save what you don't spend and use it for college." I watched him get in his truck and drive off before I headed to the bus. I was one of the first students to arrive.

When I looked in the bus, the air caught in my chest. There in his official P.E. teacher outfit stood Z. "Good morning, little *o'waci,*" he said with a cheeky smile.

I was thoroughly confused. I just assumed he'd left town when he couldn't fish on Sunday. "What? Are you going to Nashville with us?"

"Yep. The bus driver canceled, and since I have my CDL, I was volunteered."

I didn't know whether to be excited or upset. It was going to make the trip interesting if nothing else.

"Were the fish biting?"

"I didn't go Sunday, but Perry and I went on Monday. You should've seen the catfish Perry caught. I thought the pink pole was done for."

"Hrrmmp." Someone cleared their throat directly behind me. It was Beth. I wasn't sure how long she'd been there or what she'd heard. I'd been so excited to see Z that I had become oblivious to the rest of the world.

"Hey, Beth," I said. "Do you know Coach Z?"

"Hello, Beth," Z said on cue.

"Hello, Coach Z," Beth answered rather formally.

"He's driving the bus," I explained while mentally reviewing if I'd said anything to incriminate myself.

Beth and I turned around at the same time when we heard Kelsey calling for us. She ran straight to us full of energy, "I'm so excited. We are going to have the best time!" Then she noticed Z and stopped talking. The excited schoolgirl was now cool and collected. "Hello, Coach Zuzeca."

He reached for her bag. "Hello." He turned around and started piling our luggage under the bus. As soon as he wasn't facing us, Beth mouthed to me, "Les, what the heck's going on?"

I just shrugged. Now was not the time to talk about this. Thankfully, I was saved by Mr. Patton's loud, monotone voice. He was our class sponsor.

After Mr. Patton went over all the rules, we boarded the school bus. Beth and I took a seat on the right side. Kelsey sat directly in front of us. It wasn't long before Kelsey had a seatmate. Scout Weston seemed all smiles when he realized her seat was open.

As soon as the bus started rolling, Beth said, "I now see what everyone has been talking about."

"What?"

"Coach Zuzeca is different to you. He dismissed me like I was stale bread or something. Every teacher loves me. I'm completely adorable, right?"

"Absolutely."

"Coach Z wanted to talk to you but didn't even ask me about the weather. What am I? Chopped liver."

"It's pretty simple. I'm his student and you're not. Plus he likes to talk about fishing."

Still upset by the slight, Beth said, "Well, I've been fishing a time or two myself. Plus, I didn't see him talking to any of his other students. Les, you've got to admit there's some chemistry there."

I just waved her off and changed the topic to Henry Noble. It worked like a charm. She forgot all about Z, his slight, and the chemistry.

The trip from ACI to Nashville was a long four and a half hours even without stops. It would take us most of the day because Mr. Patton planned several educational stops along the way, including one in Bowling Green, Kentucky, to see the National Corvette Museum.

Many of the students were obsessed about cars and trucks. I just didn't get it. I was perfectly content driving the work truck. The truck Dad drove was fairly new. My mom drove the church van. We called it the church van, but we paid every payment on it. The fact we used it personally had been a source of contention with Brother Seeley and the other elders until Dad showed them the title and the payment receipts. He even showed them where he'd sold the old van, and the church got all the proceeds for it. So, technically the van was ours. We just kept the church sign on it as a form of witness. I hated to think what would happen to the church without my dad. He was by far the church's largest contributor. When he got blessed, then the church got blessed too.

We stopped at McDonald's on the way so we could eat breakfast. Shortly after the bus came to a stop and my classmates started rolling out, I felt my phone begin to vibrate. Thanks to all the messages Beth had sent me in the last few days, I was almost used to the pulsating of the phone on my leg. I had a message from that same number that had texted me on Sunday when I was fishing. The message was one word. *O'waci.*

I looked up to the big mirror overtop of the driver's seat. He was looking directly at me. I smiled at him to acknowledge the text but quickly looked away so Beth wouldn't become suspicious. He definitely had my number—in more ways than one.

Kelsey and Scout seemed to be hitting it off. She even sat with him at McDonald's. I could tell I was spoiling Anthony's plans of hanging out with Beth. Beth didn't seem to mind. Her mind was so full of Henry Noble that she didn't have room for anyone else. She'd made a couple of fictitious Facebook accounts and through them she was able to monitor the comings and goings of both Misty Shane and Henry Noble without anyone being the wiser. This was all the Clarksdell connection she needed.

Using her phone, we looked at every picture Misty Shane had on her account. She was the queen of selfies; there had to be a hundred or more photos. She must've felt especially pretty when she had her lips puckered. There was a bunch of those big-lipped ones. Beth really hated the ones with Aphrodite and Adonis together—especially the happy ones. It was amazing how much we learned about them through Facebook. No wonder my parents didn't want us girls to get caught up in social media.

The Gaylord Opryland Hotel was mind blowing for many of us Kentucky kids who weren't well-traveled. Kelsey wasn't nearly as awestruck as Beth and I were; she was too preoccupied with Scout to care one way or another.

Kelsey told us some of her and Scout's conversations, but I could tell she was leaving out a bunch. Beth tried to get her to open up more, but Kelsey didn't take the bait. I silently applauded her. Talking about things sometimes reduces them to nothing but words.

The next two days were filled with parks, the replica of the Parthenon, and country music. Mr. Patton made sure everything we did had an educational value to it. Coach Z stayed around the other teachers most of the time. He would occasionally text me a few one or two word messages. He went missing on Friday. He wasn't at breakfast. He didn't go on the tours. It was like he vanished. I couldn't very well ask anyone about his whereabouts either. So I just kept my eyes peeled for any sign of him.

Beth couldn't wait to go to the Ryman Auditorium to watch the Grand Ole Opry live, but it wasn't for the entertainment. She could take or leave the country music. She just couldn't wait to see me all dressed up in my new outfit. She thought I was going to give her free reign to do whatever she wanted with my hair too, but I had other plans.

We were all to meet in the lobby by five. I was grateful Beth had insisted I have new clothes. I felt my new outfit was a nice look. It wasn't very frilly or feminine but practical and businesslike. Beth wouldn't let me escape with my basic ponytail; she insisted I wear it low on my neck with a few loose tendrils framing my face. She said it was a softer look for me. I tried to inconspicuously look around to see if I could get a glimpse of Z. Then I saw *her.*

She was tall, dark-skinned, had long jet black hair and from a distance was beautiful. A feather in her hair and moccasins were all she needed to be Native American royalty. She wore a long loose cotton skirt that would've been appropriate to wear to our church, but on her it looked stylish instead of Holiness. When I saw Z behind her, I wasn't surprised. They looked like they belonged together.

It wasn't long until the lobby was so quiet that a pin drop could be heard. All eyes were on the couple. I wanted to throw up. It was at that moment when everything made sense to me. Z wasn't interested in me in anything other than a fishing partner and a basketball player. This had all been a trick of the devil. I should've known better.

I needed to get some air. I stepped outside the door with Kelsey and Beth following close behind me. I had to clear my head.

"Who in the world is she, and where did she come from?" Kelsey asked as soon as we were out of earshot of anyone.

Nonchalantly, I shrugged before saying, "They sure look good together." I wanted to go home. I wanted to be anywhere at this precise moment instead of here. I was kicking myself. *Why did I think it could be anything more?*

After a few minutes, Z and his girlfriend came outside too. I would've gone back in had it not looked so obvious. I didn't want to be anywhere around them.

Beth whispered, "Don't look now, but *she's* coming our way."

Sure enough, she had her eyes beaded on me and was like a person on a mission. Coach Z was trying to slow her down. When she was directly in front of me, I began to see all of her imperfections. Her smile looked more like a smirk. Most people's smiles only made them more attractive. Not hers. Her smile brought her down several rungs. Her right front tooth overlapped her left. Her makeup was thick making me wonder what all it was hiding.

"Are you Les?" she asked me.

Before I could answer, Z said, "Leslie, meet Emily."

I tried to cover my anxiety with sincerity. "Nice to meet you, Emily." I put my hand out to shake hers.

Slowly and almost reluctantly, she shook my hand. "This is Beth Rudder, and this is Kelsey Van Hook." I introduced her to my friends.

Clearly not interested in meeting my friends, she held onto my hand and kept looking at me. Finally, she must've seen all she needed. I could see our classmates gathering outside and peering our way. Hopefully, they were too far away from us to hear our conversation.

"Leslie," she said my name and kind of wallowed it around to make it something ugly. "So you're Les Lewis."

I wasn't sure how to respond. "Yeah?" I refused to look at Coach Z at all even though I could tell he was looking at me in some kind of desperate way.

"Has *Timothy* not told you about me?" she asked all innocently. Something about the way she said his name was almost sensual.

"No, ma'am, why would he?"

"He'd been telling me about spending a lot of time fishing with a student named Les. Of course, I assumed Les was a guy. Imagine my surprise when I received a message telling me I needed to watch out for some dyke basketball girl called Leslie."

Beth defended me. "Les hasn't been fishing with him. Tell her, Les."

"And Les isn't a dyke," Kelsey added.

When I didn't defend myself then Beth and Kelsey realized that I'd been keeping things from them. I looked to them and begged for their mercy with my eyes.

"Emily, that's enough." Coach Z ordered as he grabbed hold of her arm. Then he turned toward me. "I'm sorry, Les."

Emily wasn't finished with the show. "Okay, my *thawichasa.*"

I'm not sure what she just called him, but my bet was that it was some term for lover. She then placed her perfectly manicured left hand on the side of his face. Her bangle bracelets slid to the lower part of her arm. She only had one ring on her hand, and it was on *the* finger! *Breathe, Leslie. I am so stupid. What was that? Did Coach Z just cringe at her touch?*

Then she turned to me. "Little girl, don't go messing with fire." I knew before she opened her mouth that she was mustering up something sinister. I could tell by the evil slant of her eye. "Actually, I think I've overreacted. Now that I see you, I'm not a bit worried. I guess Timothy really does see you as one of the guys. You have the word *lesbian* written all over your face."

Coach Z was mad. "Emily, that's enough."

This woman didn't deserve to be addressed. I refused to look at her when I very calmly said, "Coach Zuzeca, please tell your *friend* that she has ten seconds to get away from me, or the *dyke* side in me is about to knock her crooked teeth out."

When she smiled, her evil came through. Instead of beautiful, she was actually the ugliest person I'd ever seen. She stood there challenging me with her eyes.

"Emily, come on!" His voice was stern.

I started counting. "Ten, nine, eight, seven ..."

"Oh, you aren't worth the trouble. You even smell like fish guts." Satisfied she'd humiliated me enough, she turned and walked away.

Coach Zuzeca didn't follow her. "I'm sorry, *o'waci*. She just showed up here today. I had no idea she was going to say anything to you."

I just looked at him. "Really? That's the best you can do. Your fiancé just completely humiliated me, and all you can say is sorry dancer? Just leave me alone."

"Fiancé?" he asked.

"Timothy, come on," she impatiently yelled.

"Go on, Timothy," I mimicked her exact tone. "Princess Crooked Teeth is calling." I didn't even care if my comment made me sound like I was Perry's age.

CHAPTER 18

I'd been so caught up in my anger and embarrassment that I forgot I'd been keeping things from my friends. Beth's arms were crossed and her look meant business. Kelsey, on the other hand, wore an expression of hurt.

"There's an explanation," I said. "I'll tell you everything when we get back to the room, truthfully there's nothing going on. Please believe me."

Neither of my friends said anything at first. Beth finally said, "Promise?" She never could stay mad at me for long.

"I promise." Then I asked, "Can either of you tell me exactly what a *dyke* is? Isn't that what the little Dutch boy put his finger in to save the town?" I kidded.

Kelsey shook her head. "Les, darling, you really are going to have to get out of your *holler* more often."

135

"Bethie, maybe you should've gotten me some ruffles after all." Then I laughed. "And to think just a few minutes ago, I was feeling like I looked *smokin' hot.*"

Kelsey said, "I think that's Emily's problem. You looked too hot to be fishing alone with her man. I still can't believe you've been holding out on us all this time,"

"I'll tell you every gory detail; every slimy fish we caught and even how the worm squished when we put them on the hooks. I'll leave nothing out."

Beth said, "Eew! You don't have to tell every detail. I'm curious though ..." She didn't give us time to read her mind before she answered herself. "I want to know who sent her that message."

It didn't take rocket science to figure it had to have come from one of two people. "Sadie in my gym class mentioned something about her uncle's cousin's brother or someone like that seeing a picture of Coach Zuzeca's girlfriend in his dorm room. My bet is that she's the resourceful little witch."

Kelsey added, "Don't rule out Paige Benton."

We were the last ones to load the hotel bus going to the Grand Ole Opry. The idea of having to face Emily again at the Ryman

Auditorium made me uncomfortable. She was dangerous. Her ugly words could completely ruin my family. It wouldn't take much more of her nasty accusations and comments for me to reach my breaking point. She was tall, but I could tell she didn't have an athletic bone in her body. Her long, bare arms weren't flabby, but they weren't muscular either.

All my life, my daddy taught us to turn the other cheek. Momma, on the other hand, sometimes let her Mississippi side come out and provided us other words of wisdom not found in the Bible. She once told me we really should turn the other cheek at least once, but after that they were fair game. On another occasion, she told me what her mother told her. She said, "Ladies don't start fights, but they better finish them."

I wasn't in the mood to fight, and I sure wasn't in the mood to see Coach Zuzeca either. I started to ask Mr. Patton if I could stay at the hotel, but I knew that would just knock one of the chaperones out of going to the show.

On the Opryland bus, Beth and Kelsey acted as my bookends, tucking me safely in between them. We talked quietly amongst ourselves. "I just don't understand why she would think you're gay. In my opinion, you look like a gorgeous heterosexual to me. Ole crooked teeth can't even compare to you." Kelsey couldn't have said anything that made me feel any better.

Vicki Blair

I was in luck. Coach Zuzeca and Emily didn't go to the show after all. Without being too conspicuous, I looked all around to see if I could spot the lovebirds. I felt I would probably hear her since she had such a distinctive voice. I kept replaying her voice honking, "lesbian" over and over in my mind. *I purposely wear pants and am somewhat of a tomboy by nature, but that doesn't classify me as a lesbian, does it?* I used my limited internet option on my phone to Google both dyke and lesbian, just to make sure I understood correctly. I must be the only long-haired Holiness dyke-lesbian in the history of mankind.

I was hopeful that my classmates didn't hear the exchange. My hopes were dashed all to pieces when Mr. Patton stopped me and wanted to know if I was okay. I'd say the rumor that I was a *dyke lesbian* was already being circulated.

I didn't want to ruin my friends' last night of our senior trip. So using the quiet time of the show, I tried to get my anger and hurt out of my system. I was more than just hurt; I was crushed. I felt like such an idiot. I had fallen for him—hook, line, and sinker (no pun intended). I'd felt special when Coach Zuzeca asked me to call him Z instead of Coach Z. Clearly calling him by Tim or Timothy was too personal and reserved only for *Emily.* From now on, I would call him Coach Zuzeca or Coach Snake, whichever popped out first. Although in my opinion, snake was too good of a name for him. By the time I left the Ryman Auditorium, I felt much better.

My entire body cried out in relief once we got back to the hotel room. I immediately changed into my jeans and pulled my hair into my normal ponytail, no more soft tendrils for me. Even though my normal attire had attributed to the names she called me, I didn't care. My jeans and ponytail were part of my safety net. Her name calling didn't hurt near as much as the betrayal that had bruised my heart. I promised myself years ago that I would never be vulnerable again. Here I am ... again. It had to be the clothes.

Beth, Kelsey, and I all gathered in one of the queen-sized beds in our room, and I began to give them the scoop on my fishing trips. I told them about Z showing up at the river and how it had become an every Sunday thing. I even showed them my picture of him on my phone. I left out a lot of the incriminating details. I sure didn't tell them how my stomach turned flip flops when he put his hands on my face. I even left out our time with the black snake. That may not seem special to most people, but to me, it was significant.

When there was a lull in the conversation, a loud single knock on our door caused us to quickly rouse. No one said a word, but I'm sure thoughts of rapists, thieves, and murderers crossed through my roommates' minds. Not mine, I knew who was standing behind the door.

Beth whispered, "Quick! Let's hide our money."

Thankfully, I was still in my jeans and was no longer vulnerable. I slowly walked to the door and looked out the peephole. I was right.

"Who is it?" Kelsey asked.

"It's Emily."

I confidently opened the door and stepped into the hallway ready for whatever confrontation was about to take place. I shut the door behind me. Emily was still in the same clothes with the addition of a trendy shawl covering her shoulders and arms. Her hair looked mussed and her red-streaked eyes were not as vicious as before.

"Don't you think you've done enough damage for the day?" I asked her.

"I think *I* should be the one asking you that."

I let her words sink into my head without commenting. *What does she mean? What damage did I do to her?*

"Did you know that Timothy's *at'e*, his father, is a bad man and will rot in prison for what he did to our tribe?"

"Why are you telling me this?"

"When others shunned him and his family—I stood with Timothy. I took him in my arms and comforted him when his sister took her life. I gave him money and food. I pledged my entire life to him." She was very expressive with her body and hands as she spoke. She seemed to be acting out what she said. Then she became very still. "He would be nothing without me. And yet he chooses you."

Did I just hear her correctly? "What are you talking about?" I looked down to her left hand. The ring was gone. Then I saw it on her right hand.

"Don't play dumb with me. You're playing with fire. Only this fire will consume you if you let it. I will pray my gods curse you for what you've stolen from me, and may you never have one day of peace."

I'd had enough. "Whoa. I have no idea what you're talking about. I barely know Coach Zuzeca. If he's chosen me like you say he has, then know this—I haven't chosen him. You can curse me all day long, but I've never had a day of peace anyway. So the joke is on you. Everything you say about *me* will happen to *you*. Your words are *your* own curse."

A breeze came through the hallway causing Emily's shawl to rise off her shoulders and fall to the ground. She gasped. I stepped forward to pick her shawl up, and she grabbed it up before I could touch it.

"Stay away from me. You, *hmuga.* You are a witch and have cast a spell over my *thawichasa."* She started slowly backing away from me while her eyes never left me. Then she turned and ran.

I scratched my head as I watched her leave. *This is too weird.* The door opened to Kelsey's gaping mouth and Beth's wide eyes. "What in the world just happened?"

"Beats the heck out of me. That woman is crazy."

Kelsey pulled me inside. "It was like a silent movie, we could see you but we couldn't hear you. Come tell us everything."

After I told them what I could remember, Beth said, "Let me get this straight. You weren't weird enough just being the jeans-wearing daughter of a snake-handling Holiness pastor? In one day's time you've been called a dyke-lesbian, jeans-wearing witch that's the daughter of a snake-handling Holiness pastor.

Kelsey asked, "So what does that make us?"

I answered, "You're the best friends any dyke lesbian witch could ever ask for."

"Aww. Group hug," Beth said as we piled on the bed together. The beep of Beth's phone stirred us as we tried to figure out who could be texting this late at night.

Beth sucked in so much oxygen and held it inside that I was afraid she would pass out.

Curiosity got the best of Kelsey, "Here, let me read it." She took possession of the phone. "Les, it's from Henry Noble. It says, 'Can't get you off my mind, Henry.'"

"Oh no, what do I say back?" This was a far cry different person than the smooth Beth from the ballfield.

My friends told me I was overly cautious and too guarded for my own good, but I had to warn Beth before she did anything stupid. "Are you *sure* the message is from Henry?" I asked.

Beth said, "It says it's Henry."

"But do you know for sure it's him?"

"No. I gave him my number, but he didn't give me his."

Playing the devil's advocate, I said, "What if Aphrodite found your number, and she decided to have a little fun with you?"

Kelsey agreed with me. "Good point. You don't want to be the object of their entertainment."

"So what should I do?"

It was simple even though I was the least likely person when it came to the ways of courtship. "Nothing. If it's him, he'll call you."

Kelsey added, "My bet is that Aphrodite has his password and goes through his phone regularly."

We ended that topic and were all settling down from the excitement. I moved over to the other bed.

Beth's mind was working in overdrive. "You know, Henry can't break it off with Misty until after prom at least. That would just be terrible. I bet she even has her dress."

"Trust me. He's going to call you. After all, how can anyone resist the beautiful and charming Elizabeth Jean Rudder?"

She didn't immediately comment. "You forgot sweet and adorable."

Kelsey sleepily added, "Smooth and smart too."

I playfully threw my extra pillow over to their bed. "Don't forget stubborn and sassy."

Things would get all quiet, I would about be asleep when someone would throw another adjective out.

"I'm coordinated too. That would be appealing to someone. Ah, appealing. I'm appealing too, right?"

Finally, I called out, "You're killing me. You're a doll. Trust me, he will call."

"You promise?" she asked.

"I'll promise if you'll go to sleep."

As I closed my eyes I felt my phone begin to vibrate with a text. Knowing who it was from, I refused to look at it. Instead, I turned over and went to sleep.

CHAPTER 19

The ride home was a long one. Beth and I slept for most of the ride, even choosing to forego the stop at McDonald's. I finally read Coach Zuzeca's text, though I told myself I didn't care what he had to say. His text was short and to the point. *I'm so sorry. Please forgive me.*

While still on the bus, he texted again. *Any chance we can fish tomorrow?*

I didn't respond. I don't care if Emily said he'd chosen me or not. I was still so hurt and confused. The pain I felt seeing them together was more than I could stand. He was playing with my mind whether he intended to or not. My head said we were just fishing partners, my heart confessed something different. I felt it shatter into a million pieces. Everyone knows that scars overtop of scars won't heal.

Every now and again, I noticed Beth rereading her text from the Greek God. I know she so badly wanted it to be from him. It was taking a lot of restraint for her not to respond to it. After the fifth time she looked at it, I patted her and said, "It's okay. He will call you. Just have a little faith."

"Do you think it would be a bad thing to go to another one of his games, just in case?"

"Just in case what?"

She thought about it for a moment. "Just in case, he needs to have a reminder of why he needs to call me."

"Maybe, but think about it first," I told her. I didn't want her to make a fool of herself or appear too desperate, but I didn't want to burst her bubble either. For whatever reason, I just didn't think the text was from Henry. This had nothing to do with my gifting; it simply didn't add up.

Scout and Kelsey talked nonstop while they were awake. They slept some too. I noticed her head leaning slightly on his shoulder. They were a cute couple. I don't know why they hadn't gotten together before now.

I didn't look at Coach Zuzeca when I walked past him as I left the bus. It was best this way. Best for him too, since he still needed his job. I could feel him watching me all the way to Beth's car. Since the Seeleys would be at our house, Beth invited me to come over until they left. The last thing I wanted to do was to be polite to Brother Seeley or play basketball with his sons. Beth said it best, when she said that a little *Grey's Anatomy* would be good for our weary souls. We watched three episodes until it was time for the Seeleys to be gone. Meredith Grey almost made me want to become a doctor. If only I could figure out how to do it while staying in Leslie County, Kentucky.

When I arrived home, the girls wanted to know every detail of the trip. I brought them all back souvenirs. Perry didn't leave my side the entire evening. She even asked if she could sleep with me. Normally, Whitley and Laurel were like two peas in a pod but not tonight. I noticed Whitley stayed in my room even after Laurel left to go to bed. Laurel said she wasn't feeling well. I noticed her eyes were a little puffy.

When I was alone with Perry, she explained that Laurel was upset because Joseph Seeley dumped her.

"Dumped her?" I asked. "I didn't realize they were an item." This news made me sick. Joseph wasn't as handsome or suave as his older brother. I guess he was good looking in a lumberjack sort of way. He'd probably spent the last four years trying to fill the void his brother left.

As I was unpacking, I noticed one of my dresser drawers was slightly pulled out. I don't consider myself to be O.C.D., but I had a real problem with my drawers not being shut properly (especially since I had money hidden in them). "Perry, have you been in my drawers this week?"

"I don't think so, I can't remember for sure."

After I made sure all my money was still safely hidden, I fell in my bed. Perry was already asleep. I must've fallen asleep shortly after my head hit the pillow. I'm not sure how long we'd been asleep before I heard a blood curdling scream coming from Laurel's room. Then she screamed again, "Help! Help!"

My feet met the floor hard as I hit the ground running. My insides were shaking as I tried to think what could have caused the desperation I heard in her voice. Perry was running down the dark hallway at my side. It didn't even register for me to turn on the hallway light. Either Momma or Dad had mind enough to do that as we met at her doorway.

Slowly, I opened Laurel's bedroom door inch by inch. As the hallway light rushed in the room, I clearly saw what the problem was. I pushed Perry out of the way. Dad was in the doorway right next to me. No one said a word.

Laurel's knees were pulled up under her chin, and she was pressed up against the headboard of the bed. She had the covers pulled up around her as a barrier. At the foot of her bed, Red Ruby's large body was coiled in a heavy heap. The odor she was giving off was strong; it was a wild and musky smell. Ruby was in striking distance. Her red rattle was singing in warning. It was almost like she was toying with Laurel. The cadence of the rattle's rhythm was slow but continued to increase steadily as she sensed a room full of our fear. Even with the covers around her as a shield, this was a deadly situation.

"Don't move." Dad's order to Laurel was calm but stern. Then he told me, "Go get the long snake scoop and the bucket in the kitchen closet."

I made as little commotion as I could as I headed out the door. I watched every place my foot landed. If Red Ruby was out, then other snakes could be loose as well. Something didn't seem right to me; there was nothing about this scene that made any sense at all. I could see that the basement door at the end of the hallway was shut and locked from the outside. The locks were just one of many precautions that Dad had taken to ensure nothing like this would ever happen. He'd made sure there were no holes or cracks in the basement ceiling or flooring that a snake could escape from. Even the bottom of the basement door had a rubber guard that would prevent one from coming under the doorway. Short of getting rid of the snakes, I don't think there was anything else we could've done to better protect ourselves from this very situation.

When I returned with the tools, I could hear Dad whistling and Mom was softly humming. He whistled often when he worked in the snake room explaining that music had a calming effect on them.

Red Ruby was conditioned to Dad's whistle. Although still coiled in striking position, her tail wasn't shaking. This didn't deter her from striking out at the scoop as it came her way. Now her focus was on Dad. She used her powerful body to thrust halfway up the six foot scoop handle. I'd never seen her act like this before; she was continuously striking out blindly toward Dad. While her focus was on Dad and the scoop, Mom went around to the other side of the bed. Laurel was paralyzed with fear and unable to move out of the striking range; even with Momma calmly urging her to come toward her slowly. Laurel could only grip the blankets tighter around her throat.

Red Ruby's body was half-on and half-off the scoop when Dad carefully dropped her into the bucket. I quickly put the lid on it. I could hear the sound of her hitting the sides of the bucket as she continued to strike. Usually she struck once and was done. At least that was how she had acted in the past when she bit those trying to handle her at various revivals. Three of the handler's she bit died, one lost several fingers, and another came close to dying. Everyone knew they'd better be prayed up before they put their hands on Red Ruby. Dad decided to keep Red Ruby in the bucket overnight so she would be less anxious when we moved her.

When Laurel realized she was safe, she screamed, "Get her out of here!" Her sobs were the most pitiful sounds I'd ever heard. They came from someplace deep inside of her and reminded me of a sound that a wounded animal would make.

Momma tried to calm her. "It's okay, baby. Momma's got you," she murmured to Laurel while she wrapped her arms tightly around her.

Even though it appeared the crisis was over, I knew we had to check the house to make sure Ruby was the only one of the snakes that made it upstairs. "Whitley, you and Perry get in bed with Laurel and Momma. Okay?"

I think the girls were still in shock. They minded me without any question. As Perry crawled up in the bed, she asked, "Laurel, why do you think Red Ruby chose you?"

Momma hushed her. "Perry, that's a crazy question. Laurel's upset enough."

Using a broom and the snake scoop, Dad and I looked under the bed and around the furniture in Laurel's room. Then we repeated this same process in every room on the main floor. After we were fairly certain no other snake was lurking around in our living space, Dad and I ventured downstairs. By now, my knees were physically shaking, my insides too. I kept thinking about how close Laurel came to being bitten. We turned all the lights on and used Dad's industrial flashlight to make sure we could see every step we made. I counted the steps during our descent. Dad had instilled in me the need to be calm. I took slow, deep breaths trying to calm myself before we made it to the snake room.

I wanted to have our gun in my hand so I could start shooting if I saw a bunch of snakes loose. It would be a lot easier. Of course, that would never happen. Dad didn't believe in using guns as protection. He wanted to live only by God's protection. The only reason he had the gun in the first place was to use as an act of mercy to put one of our farm animals out of their misery. Even then he prayed for divine intervention. I don't think he could pull the trigger even if one of these snakes were about to bite him. Dad says that sometimes the Lord allows even the faithful to be bitten. Brother Mugs, one of the Holiness preachers in West Virginia, had been bitten so many times that a snakebite was just like a wasp sting to him. They didn't even faze him. The last snake that bit him actually got sick and died shortly after the bite.

I was relieved to see that other than Red Ruby not being in her glass cage in the center of the room, everything else looked normal. Methodically, Dad began taking inventory. I had our notebook and checked each snake off as he called out to me. We had names for each of them. When he hit twenty-two, we knew the snakes were all accounted for. We checked the latches on each cage. All were intact with the exception of Red Ruby's cage. The door of the cage opened from the top, and it was still closed but the latch was unlocked. Ruby was strong enough to have pushed the lid open and crawl out, but that didn't explain how she made it through two doors. "Without help, I don't think there was any way for her to get out of this room," I told Dad.

When we emerged from the downstairs, Laurel, Whitley, and Perry were all asleep in Laurel's bed. Arms and legs were all entwined as they held on to each other for dear life. I shut the door to Laurel's room and headed to the kitchen. Momma had a pot of coffee made. I could tell she was interested in knowing what we found downstairs.

Dad explained, "All the other snakes were locked in their cages. It was just Red Ruby that was out."

"It doesn't make sense to me." Then I asked, "When was the last time you were down there?"

Mom answered, "Dad and I watered them and cleaned some cages on Friday. I don't think anyone else has been down there since then, have they?" she asked my dad.

"Not that I know of," he answered.

"I can't imagine the girls being down there without one of us. Can you?" Momma directed her question to me.

"I know Laurel and Whitley wouldn't go down there, but I wouldn't put it past Perry." I paused and took a deep breath before I ratted on my little sister. "The other day when the copperhead had the babies, Perry had been downstairs alone. She was the one who discovered them."

Dad answered, "I don't know. Even if she did go down there, I can't imagine her opening Ruby's cage. She likes to act like she's a tough snake wrangler, but she really is afraid of 'em."

Then it hit me like a lead balloon, "What about the Seeleys? Did any of the boys go down to the basement?"

"The boys never showed any interest in going downstairs. I showed Brother Seeley around the snake room the first time he came for supper, but he didn't go down there yesterday," Dad explained.

"Could one of the boys have snuck and done it as a prank?" I asked.

Momma answered, "I don't think so. The only time they were in the house was when they ate. They played basketball or were at the barn the rest of the time." Then her eyes widened. She looked at Dad. "Oh, Clay, it had to be Brother Seeley. You remember when we were sitting on the porch after supper, and he said he needed to use the bathroom."

Dad closed his eyes. I could almost see him replaying the scene in his head as his color turned from a healthy pink to a sickly white. "I remember. We even joked about him taking so long."

"I knew he had some meanness in him by the way he treated Sister Seeley when he thought no one was looking, but to try to hurt one of our girls. I just can't believe it." Every word Momma said was labored.

I knew Brother Seeley was the one who let Red Ruby out. It was the only thing that made sense. He was probably hoping she would bite me. *My dresser drawer!* "That explains why my dresser drawer was ajar when I came home tonight. He was trying to hurt me. He put her in my drawer, but he didn't close it all the way and she got out."

"Clay, honey, what do we need to do?" Momma asked. "Do we need to go to the police or the church elders?"

"Ruth, darling, we can't call the police, or the only people going to jail would be me or you. We have to think of our girls. They would put them into protective custody as soon as they got one look at our basement." He paused before he said, "We can't tell the elders either. We can't prove he did it. I think they would believe Brother Seeley over me anyway."

Momma started crying. "We've got to get out of that church, Clay. He was trying to kill us. If he would do that, then he would do anything."

My dad explained, "You know he blames us for Jeb's accident."

"It was an accident. Leslie ran her little legs off to get you to help him after he hit his head. Both you and Leslie did everything you could to save him."

Dad looked at me to see my reaction. I didn't say anything. I couldn't.

Dad said, "Les, you told me the other morning that you had a bad feeling about the Seeleys coming over. I should've listened to you. That's what I get trying to please man and not God."

CHAPTER 20

After such a horrific night, my few hours of sleep were restless—Red Ruby's yellow eyes haunted me. I doubt my parents slept at all. Before I ever made it to the REM stage of sleep, I was interrupted by a noise. Instead of waiting for my body to receive all the signals and impulses from my brain, I jumped up in fight mode, though it took me a few minutes to realize who I needed to fight. After the second series of light knocks to my door, I was fully awake.

Through the process of elimination, I figured the knock had to belong to Whitley. Perry didn't believe in knocking, Laurel would still be too afraid to venture this far through the house, and my parents would knock once before barging on in. "Come on in, Whitley."

She was still in her gown. "Are you awake?" she asked.

"I am now. Everything okay?"

She gently shut the door before answering me. She was such a polite and mannerly thirteen-year-old. "No. It's not." She started crying.

"Whit, what's wrong?"

She couldn't talk. She just kept crying. I waited her out without interrupting her. Finally able to speak, she said, "It's all my fault."

"What's your fault? Were you the one who let Red Ruby …?"

"No, no." She shook her head back and forth. "That's not it."

"Well, what is it? I don't understand."

"You know when Perry asked why Red Ruby chose Laurel …" She let her words dangle.

"Yeah. I remember Perry asking that?"

"I know why Red Ruby chose Laurel."

"Whit, Red Ruby just got in the first door she could. It could've been any of us."

"Les, you know Red Ruby's special. She knows things."

"She's just a snake, that's it. Don't go giving her special powers." Even though I sometimes wondered about Ruby knowing things, I wasn't going to own up to it. "What does that have to do with Laurel anyway?"

"Well, I know Laurel is sinning. If Red Ruby would've bitten her, she would've died." Once again, her tears starting running out her lids and down her full cheeks.

"What's Laurel doing?" Whitley had a flair for the dramatic so Laurel's sin could've been a range of things from using the computer when it wasn't her turn to putting up the dishes wet.

"Les, I saw something the other day. I know I should've told, but I was afraid to get Laurel in trouble."

"What did ya see?" From the look on her face, I had a feeling it wasn't about wet dishes.

"While the choir was practicing before church last Sunday night, I heard something in the nursery. I opened the door and saw ..." She stopped talking. She closed her eyes.

"And what did you see?"

"I saw Joseph Seeley and Laurel kissing."

That wasn't so bad. I was starting to breathe a little easier. Then she started describing what else she saw.

"Her dress was pulled up, and his hands were under her skirt."

"No!" I didn't mean for the scream to come out. I put my hand over my mouth to prevent further slippage. *Not Joseph Seeley. This wasn't good.* "Did she see you?"

"No. She was too busy with the kissing to be worried about anything else."

"Did you tell anyone else?"

"No. I didn't want Laurel to be mad; but, I had to tell you. I love Laurel; she's my best friend. I don't want her to die. It would've been all my fault."

"Whit, it's not your fault. You aren't responsible for Laurel's life, she is. But, you were right to tell me."

"Think about it, Les. You know it too. Red Ruby chose Laurel. Mine and Perry's rooms are closer to the basement door, but she didn't choose us. She chose Laurel for that reason."

"I thought Perry said Joseph dumped Laurel."

"They've never been going out. He told Laurel that he had a girlfriend at his school, but that she could be his secret girlfriend at church if she wanted. She was just happy that he's paying her any attention. You know she's loved him for so long."

"That sounds about like a Seeley. I'm going to talk to her. I may have to tell her what you saw, but I'm going to try to get her to tell me without mentioning your name. Okay?"

"I don't want her to hate me, but I don't want her to die. Daddy says that sin leads to death. She needs to repent."

"You're exactly right." I had tried to repent so many times myself, but it's kind of hard to ask for forgiveness … when you're not sorry.

CHAPTER 21

The smell of breakfast called to me. Meaning Mom didn't sleep at all.
I guess a Sunday morning treat for the family was in order to help us
not dwell on the horror we felt last night. I could hear her singing one
of her Gaither songs. "Hold on my child. Joy comes in the morning.
The darkest hour means dawn is just in sight." I stood in the hallway
watching her. Her eyes were shut tightly, and her voice was powerful.
Chill bumps just like I was freezing formed up and down my arms.
I knew she was right. Morning light always had a way of making the
fears of the night seem less threatening.

After Dad prayed a morning prayer of thanksgiving for God's
protection, he blessed the food. No one mentioned what happened
last night. Everyone, including me, was trying to pretend it never
happened. Laurel had yet to speak. She didn't eat, either; she just
moved things around on her plate.

I could tell Dad was about to say something profound just by the seriousness of his countenance. "I'm not sure how Red Ruby got out of her cage and got in Laurel's room." He looked over at Laurel as he talked. Laurel began to tear up. "We're still trying to figure that out, but all the other snakes were in their cages. It's important that none of you girls go down to the basement without either Les, your momma, or me with you. Understand?" He looked directly at Perry as he said this.

Perry looked over at me. I put on my best poker face so she couldn't tell if I had told or not. She just nodded her head that she understood.

"Remember it's critical you don't tell anybody about last night. It's bad enough that it happened, but if anyone found out, then we'd have social services crawling all over the place, and you'd all have to go to foster care. Understand?" This was about the hundredth time we'd had the foster care talk.

Since no one wanted to live with foster families, we all said, "Understand."

"Laurel, honey, are you okay?" he asked.

She shook her head no.

Momma asked, "Do you want to stay home with Leslie Esther today?" It wasn't often that she used my first and second names together unless I was in trouble.

"Please, can I stay home," she begged. "I just don't feel like being around *everybody.*"

My guess is that her *everybody* that she was referring to meant mainly Joseph Seeley. "Let her stay home with me."

"Aren't you going fishing?" Perry asked.

"Not today. I think I'll just hang out here with Laurel."

Laurel smiled at me. "Thanks, Les."

As soon as the rest of the family was out of sight, Laurel and I put *The Sound of Music* in our DVD player. I knew that was her favorite movie. As corny as it sounds, our family would have a sing-along as we watched it. We all knew every word to every song. Today when we got to the "Sixteen Going on Seventeen" song, I thought it was a perfect opportunity to bring up what Whitley told me. "When I asked Perry why you'd been crying yesterday, she said you were crying because you got dumped."

She didn't respond, so I asked, "Well, did someone dump you?"

"Kinda," she answered.

"Was it Joseph Seeley who *kinda* dumped you?"

I could see the puddles starting to form in her eyes. Before she sulled up on me completely, I began imparting some words of my seventeen-year-old wisdom to her. "You don't need Joseph Seeley. He's trouble. He only wants one thing from you and then he'll be done."

"He may be trouble, but I've loved him for so long, and now he's paying attention to me like I'm a real person," she answered.

"Please tell me you've not had sex with him?"

She was quick to answer, "No. It's not like that."

"Sure it is. It's always like that when you're dealing with boys. I'm going to ask you one more time, and you better tell me the truth. If you don't, I'll know." I paused to make sure she was looking straight at me. I said each word slowly and clearly to emphasize the importance of my question. "Have you had sex with Joseph?"

"No!" She answered a little too fast and a little too loudly.

"Have you kissed him?"

Reluctantly, she said, "Yes, we've kissed a couple of times."

"Has he made it past first base?"

"Oh no. He's much too respectful to do that," she lied.

"Laurel, are you telling me the truth?"

"Yes!"

I knew she was lying, and it was important that I understood the extent of her lies. "I've got an idea," I said as I got up and headed toward the basement door.

"Where're you going?" she called out to me.

"I'm going to go get the bucket with Red Ruby in it. She'll be able to tell me if you're telling the truth or not."

"No, no, no, no. Don't get her, please. I'll tell you the truth. Please. I don't think I can handle hearing her rattle."

"Okay. Then tell me the truth."

"You can't tell Mom and Dad, but one time, we got a little carried away, and I let him touch me places I shouldn't."

"And?"

"That's it. I made him quit as soon as I got my head back on straight. Please, please, you can't tell Momma and Dad. Please, I'm begging you!"

I didn't answer immediately. I didn't exactly believe her, but at this point I wasn't sure if I really wanted to know. "Here's the deal. When you're at church, I'm going to ask Whitley to stay with you and follow you everywhere. If I hear of you being alone with Joseph Seeley or any other boy for that matter, then I'll tell our parents all about your little make-out session with the head elder's son. Got it?"

I couldn't read the look on her face. It was a mixture of defiance, remorse, and possibly relief.

CHAPTER 22

Laurel was asleep before the von Trapp family sang the last rendition of "Edelweiss". Bless her heart. She'd been through so much in the last few days. I know Red Ruby practically scared her to death, and I still don't have a good feeling about this thing with Joseph Seeley either. He always seemed like a nice enough boy, but then again, so did his brother.

I felt Brother Seeley was evil through and through, but it was only a feeling. I had no tangible proof. Even this mishap with Red Ruby—just another thing we couldn't prove. When you first meet Brother Seeley, you'd think he was the nicest and most Godly man ever. As long as Dad was doing everything he wanted him to do, he was nice as pie to him. Let Dad go against his wishes, and it was war. Only Brother Seeley wouldn't outright fight with Dad. To his face, he would still be nice, but he would sneak around, saying half-truths and planting seeds of doubt to try to discredit anyone who opposed his way of thinking. Mainly my dad.

At times, Momma would get so fed up with always having to explain our every move to the elders. She begged Dad to give up his position as the pastor. He said the Lord hadn't released him.

Being idle only gave me more time to think about things. Wasting one more minute thinking about Coach Zuzeca wasn't something I was willing to do. While Laurel slept, I used the computer to research colleges. For the first time, the thoughts of going far away from Leslie County appealed to me. I wanted to be anywhere but here. It was bad enough having folks whisper about me because of my religion or lack thereof. Adding the question about my sexual orientation was more than I could stand.

The river had called out to me today. Part of me wanted to go, but my favorite spots were now tainted with too many memories. I wasn't ready to talk to Coach Zuzeca who could possibly be there. The river and Coach Zuzeca would just have to do without me. It was best I end this infatuation while I still could. I knew I was a lot like my sister, Laurel. Once I gave Coach Zuzeca my heart, there would be no walking away unscathed or untarnished.

I tried hard not to think about *that* woman calling me a dyke, lesbian, and a witch. Her calling me a lesbian was about the equivalent of her calling me an alien from Mars. Other than our clients, two very nice men from Hazard, I had no personal experience with being around gays. There'd been a rumor going around about a couple of the girls on the basketball team caught kissing, but I just dismissed it as just that, a rumor.

Going to a Christian school, I had very limited experience with lifestyles that were contrary to the one called about in the Bible. Coach Zuzeca's revelation about practicing the Sioux's religion made him one of the few possible non-Christians I'd ever known. Many of the new troubled kids coming in to the school would be full of the devil, but it didn't take too long for an exorcism to take place. In my world, it was a given that I would grow up and marry a Christian man, not a woman or a nonbeliever. Anything different from that would make me unequally yoked and subject to the Master's judgment.

In the mirror overtop of the computer desk, I studied my face. It told a story I didn't want to hear. I looked rugged. Even with the help of *my stylist* and soft ponytail, I'm sure I looked rough and rugged when Emily saw me. I had no time or energy for being soft and feminine. It had been so long since I'd taken any interest in how I looked. I had no desire to look pretty. In some ways these last four years had been safe and liberating. In other ways it felt like a prison. As an experiment, I took my ponytail down and brushed my long hair out. My dark brown hair fell past my shoulder blades and had a nice wave even without using a curling iron. Having my hair down completely changed my looks. I immediately pulled it back up in the tightest ponytail I could make.

When the house phone rang, I knew I had to answer it. I couldn't figure out who would be calling our house on a Sunday afternoon. Before I placed the phone to my ear, it dawned on me who it had to be.

"Hel-lo." The last part of my greeting fell flat.

"Hello, *kitala o'waci*. Please don't hang up," Coach Zuzeca begged.

I silently kept the receiver at my ear while I contemplated what to say. "Why are you calling me?"

"You should've seen all the fish I caught without you this morning." I could hear the smile in his voice.

"Wonderful. I'm really happy that I gave you my best fishing spots. They're yours. I hope you catch Moby Dick there." I sounded like a ten-year-old.

"Please don't be mad. I didn't know Emily would come to Nashville. I should've ended it with her a long time ago. It's entirely my fault."

"Listen, Coach *Zuzeca*." I emphasized his name. "I've had a nice time fishing with you. You seem like a nice guy and all, but it's hard enough coming to school with the stigma of being a Holiness preacher's kid. I don't need more complications in my life. Especially now that half the school probably already knows what your girlfriend called me. Not to mention, our secret fishing partnership would be frowned upon by ACI."

"Would it make a difference if I told you that I've already decided not to teach here next year anyway? I've applied for several other coaching jobs."

"That's a decision you'll have to make. I accept your apology. It's just not a good idea for us to …" I was struggling with what to say next since the only relationship we had was in my mind, anyway. "Be sneaking around fishing together. Let's just leave it at that. There are plenty of guys who would go fishing with you." For good measure, I added, "and some girls too. I'll see you at school." I hung up before he could reply.

I really need to understand how he is getting my phone number.

CHAPTER 23

Laurel still wasn't feeling well enough to go to school on Monday. She wouldn't eat or talk. Mostly she just slept. Sleep is a time when one's soul can heal. Any other time, I would've volunteered to stay home with her, but I couldn't today. It would only make me look like I had something to hide. Perry wouldn't stand for me to stay home either since Dad had already given me permission to drive to school.

As usual, Perry rushed me to get ready and even had my coffee waiting for me in the truck. "What's that smell?" I asked when I recognized my perfume.

She looked up at me with those big, puppy-dog eyes and said, "I've been doing a lot of thinking. I've decided it's time for me to look for a boyfriend. I put a dab of Mom's perfume on so I could drive the boys *wild* today."

"What's your hurry? You're only ten years old. You have plenty of time to drive boys wild."

"Well, the way I see it, my life's about to change when you go off to school and leave me behind. I figure a boyfriend would at least like to do the same things I like to do. I think that's my best option."

I rolled my eyes. "Not that again. I told you I'm waiting until after I graduate before I make my mind up about where I'll go to college."

When Perry crinkled her forehead, I knew she meant business. "So tell me, Leslie Esther, if you were so serious about waiting until after graduation, then why were you looking at colleges on the internet while we were at church yesterday?"

"Okay, you little internet Nazi, just because I looked at some school websites doesn't mean my mind is made up to leave. There is a community college close by you know."

"I just need to be prepared, because if you leave me, then I won't have anyone who likes to do fun stuff. Laurel and Whitley will just want to curl my hair and make me read books and girly stuff like that. I need to have a plan B. Just in case."

I laughed slightly before saying, "So a boyfriend's your plan B to replace me."

"Well, it's the best option I can think of right now. The Seeley boys all like fishing and basketball. Maybe one of them can be your replacement."

"Perry Gail Lewis, I better not hear about you replacing me with one of the Seeley boys or any boy for that matter. Do you hear me? You don't need a boyfriend for a long, long time—at least until you're in college."

"Is that why you've never had a boyfriend?"

"Partly. Boyfriends take way too much time. Plus, I've never found a guy that could beat me at fishing or basketball." For good measure, I added something only she could truly appreciate, "Or a guy who wasn't afraid of snakes."

"You're exactly right. I bet every boy in my class would run if they saw a little garter snake. I guess I wasted Mom's good perfume for nothing."

I loved all my sisters, but it was different with Perry. I felt like she was partly my daughter, my sister, and my friend. I watched her as she walked all the way into the school building before I drove off.

As I turned my attention away from Perry, I had one of those bone-chilling feelings. It started in the pit of my stomach, worked its way up to my diaphragm, and it stopped in my throat. I could barely breathe. My lungs felt like a grizzly bear was sitting on top of my chest. What air that made it to my windpipe came in spurts. I felt like I was going to choke to death. My eyes even watered.

The honks of rushed parents caused me to realize I'd come to a complete stop. Thank goodness I hadn't been on the main road when

I had my episode. I pushed the accelerator a little too hard as I left the drop-off loop causing the old truck to leave some rubber on the road.

I didn't see a vision or hear God's voice. It was just a weird feeling. Most of the time it only lasted a few seconds then the feeling was gone. Today the feeling was stronger and lasted longer than any of my other episodes. I felt it was a warning to me that something was going to happen. And it was going to happen to Perry.

By the time I got to my school, I had one of the sick headaches that usually followed the feelings. This one was a doozy. I knew better than to look for medicine in my dad's truck. There wouldn't be even a trace of aspirin in the glovebox. The only medicine my parents believed in was the supernatural kind that comes through faith and prayer. My dad would often say from the pulpit, "How can you ask God to heal your cancer when you don't have enough faith to ask him to heal your headache?" It worked too. I can't remember the last time any of us went to the doctor. Before leaving the truck, I put my hands on each side of my head and squeezed.

Today, I decided against parking in the faculty lot even though it would mean a longer walk. I didn't want to take any chances of running in to Coach Zuzeca. I still couldn't bring myself to shorten his last name; using his initial would be much too personal and informal. I needed to keep everything on a professional student-teacher level. I could still hear the way *Emily* said his name, "Tim-o-thy." The "T" exploded off her tongue, and her heart-shaped lips would almost pucker while emphasizing the "o" sound. The sound of her voice was carnal and raw. There was no way I would be able to say his name like that even if I practiced in the mirror.

Get a handle on things, Les. I was officially delusional. Why would I even care who calls him what? He's my gym teacher, for Pete's sake. The sooner I get that little fact in my brain, the better. I had at least four more weeks of school. After that, I would probably never see him again. *But she said he chose me!* I put my hands over my ears to try to shut up the voice in my head. It was then when I realized my head was no longer hurting.

I changed my thoughts to my friends. I really wanted to tell them about Red Ruby getting out and our suspicion about Brother Seeley, but I couldn't. It was way too risky for anyone outside our home to know. Our secrets were big ones. In the wrong hands, they could destroy us.

Even though I was early when I arrived to school, I was the last one of my friends there. Kelsey and Beth were in the front foyer. Only they weren't alone. Paige Benton was in the center of the three girls. They were so preoccupied with their conversation with Paige they didn't even notice my arrival. I thought we were shed of her, but evidently I was wrong. It looked like she was once again trying to reinsert herself in our group. I didn't like it.

"Les, come here. You've got to hear what Paige heard about Henry and Misty Shane. Paige says that the lovebirds are having problems because Misty found Henry's text he wrote to me over the weekend."

I immediately smelled a rat. Although I was skeptical earlier, now I was certain that the Greek God was not the author of the text. Paige couldn't have sent it from her own phone since we all had her number, but she had to be behind it. Maybe she enlisted her new accomplice, Sadie, to send it. It almost made me mad that Beth was so gullible and was playing right into her hand.

I'm pretty sure Paige knew I was onto her. She kept looking directly at me trying to assess what I was thinking. Finally, I asked her, "How did you find out about this latest newsflash?"

There was no hesitation when she answered. "I still keep in touch with my Clarksdell peeps."

"Which one of your peeps told you this?"

"Why does it matter?"

"It doesn't. I just wanted to make sure the person telling you this was credible."

Always the peacemaker, Beth rationalized with me. "Les, it doesn't matter. I really hate that Misty knows. I think that will hurt my chances with Henry in the long run."

Even though my back was to him, I smelled Coach Zuzeca as soon as he came through the front door. The noisy chatter from the foyer ceased as Coach Zuzeca walked through. The silence was proof that everyone knew about the interaction between Emily and me. Their stares felt like lasers; I could feel the heat. I didn't turn around. I pretended I didn't realize he was anywhere near. Even without turning around, I knew the minute he passed through—his scent faded and the buzz of conversation resumed.

Paige's eyes challenged me when she said, "I heard you got to meet Coach Zuzeca's *beautiful* girlfriend."

Kelsey came to my rescue. "Trust me. Up close, she wasn't a bit pretty."

Beth agreed, "I didn't think she was beautiful at all."

Once I noticed the time, I knew I needed to get to first period. I contemplated purposely going in late but decided against it. Instead, I peeked through the narrow pane in the gym's hallway entrance to determine Coach Zuzeca's location. I waited for him to move to the other side before I quickly headed to the girl's dressing room. The bright locker-filled room smelled like a mixture of onions and baby powder. There was one lone person still getting ready.

Sadie was sitting on one of the benches wearing only her bra and panties while looking at her phone. Her appearance on the ACI scene wasn't cause for much excitement or speculation. A new student usually generated a lot of buzz as the various cliques tried to size up the newcomer. Even the loners who didn't fit into one of the established factions would look to the new student as a possible alliance. Since Sadie wasn't a dorm student, she wasn't cause for a lot of speculation. A new dormitory student during the middle of the school year meant some horrible deed resulted in the student's court-ordered banishment to *the farm*. Sadie just showed up one day. I didn't even know her name much less her crime. Without looking up from her phone, she said, "Heard you had an interesting senior trip?"

"It was okay."

"That's not what I heard." She was still playing with her phone.

I knew some type of confrontation was inevitable so I sat down next to her while there was no audience. "So, Sadie, what *exactly* did you hear happened in Nashville?"

Finally she looked away from her phone. She sat straight up on the bench; her large bra-clad breasts were erect and intimidating. She wielded them like she'd used them as weapons of war before. "I heard the coach's girlfriend called you a lesbian."

"Is that all?"

I could tell she enjoyed toying with me. "Isn't that enough?"

"Do I look like I'm a *dyke* lesbian to you?" I figured that I would at least get an honest answer from her.

She took her sweet time as she looked me over. "Well, maybe a little. Either that or you are completely crazy."

"Why would you say that?"

"If I had a good-looking teacher like Coach Z looking at me like he looked at you, then I would be doing much more than fishing with him."

The sirens in my head went off in full warning. *If Sadie knew I'd been fishing with Coach Zuzeca, then that meant there was a good chance that Sister Ruth Lewis would know it too, before the day was over. I was so busted.*

CHAPTER 24

I'd always heard about the importance of keeping your friends close and your enemies closer, but I never understood the significance. Until now. Other than Brother Seeley, I didn't have any enemies that I knew about. This wasn't because I was such a warm and wonderful person but mainly because I stayed under most people's radars. It was a relatively easy feat to do since most enemies were formed because of boyfriend issues. Since fishing with Coach Zuzeca, I had more girl drama now than in my whole high school career.

I hung out with Sadie, my new "frenemy," the entire first period. In some ways, I saw a lot of myself in her. Just like me, she too was incapable of small talk. She said exactly what she was thinking and didn't make any apologies for it. I liked her confidence; I just didn't like her cruelty. I now knew her as Sadie Long. Sadie Long may've been a somewhat likeable and entertaining character, but she wasn't particularly smart. I left class with her phone number entered into my phone.

For the next two periods, I tried to come up with discreet ways of finding the "Henry" text number without making Beth suspicious. Hopefully, I wasn't right. After all, there was a remote possibility that Henry Noble really did text her; however, there was also the possibility that someone was messing with her. I'm no psychologist, but I feel if Misty Shane really did know about the text, then by now she would've made her displeasure known. Girls like her don't let things go unpunished. And guys like Henry Noble don't leave incriminating texts on their phones either.

I was a little nervous as I headed to our lunch table. Thankfully, Paige wasn't there. She and Sadie had their heads together sitting in their corner table. This table still gave them a direct view of us; it was far enough away so we couldn't hear their conversations but close enough for them to read our expressions.

Kelsey was all smiles when she saw me heading her way. "So, you don't look like you've been beaten up too badly," she kidded.

I added, "Just wait until tonight. I bet Sister Ruth has already heard all about my fishing partner by now. I'm so busted."

Beth started cackling. "No! You are *so* in luck."

"What're you talking about?" When Beth continued to laugh, I reminded her. "This really isn't a laughing matter."

"Yes, it is. You just haven't thought it through."

Without speaking, Kelsey let me know she wasn't following Beth either.

In an exasperated tone, Beth said, "Come on, it's not that complicated." She pointed at her head, "Think. If your mom has heard the rumor about you being all alone fishing with the good-looking teacher, then she's probably also heard the rumor about you being a lesbian." Beth actually snorted before she continued. "Then my bet is you have nothing to worry about. Sister Ruth will be too worried about you going to hell in a handbasket as a lesbian than worried about you being alone with a single man even if he is your teacher."

"Oh," I said as I thought it through. Momma *would* probably be more mortified about the lesbian part than the fishing part. In the back of her mind, she'd probably already questioned why I'd never had a boyfriend. This would play into her fears. "You know, Bethiepoo, you may be right."

By this time, Kelsey was sniggering too. "This may be your lucky day after all."

It was a lot easier for them to laugh since they weren't the ones going to get *the talk* tonight. I didn't leave my parents a lot of options. I'd be an abomination either way I went. Being gay or having an affair with an older man would both weigh equally on the sin scale, but the older man sin would be the easier of the two for them to deal with.

Beth said, "I'm so sorry, Les. I just keep seeing Sister Ruth in bed with a cold washrag over her face while Brother Clay walks around and around your bed tonight praying the devil out of you."

Kelsey said, "Ten dollars says they're both fasting before the nights over."

I noticed Paige and Sadie looking our way. I decided to go ahead and test my theory. "Beth, would Henry Noble's phone number be 606-682-9441?" I held my breath until she answered. *Say no! Say no!"*

She pulled her phone out of her purse. "How did you know?"

I blew out the breath I'd been holding. "Just a hunch."

Kelsey eyed me suspiciously before asking, "What's going on, Les?"

When I didn't answer fast enough for her, Beth said, "Tell me how you knew the number? Just tell me what's going on. I'm a big girl."

"That's Sadie Long's cell number."

"What?" Both Beth and Kelsey said loudly in unison.

"Sadie as in, the girl sitting over there with Paige?" Beth asked before she headed straight to confront them. Before she took her fifth step in that direction, I put a chokehold on her while I disguised it as a hug. I tried to inconspicuously drag her back to her seat. "Sit down, and listen," I whispered in her ear.

"I don't want to listen. I'm so mad. I want to break Paige's face! Why would she do this to me? I was so nice to her."

Although Kelsey's face was flushed with anger, she was still the voice of reason. "Bethie, some girls are just mean. You can't stoop to their level. Plus we only have four weeks left, and you can't get in a fight now. It would ruin everything. Paige Benton is a miserable person and would like nothing better than to see you sink to her level."

Beth took three deep-cleansing breaths. "You're right." She sat straight up in her chair, closed her eyes, and lifted her nose in the air. "I guess this means Henry really didn't text me."

I reassured her. "Henry will call that smart and smooth girl from the parking lot. Trust me. He thinks about you every day, but he's busy trying to get through his last year just like you are. Plus what kind of guy would he be if he dumped Misty Shane right before prom."

Kelsey didn't add any more words of wisdom, but her head was nodding up and down with each point I made.

"Okay, I'm done being the victim. I'm ready to get even."

CHAPTER 25

I talked on my phone all the way home. First to Beth then to Kelsey. Beth was determined to hit Paige Benton where it hurt. Problem was, we didn't know exactly where that was, or how to do it. It wasn't that any of us were perfect little angels; we just never faced this kind of situation before. We were having fun trying to come up with ideas though.

Kelsey's assignment was to find out why Paige was banished from Clarksdell High School. There had to be a story there. They had her working at the farm. There had to be some way to find out what sent her packing short of breaking into the file room. We needed to make a Clarksdell connection and fast.

Making these plans at least kept my mind occupied on the ride home. When I saw our driveway, my stomach did a few flip flops with dread. I knew that in a matter of hours, I would be getting *the talk.* Since I already caused my family a lot of grief over my need for all my sanity boundaries, I vowed not to cause them any more issues—especially my dad. I was almost home free too. After children graduate from high school, the bulk of their raising has been done. Any mistakes children make after graduation didn't reflect as negatively on the parents as before. Or, at least the mistakes were much easier to hide from the church after graduation.

Momma wasn't home when I arrived. Laurel said she'd run out to get something. I figured it was a book on how parents could pray the demons out of their gay or promiscuous children.

Laurel was still wearing her nightgown, and her auburn hair hadn't been brushed all day. Underneath her eyes were dark and puffy. She was a mess. Her face was expressionless. It seemed as though the weekend had sucked the life right out of her.

Whitley was at the barn with Perry. Ordinarily, Whitley and Laurel would be joined at the hip, and Perry would be the odd girl out. Whitley seemed to be purposely avoiding her older sister, probably out of guilt. I sat down on the couch with Laurel. She kept looking at the book she was holding. At first, I didn't say anything to her because I didn't want to disturb her reading. When I realized she hadn't turned a page in over fifteen minutes, I suspected she was just using the book as a prop. I began to inch closer and closer until a dollar bill couldn't fit between us. Although I was practically in her lap, she was trying hard to act like it wasn't bothering her. After I reached over and stole her book, I saw a little life come back in her face when she tried to take it back from me. When I ran down the hallway with it, she followed me. "Give it back!" she ordered.

"I will if you can tell me the title of the book."

"*The Long Road Home?*" she said like she wasn't certain.

"Wrong. Try again."

Her earlier paleness was now flushed with a healthier pink. "*The Longest Road Home?*"

"Guess again."

"Just give me my book back."

I held it so she could see the cover. "I'll make a deal with you. I'll give your book back *if* you'll help me decide on my hairstyle for prom."

That did it. She grabbed my arm and pulled me toward her room like she was on a mission. "I've been waiting a lifetime to hear you say that."

For the next hour or so, I let her curl, twist, tease, and spray to her heart's content. It was pure misery for me, but Laurel seemed to be enjoying every minute of it. When I didn't think I could stand one more brush or curl, Perry and Whitley came bouncing into the room and saved me.

"Please tell me you're not gonna wear your hair like that," Perry said. She was not amused.

"Perry, I don't know what I'm going to do, but I can't wear a ponytail with that black prom dress."

Whitley seemed to be relieved when she said, "Les, I'm so glad to hear that. I've been so worried you would have that beautiful dress on and ruin it by not fixing yourself up."

Whitley began lifting strands of my long hair, first this way, then that way. "You really have pretty hair, Les."

"Les, I think you're beautiful even with a ponytail," Perry said this like she was defending my honor.

Laurel ignored Perry's comment and asked Whitley, "Whitley, how do you think she should wear it?" She turned to me. "Whitley is really good at fixing hair. Fixing hair is her gifting."

Perry sulked against the wall. She wasn't used to sharing me with the curling iron queens. Whitley and Laurel finally came to a joint decision about my hairstyle. It was a good thing too, because my head was starting to feel sore.

"Momma's home," I said. I could smell the fried chicken even before I heard the screen door slam.

"Girls! I've got supper!" Momma called out loudly.

I heard the door open and close again. I could hear my parents talking before we made it to the kitchen. Perry and Whitley led the way with Laurel and me bringing up the rear. Dad seemed pretty normal, but Mom was trying way too hard. *They knew.*

It'd been a while since Mom let Colonel Sanders do the cooking. She was a planner and normally prepared a lot of our meals ahead of time and froze them. This meal provided by KFC was actually a treat for us. If I had to endure a painful lecture, then at least I was going to have to endure it on a full stomach.

Perry said, "Momma, aren't you hungry?"

I looked over and my mom didn't even have a morsel on the plate in front of her. Kelsey was right about me causing a fast. I disguised my laugh with a cough.

"Leslie, are you okay?" Mom asked while I continued to cough and sputter.

"I'm fine."

Laurel even ate a few bites before she started moving the food around on her plate again. As soon as dinner was finished, we all helped with the dishes before we took our showers. Momma runs a tight ship, and we are all conditioned to the nightly routine. I went to my room as soon as I could and waited.

I heard Dad's steps slowly coming toward my room. My heart raced and my whole body felt like it had the tremors. Dad knocked once and came on in before I had time to answer. He didn't immediately sit down; he fiddled with some of the whatnots I had on my dresser. I braced myself.

"Les, I know you've had a hard few years, and when Jeb died, well, we about lost you too. You've kept everyone at arm's length ever since then. Your momma and I were not experts on how to help you get through your experience. We thought we were doing the right thing by letting you quit church and wear your britches in order to help you cope. We were certain all you needed was a lot of love and understanding and some space and time in order to help you heal and forget. Now, I'm afraid we were wrong."

"Dad, just go ahead and spit it out."

I could tell he was trying to be as delicate as he could possibly be. "Ruth said that there was a rumor about you liking girls instead of boys." Those words sounded foreign coming from my dad's mouth.

"Dad, there's nothing to those rumors." I paused to collect my thoughts before trying to explain how I knew I wasn't a lesbian. While in Nashville, I had a similar dialogue with myself just to make sure Emily didn't know something about me that I didn't. It took one look at Coach Zuzeca for me to know that I was heterosexual all the way. "Dad, I'm only seventeen years old, and I don't have everything about me figured out. I'm not sure I ever will. I'm not going to lie to you. That thing that happened, you know, it scarred me. I don't know if I'll ever get that girl back, but I'm trying. I may wear jeans and like fishing and basketball, but I promise you that's as far as it goes. I plan on one day marrying a man and having a family. I'm just not ready to give my heart away to anyone just yet."

I could see the relief all over his face. He asked, "Are you sure? You know I'll always love you, and you'll be my daughter no matter what."

"Yes, I'm positive." This made me love him all the more. Having a lesbian daughter just wouldn't fly in our church. His acceptance of his gay child would, with certainty, be the end of his ministry at our church or any other Holiness church.

"So, what about these other rumors about you sneaking around with this teacher? Is that rumor true?"

"Partly, but I can explain."

He said in his preaching tone, "I'm listening."

"Coach Zuzeca saw your old Chevy parked on the side of the road at my river fishing spot. He recognized it from the faculty lot and thought I was having car trouble and came to the riverbank looking for me. He ended up staying and fishing with me for a few hours. It was fine. I just didn't want to make a big deal out of it."

He looked intently at my face, like he was studying it. "Why didn't you tell anyone about him showing up? You know that not telling can be just as big of a sin as lying. They're no difference in God's eyes."

"Because I was afraid people wouldn't understand, and they would try to make something bad out of it. It's just fishing. That's all. I think he led his girlfriend into thinking he'd been fishing with a guy, and she got all torn up when she realized that I was the one fishing with him. She was really nasty."

"How old is he?"

"I don't know. Maybe twenty-three?"

"Do you know if he's a Christian or not?"

"Dad, we're fishing. Not getting married."

Dad didn't speak immediately. He always made his words count. "I don't want you fishing alone with that teacher anymore. You're still a girl, and he's still a guy. It doesn't look right even if he is a teacher. You could get him in all kinds of trouble with his job. You'll have to take Perry or Beth or somebody with you to chaperone. Little girl, your scars may be healing better than you think they are, but you don't need to be naïve either. You remember fishing caused you a mess of trouble before."

CHAPTER 26

It was probably best that I rode to school with Momma and the girls today. I think Laurel kind of needed me to walk into school with her. She seemed much better this morning, but she still wasn't acting right. I understand how scared she must've been to wake up to Red Ruby wagging her tail at her. But this was going on four days. With some antivenin, she would've recovered sooner from a snakebite.

I noticed Momma ate breakfast this morning. Her fast was short-lived since I imagine her prayers were answered right after Dad's *talk* with me. Life in the Lewis household seemed to be back to normal even if we were slightly off kilter. We left the house five minutes later than normal. Then the drop-off line at Perry's school was longer than usual. I kept looking at the time on my phone praying that Mom would drive faster. I didn't want to go into gym class late.

The foyer was completely empty when Laurel and I walked into the high school building together. I could feel beads of sweat beginning to form on my forehead. My pace was slow as I tried to will my heart rate to decrease.

Making sure my breathing was slow and easy, I continued down the hallway leading to the gym. Even the second bell had rung making me very late. I looked through the glass pane to see if Coach Zuzeca was looming nearby. Everyone had gathered in a circle at the end of the court. It appeared someone was hurt. I kept looking through the window like I was watching a television show. Up from the midst of the circle, Coach Zuzeca emerged. He was carrying someone. I could see hands locked around his neck; the hands definitely belonged to a girl. I didn't know the identity of the girl because her face seemed to be pressed into his chest.

Just like he was holding his bride, he carried her over to the bleachers and carefully sat her down on the bottom row. Finally, I could see her face. "No!" I screamed when I realized that the injured girl was none other than my new "frenemy," Sadie Long. I didn't like the way she slid her hands across his chest when she moved them from around his neck. I wouldn't consider Sadie a beauty queen, but she wasn't ugly either. Her mousey blond hair was dull, and her nose turned up too much, however her body protruded and curved in all the right places.

I knocked a couple of times on the gym door, but no one heard me. It seemed like everyone was caught up in Sadie's injury, including the teacher. Coach Zuzeca kneeled before her and assessed her ankle. Even from the distance, I could tell she was fine. I wasn't able to smile coyly like Sadie was doing now when I sprained my ankle several years back. I remember trying hard just not to cry in front of everyone. In my opinion, smiling and flirting wouldn't have been an option with a true sprain or break. I could tell from my narrow glass pane view that Sadie was putting on quite a performance. While Coach Z was touching her ankle, I thought for sure she was going to swoon. Not from pain but from pleasure.

The dam broke on my emotions. Anger boiled over starting at the pit of my stomach, and I just wanted to choke Sadie Long. Each time she touched Coach Z, my skin burned in the exact spot she was touching him. I pushed the metal bar of the hallway door as hard as I could to expend some of my angry energy. To my surprise, the door opened. It hadn't even been locked. I felt very foolish until a plan fell into my head just like manna fell from heaven.

I ran up the hall to the front secretary and told her we had an injured student in the gymnasium that would need a stretcher. She immediately called for medical assistance. I waited until I saw the stretcher being rolled through the entranceway. When we got to the gym door, I moved to the front of the gurney and ushered it in with gusto. "Over this way," I ordered the medical staff. The look on Sadie's face was priceless as she saw me heading toward her leading the medical brigade to her rescue. "Is she okay?" I asked Coach Z when I squatted down next to him.

"What happened?" I directed my next question to Sadie.

She started to explain when Coach Z interrupted and said, "You would've known if you were at class on time." His smile wasn't lost on me.

I stayed with Sadie in the infirmary for the rest of first period and most of second too. Sadie was not happy that she had to leave Coach Zuzeca's care. I fluffed her pillows and tried to anticipate her every need. She kept telling me she was fine and that I could go on back to my class anytime. The more agitated she became, the more I wanted to stay.

I'm not sure if Sadie's staged accident was part of their overall scheme or not. For all I know Sadie could've been acting alone—she simply saw an opportunity and took it. It didn't matter. I didn't like her fondling all over Coach Z, and I didn't like seeing him all cozy with her either.

By lunch, Sadie had recovered enough to eat in the cafeteria. I helped her over to her corner table while she waited for Paige to arrive. After Sadie was settled, I headed to my usual table and my usual seat.

"What in the world are you doing?" Beth wanted to know.

Kelsey eyed me suspiciously when she asked, "Why are you consorting with the enemy?"

"I can explain." Then I gave them every detail of what I saw in that gym window and how I thwarted her attempts to get closer to Coach Z by getting her placed in the infirmary.

Kelsey's expression showed she was puzzled. "So, why do you care if she gets close to Coach Z? He's just your fishing partner, right?"

"Yeah, Les. OMG. You really have a thing for the coach." Every syllable Beth spoke went up an octave.

I didn't know how to respond. I shrugged my shoulders. "Maybe. I sure don't want Sadie to cause him any problem." Changing the subject, I laid a ten dollar bill in front of Kelsey.

Kelsey said, "What's that for. Oh. The fast. So I was right." She took the money and put it in her small Coach purse."

Beth said, "We have some news for you too. Kelsey, tell Les about our possible Clarksdell connection."

"Well, I was talking to Scout last night about wanting to find the goods on Paige Benton. Scout is *so* sweet." Her pause was slightly dramatic as she gave one of those smitten, love-torn sighs before she continued. "Scout told me he went to basketball camp with a boy from Clarksdell. He's going to reach out to him to see what he can find out about Paige."

I asked, "Are you sure you can trust Scout?"

Kelsey was quick to defend him. "I think so. He gave me his word."

"What if this guy is a relative or close friend of Paige?" I asked.

"We've got that covered too. Scout's going to pretend he's interested in taking Paige out and that he's calling to make sure she's not a complete psycho."

I gave her a nod of approval before saying, "That should work."

Beth was biting her bottom lip and had her head cocked. She was definitely in thinking mode. "I feel rather crafty and conniving right now. Can I make 'em squirm just an itty bit?"

It was way too early to show our hand. I asked rather guardedly, "What do you have in mind?"

"Watch this?" Before I could protest, she was gone. Like a spider monkey gliding through the jungle, Beth zigzagged her way through all the tables until she was standing right in front of Paige and Sadie. Then, using the same spider monkey moves, Beth weaved back and forth through the array of tables and students and back to her seat. Her toothy grin told us she'd accomplished her mission. Whatever that was?

Beth explained, "I told Paige I was ready to text Henry back and asked her when she thought, since she knew all about him, would be the best time for me to text the Greek God?"

"So what did she say?" I asked.

"She said the safest time would be at the end of the school day. He would probably be on his way to the baseball field or a game, and Misty Shane wouldn't be around."

Kelsey rationalized, "Hmmm. Either Beth has it all thought out, or at least, she can think on her feet." I could tell Kelsey liked the thought of going toe to toe against a worthy opponent.

CHAPTER 27

Our house was all abuzz about traveling to West Virginia for the Spring Revival this coming weekend. It was being held in a big tent on Brother Mugs' farm. They were expecting more than a thousand people to attend. It was a scary and powerful thing to have a thousand Holiness folks in one place. The Spirit would be flowing so freely that we were bound to see miracles. I didn't even worry about someone being snake bit this weekend. The snakes were usually powerless when the Holy Ghost was as thick as fog.

Although churches as far as Canada practiced serpent handling, it remains most popular in the Appalachian and southern region of the country. Since the practice isn't illegal in West Virginia, the state has become the snake handling "Mecca" of America. Brother Mugs is the unofficial leader and organizer of the snake handling community.

Perry was crazy about Brother Mugs. Even in normal conversation, his voice box was stuck on the loud and booming setting. At first, kids were usually afraid of him, but as soon as they got over their fright, they loved him. He always kept his pockets full of bubble gum and candy and could expertly pull coins out of ears and make his finger disappear. He had many tricks up his sleeve. Since he and Sister Paulette had no children of their own, they adopted all of the children of the church. He especially loved to prank with my little sister because she would give it right back to him. The weekend would be filled with the two of them trying to out prank each another.

Even if I didn't want to go, staying home would not have been an option. We treated this long weekend as our vacation. We stayed in a Holiday Inn Express that had an indoor swimming pool. Even Laurel seemed to be excited about the much needed getaway. I'm sure the Seeleys would be there as well, but they wouldn't stay in a hotel. I'd bet money on that. Brother Seeley was too cheap. He'd find some good-hearted West Virginia family that would open their home up to him and his big boys. He'd mooch all weekend.

Even the excitement of a weekend in West Virginia wasn't enough to make Perry a happy camper on Sunday evening when Laurel asked if she could ride with us to school the next day. Perry didn't hesitate with her answer, "No, you can just ride with Momma and Whit.

There's not much room in the truck, and we leave too early for you. You'll never be ready in time."

The next morning Laurel was completely ready and waiting for us in the truck. She was wearing her hair in a ponytail that matched Perry's and mine. Perry was mad the entire duration of the trip. She made Laurel scoot to the middle so she could sit next to the window, but when she saw Laurel lean her head on my shoulder, she was mad she wasn't the one sitting in the middle. For some reason, Laurel seemed to cling to me right now like I was her lifeboat keeping her afloat. Lord knows, I was not a good one to cling to; I was barely keeping myself from drowning.

When Perry was getting out of the truck, she said, "Laurel, I know you're sad about being dumped and about Red Ruby and all, but we just don't have enough room for you to ride with us anymore." Then she stomped all the way into school. I said a little prayer for her teachers today.

I parked in the faculty lot again. Maybe part of me subconsciously wanted a glimpse of Coach Z on this fine Wednesday morning. Laurel didn't seem in a hurry to get out of the truck. She just sat there staring at the front window with her truck door open.

"What's wrong?"

With one foot out of the truck, she said, "You were right."

"Right about what?"

Completely out of the truck, she said, "You know." Then she quickly walked on ahead while she let me try to figure it out.

I just sat in the truck trying to make sense of what she was trying to tell me. Then it dawned on me what she was talking about. I felt sick.

CHAPTER 28

Kelsey hit pay dirt—she had the goods on Paige Benton. She was grinning like an opossum while Beth's eyes were wide in anticipation. Evidently Kelsey was waiting for me to arrive so she'd only have to tell the story once. I didn't have any smiles in me right now. I felt like someone had sucker punched me. Maybe I was wrong about what Laurel was trying to tell me. I sure hope so, but right now I didn't want to think about it. I'd become pretty adept at compartmentalizing my feelings. I really just wanted to fully concentrate on what we'd dubbed, "Operation Revenge."

"Can we go to your mom's classroom to talk?" Kelsey asked while looking suspiciously around the foyer.

I looked to make sure Mom's duplicate school keys were included on the truck's key ring. "Yep, I have her key." She always kept her room locked because of all the expensive musical instruments that were stored there.

"Hurry up!" Beth called back to us since she was several steps ahead. "I think I'm going to bust if I don't find out this news."

As soon as we were safely tucked inside Mom's music room away from any prying eyes or ears, Kelsey began. "Well, Scout called his friend and told him that he was thinking about asking Paige Benton out but wanted to make sure she wasn't a freak."

"And?" Beth continued to try to speed her up.

"You're just making it worse. Just sit there and listen. Now, where was I?" I could tell Kelsey was enjoying tormenting Beth.

Beth repeated, "Scout talked to that guy to see if Paige was a freak."

Buying some dramatic time, Kelsey turned her head first to me then turned to look at Beth before saying, "Well ... she *is* a freak!"

Beth even hopped up and gave me a high five. "I knew it, I knew it."

"Evidently, she's had sex with every guy in Clarksdell that would have her. She even had her own nickname. Scout was too much of a gentleman to tell me what it was but he gave me a few hints," Kelsey explained.

"What was her nickname?" I asked.

"He said she was called Free, another word for cat, Paige."

I knew immediately what her nickname was but wasn't going to say it out loud. Beth was still trying to figure it out. "Free Kitty Paige, Free Feline Paige, Free Kitten Paige."

We were really too naïve to be going off to college in a few months. Finally, I helped Beth out a little by saying, "Think Shrek. What was the cat's name in the movie?"

"Oh! Free Puss in Boots Paige? That doesn't make any sense."

Kelsey said, "Take off the *in boots* part, and you will almost have it."

I could tell Beth was a little embarrassed that it took her so long to figure it out. "Oh, that makes me almost sad for her."

"Don't feel too sad about her since she's the one trying to set you up," I reminded her.

Kelsey got our attention back. "That's not all. Evidently she was a stalker too. She would sleep with the guy and then would taunt his girlfriend. Until she stalked and taunted the wrong girl."

Beth asked, "Misty Shane?"

"Close. It wasn't Aphrodite, but it was one of her best friends whose Dad just happened to be an attorney. He filed charges against her for harassing communications."

I said, "So this is the reason she was banished to the farm. I guess old habits really do die hard."

Beth was mad again and up on her soapbox. "Looks like she would have learned her lesson, but here she is trying to play mean games with me. I really was nice to her."

Kelsey said, "Beth, you're nice to everyone. She's just got problems."

"So maybe we should just leave it alone?" I said.

"No way." Kelsey said. "I'm having too much fun. Plus Paige and Sadie had to be involved somehow in all of your Nashville drama."

Then Beth chimed in. "Heck no! These girls need to learn their lesson. Since she and Sadie will be seniors next year, they may try to be mean to others. We need to let them both know that we aren't gonna sit back and take it from 'em."

"Okay. So what're we gonna do?" I asked while looking at Kelsey.

"Don't look at me. I completed my homework, now it's up to you two to figure out the revenge part."

Beth said, "Let me think about it. I can't let little Puss in Boots get away with messing with me."

I was still laughing at Beth as I headed toward the gym. I still had several minutes to spare before the first bell rang. My happiness quickly dissipated when I saw Sadie sitting on the bleachers with her crutches placed next to her; they were all that separated her from Coach Z. They were talking and laughing like they were the best of friends. As soon as Sadie noticed me, she waved her arms over her head like she was signaling for an airplane. I didn't smile when I slightly waved back.

Laurel was waiting at the truck after school let out. "I told Momma that I was going to go with you to the building supply store. Hope that's okay?"

"That's fine." I said as I opened the driver's door. Actually, I was happy to see her and hoped we could talk more about what she'd said earlier,

Both of us seemed too quiet for the first few minutes of the drive. I didn't know whether I should dive right into where we left off this morning, or let her mention it when she was ready. I decided to wait her out. To break the silence, I asked, "Anyone notice your ponytail?"

"Actually, I had a few friends say they liked it. Can you believe that?" She smiled.

"We may've created a monster. You may never wear hairspray again."

"It sure makes getting ready easier."

"It's a good thing that we're Holiness, or y'all would never be to school on time if you and Whitley had to put your makeup on each morning too."

"Les, wouldn't you like to just try to wear a little make up? I've looked all through the Bible and can't find anything that says 'thou shalt not wear makeup.' What do you think?"

"I asked Dad about it once, and he told me a little about Jezebel and quoted a couple of verses about painted eyes, but he said it was more of a personal thing between a woman and God. He said while we were under his and Mom's care, they had an obligation to teach us to be modest and Godly women. That was the reason he expected us to conform to the Holiness dress code. But as we got older, we would have to be the ones to determine God's plan for us and be responsible for walking in the light the Lord personally shows us."

She gave her best Brother Clay Lewis imitation as she said, "Take that plank out of your eye before you go trying to get the sawdust out of someone else's."

"Dad also said that we all have different walks in life. If God tells me to keep my hair long and I cut it, then that would be a sin. It's just like wearing pants. I don't think it's a sin for me. Dad always says we have to be careful not to listen to man but to listen to God."

Like Dad, I noticed how Laurel also carefully weighs things out before she speaks. "Has God ever spoken to you?"

"I've never heard God audibly speak to me, but I've heard him speak inside my head. Plus when I get those feelings from time to time, I think that could be from God."

"Do you think he can forgive me?" she asked.

Oh boy. Here it comes. I braced myself for this conversation because I knew immediately what she needed forgiveness for. I took a deep breath. "Of course he can, and he will as long as you repent. Could you be pregnant?"

She started crying. "I don't know."

I gave her a little time to squeeze off her tears before I asked, "How long ago did it happen?"

"Which time?"

I tried not to act shocked, but I was. After all, she was only fifteen years old and the pastor's daughter. "The first time?"

"Three Sundays ago." She began using her fingers to count. "Sixteen days ago, to be exact, was the first time we actually went all the way. Then we did it again on that Thursday night and again Sunday before last." Her head dropped slightly.

I managed to keep the vehicle in the road as I barely squeaked out the next question, "Did he wear protection?"

"No. He said it was up to me to protect myself. He said wearing a condom was the same as spilling his seed on the ground, which was a sin."

I pulled the truck over when I saw a wide spot on the side of the road. My knees were so weak and wobbly—I barely could press the brake. "You can tell me the truth. Did Joseph force you?"

"*Kinda.*"

"What do you mean, *kinda*?"

"One minute he had his hands down *there* and then the next minute he was on top of me. I couldn't say anything because he put his hand over my mouth so no one would hear me cry."

I was sick. I felt sure it was rape. "What about the other times?"

"I told him I didn't want to do it again, but he told me if I loved him I would let him do it whenever he wanted. He also told me that I better do what he said, or he would have Brother Seeley throw Dad out of the church because I was such a Jezebel."

I wanted to hurt Joseph Seeley, but I tried to keep my anger in check. Instead of going off on a tirade, I asked, "Do you love him?"

"Sometimes. It's like he's two different people. He can be the nice Joseph one minute and then he can be so mean the next. I think I kinda love the nice one, but I hate the mean one. Does that make sense?"

I probably knew better than anyone what she was trying to say. "It does."

"He would say stuff to try to get me to do things. He would call me a baby and say that his other girlfriend didn't cry when it hurt. He said some other things that were so horrible that I can't even say them out loud." When she looked up at me, I could tell she was broken. She was between a rock and a hard place. Joseph not only raped her, but now she feels like she has to continue to let him abuse her so Brother Seeley doesn't hurt Dad. *I'm not going to let him by with this!*

I held her, and we both cried.

"Are you going to tell Mom and Dad?"

I just sat there and looked at her. "I don't know what we should do. But Joseph has to be stopped. Are you late?"

"Not yet."

"Let's wait until we know if you're pregnant or not. *I'll* take care of Joseph Seeley myself. If I even hear that you've spoken to him, then I'll tell our parents. Got it?"

"I don't want to get around him, but I'm afraid not to. I don't want him to tell Mom and Dad all those horrible things about me."

"Don't worry. He can't afford to tell anyone because it would only incriminate him. He's just trying to control you."

A random picture of Sister Seeley's sad face came into my mind. "No wonder Sister Seeley drank the poison." I knew apples didn't fall far from the tree.

Laurel agreed. "Poor Sister Seeley."

CHAPTER 29

When we crossed over into West Virginia, I almost cried in relief. I wanted nothing more than to leave all my worries behind at the state line. I felt like the piece of meat in the middle of two wild dogs while Perry and Laurel continued to compete for my attention. All Perry could see was Laurel was trying to take her place. She couldn't understand that I was the only glue holding Laurel together right now. It wasn't that Laurel *wanted* to hang out with me—she needed me.

Laurel just couldn't be pregnant with the spawn of Joseph Seeley. Being bound together forever with the Seeley family was the worst possible thing I could imagine. Plus, Laurel was only fifteen-years-old. She wasn't old enough to drive a car and had to be reminded to do her homework. I can't even imagine her taking care of a baby.

Not only did I have the mental drain of Laurel's issues, I also had my own problems. Coach Z pretty much acted as though I didn't exist all week. This was exactly what I wanted him to do a week ago. Now that he was honoring my request, I was even more miserable. He'd quit texting me, quit giving me weather forecasts, and was now treating me with the same indifference he did to his other female students. He'd moved on and was very attentive to another student—Sadie Long. While the rest of our class completed the exercises and ran laps, he would sit with injured Sadie on the bleachers. I couldn't hear what they were saying, but they sure were enjoying each other's company.

Sadie loved every minute of it, and it was driving me insane. I still didn't believe she was hurt. I couldn't blame her for faking it. If I had to choose between gym class and sitting and talking to Coach Z, then I'd choose the second option too. I only had to contend with this for thirty more days. I also changed my mind about Sadie. She wasn't likeable or entertaining at all. Just the opposite, she was despicably evil. I really think I hate her.

The only reprieve from my tormented life was when I worked on *Operation Revenge* with Beth and Kelsey. Beth was the one who came up with the final plan. It was relatively simple—but a good plan. It only involved one act of espionage and one act of breaking and entering.

Beth began sending texts to Sadie's phone number like she was sending them to the real Henry. She would work all day trying to figure out the exact words. She even enlisted Paige and Sadie in helping to craft the messages.

In my opinion, Henry's return messages were sloppy and just showed that Paige didn't really know him. Beth would read the texts with dreamy eyes pretending they were really from the Greek God. I kept reminding her. "He will call. Just you wait and see."

She would always respond the same way. "Because I'm adorable and he can't resist me, right?"

Meanwhile, as we continued our Lewis mini vacation, I couldn't help but notice the mountains. The farther into West Virginia we drove, the higher the mountains loomed over top of us. As we headed into some of the highest mountains I'd ever seen, I decided this weekend to focus only on the mountains of my life and forget the valleys. I wanted to enjoy being with my family. After all, I didn't know how many more spring revivals I'd be able to attend since I may be away at school.

Perry was practicing her tricks she was going to play on Brother Mugs. She'd conned me into giving her enough money to buy a battery-operated whoopee cushion that made all kinds of strange sounds. She also bought silly string and slime. She was ready. Brother Mugs would love it.

Whitley was having a tough time without having her best friend and fellow curling iron queen at her side. At one point while in the van, she whispered in my ear. "Did you tell Laurel that I was the one who told you?"

I whispered back, "Your name was never mentioned."

"Promise?"

"It's going to be okay." I tried to reassure her. I recognized Red Ruby's rattle in the back of the van about the time those words came out of my mouth.

Dad only brought Red Ruby and a couple of our newer snakes with us on this trip. Although we didn't want people to be bitten, it defeated the entire purpose of taking up serpents if the snakes were tame or sickly. God's true glory couldn't shine through.

Red Ruby received a lot of attention at the annual revival. The kids would normally come by to see Ruby and the red buttons on the end of her tail. They marveled at the large, marble-sized jewels on her box and would say that they were real rubies and that she and her box were worth thousands—maybe millions.

As soon as we saw the green H of the Holiday Express sign, Dad announced, "We're here." Sometimes he still treated us like we were all little girls.

Perry couldn't wait to get in the pool. "Momma, can we please swim just a little before we have to go to the revival?"

"Les, can you take her?"

"Sure. Laurel, Whitley, you want to swim too?"

Whitley's comment was typical, "I won't have time to fix my hair back."

Laurel almost laughed at her own inside joke before she said it, "You can always pull your hair back in a ponytail."

Perry, Laurel, and I laughed, but Whitley didn't understand what was so funny. Momma said, "Whit, you can always use one of those shower caps in the room to swim in if you don't want to mess up your hair."

We already looked freaky enough with our *modest* bathing suits without adding shower caps to the list. Mom special ordered our bathing suits this year from a company out of Jerusalem. They were made out of bathing suit material, but they didn't resemble the bathing suits from Sports Illustrated in the least. The long-sleeved tops are tight fitting enough to keep them from showing any skin. The bottom is a long skirt with built-in leggings. It's all about modesty.

CHAPTER 30

Since Dad was scheduled to preach tonight, we had to end our swim session early so we could go to the revival. Momma packed a cooler she'd leave in the van in case anyone got hungry later. Sometimes these revivals would last all night and continue right on through the next day without a break.

The tent was set up in the middle of a big pasture field on Brother Mugs' farm, and the anticipation in the air had a carnival feel. It was refreshing seeing so many people congregated in one place that looked and dressed like our family. The men all wore varying combinations of the standard Holiness uniform consisting of black pants, black jacket, white shirt, with a vest and a tie of varying colors. Before the night was over, most of the jackets and even the vests would be removed with the ties dangling freely from their necks. It didn't matter what the women wore as long as the skirts and the sleeves were long and the colors were not loud or offensive. I left my jeans at home and blended with everyone else.

Just like my dad, the men with hair wore the same swoop hairstyle that Elvis made popular. Many of the women, including my mom, wore their long hair in what I affectionately call the Holiness bun—a bun wrapped round and round at the base of the neck. It was still nice to be with other people who had the same heritage. It was like we were from a foreign planet and found our mother ship here in Jolo, West Virginia.

The tent was one of the biggest ones I've seen. The sides were pulled up. The stage was large enough for a small praise choir, a full band, the snake boxes, and a preaching podium. Brown wooden chairs were lined up in rows. I stopped counting when I got to five hundred and that was about halfway to the end. The musicians were already playing. The makeshift altar in front of the stage was already full with prayer warriors on their knees.

Laurel saw them before I did. She stopped in her tracks and grabbed my arm. I'm not sure if she grabbed it to get my attention or to steady herself. Perry started waving her arms. "Look, guys, it's the Seeleys!" She yelled to get their attention. They noticed us and were coming our way. I thought Laurel was going to start running. I held onto her arm and wouldn't let her leave my side. "It'll be okay. I'm here." Whitley stood on the other side of her.

"Hey, Joseph, James, Jacob, Brother Seeley." Perry was oblivious to the rest of her sisters' unease. "We're staying at the Holiday Express, where y'all staying?"

"We're staying with Brother Hensley and his wife. They were kind enough to take us in for the weekend," Brother Seeley explained.

"You'll have to come to our hotel and swim with us," Perry started extending the invitation until I pinched her. "Oww!"

"Dad, can we go swim with them?" Jacob, the youngest of the Seeleys asked.

I could tell Brother Seeley was ready to pawn his spawns off on us, so I stopped him before he even started. There was no way I was letting Joseph Seeley anywhere around Laurel, especially in a swimming pool. "I'm sorry, but I'm not sure how much we'll even get to swim this weekend since our hotel is over in Logan. More than likely, we'll have to sleep in the van if we get any sleep at all tonight."

Brother Seeley's nice voice and understanding expressions matched each other when he said, "That's okay. We've been praying for two hundred souls to be saved over the weekend. Haven't we, boys?" But his eyes told a different story. His eyes told how he really felt about me and my entire family. They kept shifting from one girl to the other. Perhaps he was trying to determine if any of us had evidence of a snakebite.

Joseph never took his eyes off Laurel. I could tell he was willing her to make some kind of eye contact with him, but thankfully she didn't take his bait. She either looked at the ground or in another direction.

As they started to turn away, Perry said, "Sorry, guys. If we get to go swimming, I'll let you know. Bye James, Jacob, Joseph."

As soon as they were far enough away, Perry asked, "Why did you pinch me?"

"Perry Gail Lewis. I don't want to be around those Seeleys. Do you understand me? Laurel doesn't either."

"Well just because y'all don't like them, doesn't mean that me and Whitley don't like them. Does it, Whit?"

Even though Whitley once had plans of marrying one of the Seeleys, she'd seen enough in that nursery room to make her leery of them too. She said, "I don't want to be around them either."

Perry started with more of her sass until she saw Brother Mugs. She made a beeline straight to the big man. He was a big man in both height and weight. He had a head full of brown mixed with gray hair styled in the Holiness swoop. His suit was black and his tie was already dangling. "There's my girl," he said as she jumped into his arms.

After he let Perry down, he said, "Now, let me take a good look at the Lewis girls." He went down the line and hugged each of us. It wasn't one of those creepy old man hugs. His hugs were sincere. I noticed when he got to Laurel, he held onto her longer. Then he asked her, "Are you okay?"

Laurel just nodded her head. He must have sensed something wasn't right. I could see it in his eyes. He then hugged and released Whitley, but she got the short end of Brother Mugs' attention since he was no longer jovial. He seemed concerned.

Perry brought his attention back to her. "You just wait. I'm going to pay you back this year when you least expect it."

This caused his smile to return. "Perry Gail, you can't get anything over on me." His big voice boomed loud enough for everyone under the tent to hear him. "Brother Clay brought Red Ruby, didn't he?"

I said, "Oh yeah. He doesn't take her to regular church services much anymore, but he loaded her up first thing this morning."

"Oh, I can already feel it. Little ladies, tonight's going to be good. It'll be a Red Ruby kind of night. The Lord's gonna show up and show off." As he turned away, he said, "Mark my word."

I could see Mom up on the stage playing the keyboard. The music was so loud that I felt the bass vibrating clear through to my bones. Some of the prayer warriors from earlier were dancing while others were running up and down the aisles speaking in tongues. Some had already been slain in the spirit and were flat on their backs or bellies on the ground. From where I sat, I could see no one rolling anywhere. I still didn't understand why we were branded with being "holy rollers."

"Let's go find a seat up front. I don't want to miss anything," Perry said.

Laurel was still holding on to my hand. She hadn't said a word since our run-in with the Seeleys. She was still trembling.

Brother Mugs started the revival off. He screamed into the microphone, "Anybody huuunngggrrry?" He waited on a response before he said, "Well, supper's ready. Come on in and feast at the Master's table. We're serving up a good mess of Holy Ghost revival to anyone whose soul is hungry for more. Wooo," he proclaimed while he shivered like a wet dog. "Do you feel it? Do you feel it?" He looked out to see if he got any nods of confirmation. "I sure do. Children, we're gonna see miracles this weekend. We may not get a lot of sleep, but we're gonna experience changes. How many of you want to be able to tell your grandchildren that you were part of the Bible-thumping, holy-rolling, snake-handling, miracle-filled revival in Jolo, West Virginia?" He then held the microphone out to get our response. Everyone was on their feet hollering. It was so loud I could barely hear my own thoughts.

The music started playing, and it all began. We all sat mesmerized by what we saw and heard. Even though my dad didn't know what was going on with Laurel, he preached straight to her. Both of us cried during his entire sermon. Then we cried again when the little man in the wheelchair got up and danced around. I'd been to some services when some of the healings seemed staged. I could tell this one was real.

Brother Mugs was the first one to take up serpents. The lights caught the red jewels, and the color scattered across the tent. Red Ruby came out fighting. She was mad. When he laid her on the table, she immediately coiled up. "Children, let me introduce you to Red Ruby. She's been around a long time. She is a work of the devil. Just like the ole devil, Ruby wants to kill me. Look at that big red tail shake. Do you hear her talking?" He placed the microphone so everyone could hear the eerie noise of her rattle. "If she could talk, she'd be saying …" He squinted his eyes and narrowed his shoulders in his best Red Ruby imitation. He even stuck his tongue out a time or two before he said, "Sonssss and daughtersssss of Eve, I will forever hate you. I missssss my beautiful legsss.'" He hissed each time he made the "s" sound. "You know the serpent once had legs, don't you?" Then he began to pray loudly in tongues. He leaned over so he was only a couple of inches from Red Ruby's head and said boldly in an even louder voice, "Satan, you can't touch me."

Everyone else was watching Brother Mugs, but I was watching Ruby. I expected her to strike anytime. Instead, her tail fell flat, and she uncoiled like something had just hit her over the head. I thought she was dead.

Brother Mugs started jumping up and down. "Children, Red Ruby was just slain in the Spirit!" Then the revival really got jumping as everyone sprang to their feet and began praising the Lord. I'd never seen Ruby act like that. I knew for a fact that was not staged. I worried she was dead. Then as soon as Brother Mugs stepped away, I saw her rattle pop up. I was relieved. *I think.*

Later, when the altar call was made, Laurel was one of the first ones there. Perry and Whitley followed right behind her. I stayed at my seat. I discovered a few years back that I could make an altar wherever I was and didn't have to go up front. I'm sure if I did go up, then I'd be bombarded with everyone trying to pray the devil out of me. Out of the corner of my eye, I saw Joseph Seeley make his exit from the tent. Realizing this was a perfect opportunity to have his undivided attention, I followed him. I found him leaned up on a truck smoking a cigarette.

"I didn't think football players were allowed to smoke."

"I didn't realize preacher's daughters were allowed to wear jeans, so we're even," he said while continuing to puff on the cigarette. He even offered me one.

I just shook my head. I was trying to figure out how to start my talk. I'd not had much experience giving talks—my expertise was more on the receiving end. "Joseph, I know all about you and Laurel."

Without missing a beat, he replied, "Well I would hope so since you've known us both all your life."

I changed my tone and narrowed my eyes like I meant business. "You know exactly what I'm talking about. You better never come near her again. Do you understand me?"

He stood up to his full height of over six feet and mashed his cigarette with his foot. "Listen here, you little Ms. Jezebel. I don't know what your sister has told you, but if I were you, I would march right back in the tent and go pray for her soul. She is nothing but a two-bit slut. She's banged every guy at church and even tried to get my little brothers to do her. So yeah, I took her up on her offers. I'm a man and God understands our weaknesses, but your sister, Laurel, is on a one-way ticket to hell."

He took me off guard. When he spoke, pure evil sprang from his mouth. "Joseph Seeley, you are such a liar. I'm warning you—you better stay away from her."

He took a step toward me and pinned me up against the truck. Fear rose up in me because he was a big boy. My chances of fending him off were not good. A calm came over me as soon as I knew what to do. I put my hands on his chest and seductively rubbed on his nasty wet with sweat shirt.

"I guess it runs in the family," he said as he pressed his body up against mine.

As soon as he did, I pulled my knee up as hard as I could into his groin. Only a guttural grunt came out of his mouth, but it gave me time to get away from him. I moved out of his grasp and ran as fast as I could back to the tent.

I heard him call out, "This isn't over, you jeans-wearing Jezebel!"

Great, another enemy to worry about. I was getting pretty good at making them lately.

Just when I thought he was finished with hurling his threats and insults, I heard him call out in his normal friendly tone, "I'm glad Red Ruby's doing okay. I really worried about her last Saturday night."

I wanted to go back and punch him. My mind was racing trying to figure out if it could've been him that let Red Ruby out. Somehow I didn't think so because Joseph had always been afraid of the snakes. My bet is that Brother Seeley brought her upstairs, placed her in one of my drawers, and then bragged about it to his boys.

Instead of going back inside, I saw our parked van only a few steps away. I felt the bile rise to my throat and held on to the side of the van as I heaved. I then locked myself inside the van just in case Joseph followed me. I knew my mom kept every emergency supply known to man in the big box in between the two bucket seats. I could smell his perspiration all over me. It smelled just like the smell of my nightmares. Using wet wipes, I was able to rid myself of his odor. I also found some peppermint candy for my vomit breath and some good-smelling lotion to help at least cover up the Seeley stench.

My sisters were still at the altar when I returned to my same seat in the tent. Brother Mugs was down on his knees praying with Laurel. Whitley and Perry were slightly behind her. I could see him talking, and then I saw the back of her head go up and down like she was agreeing with something he said.

I could feel the heat of Joseph's eyes on me even though he was seated on the other side of the tent. I refused to look his way. I would not give him any power over me. I closed my eyes and prayed. I was so lost in prayer I didn't even hear when my sisters returned. When I looked at Laurel, I was certain I was looking into an angel's serene face. She was no longer the uptight mess of only a few minutes ago. "Are you okay?" I asked.

She hugged my neck and during the embrace, she said directly into my ear. "He spoke to me."

"Who? Brother Mugs?"

"No, silly. God did. He told me I was forgiven and that everything would be okay. I only had to look up when I had bad days, and he would be there."

I hugged her tighter. "That's great. I'm so happy for you."

"There's more. As soon as I heard God speak, Brother Mugs came and told me word for word what I'd just heard in my head."

"You got your confirmation. That means you're not pregnant." I continued to speak directly into her ear mainly because that was the only way we could hear each other.

"We'll see," she said like she knew more than she was telling me.

CHAPTER 31

As a family, we all came back to Kentucky revived but tired. We didn't get back to the hotel until five in the morning on Saturday. We slept until noon and then got ready and headed back to Brother Mugs' farm Saturday afternoon. Sister Paulette had prepared us a feast. Perry had the time of her life pulling pranks on Brother Mugs. She put slime in his handkerchief and got him a time or two with the sound machine. He just laughed and laughed.

We didn't make it back to the hotel until three on Sunday morning. Only Dad went back to the Sunday afternoon session. The rest of us slept in and swam until it was time to head home. Perry had swum herself into a vegetative state. She was so tired she could barely put two words together. Even the snakes were tired. I didn't hear one rattle out of Ruby the whole way home. Perry made it a point to sit with Whitley on the way home and ignored me as much as she could, still mad about Laurel.

Over the weekend, I'd done a lot of thinking, praying, and soul searching. I'd come to terms with a few things regarding my situation with Coach Z. First—and most importantly—I allowed myself to recognize that I liked Coach Z more than just a teacher or just a fishing buddy. I needed to learn to be honest with myself about my feelings. The second thing I recognized was the fact he would be my teacher for just a few more weeks. I couldn't be involved with him no matter how much I wanted until after I graduated, for his sake more than mine. Lastly, I'm not sure if how I felt about Coach Z was right or wrong in God's eyes. I just needed to be honest with God and with myself about how I felt.

I wish solving the Seeley problem was as easy as solving the Coach Z problem—it wasn't. Anyway I played it, the deck was always stacked in Joseph's favor. His evil accusations against my little sister caught me off guard and made me second guess her. Of course, it was only a matter of minutes before I completely ruled out his lies. But if he caused me to falter and mistrust Laurel, my little sister who I'd known all my life, then how many of the rest of the congregation would choose to believe him. I was not only dealing with just Joseph; I was dealing with the entire Seeley family. If I waged war with one, then all four of them would come out with guns blazing. The stakes of this war were high. With their Red Ruby stunt, they'd already proven they were capable of anything—even murder.

The wheels of my mind were turning as I alternated between speed walking and jogging down the hallway on Monday morning. I surely didn't want to be late. When I turned the blind corner, it felt like I collided with a wall. It occurred so fast that at first I didn't even realize what was happening, until I was already on the ground writhing in pain. I heard Coach Z say, *"O'waci*, what have you gone and done now?"

This is not happening. I was trying not to cry. "My ankle."

"Do you think it's broken?" He asked.

While in the middle of the hallway floor, I attempted to assess my injury. "I can move it." He began to feel around on my lower leg. His hands were warm and his fresh smell was causing me to focus more on him than on the pain.

"I don't think it's broken. You want to go to the infirmary?"

My words were labored, short and choppy. "Absolutely not. I have too much to do to deal with a sprain right now. Can you help me get to the trainer's room? If I can get some ice, then I'll be okay."

"Sure," he said. Instead of helping me to my feet, he carried me just like I'd seen him carry Sadie the other day.

"No, no. I can walk, put me down." I looked down both sides of the hallway to make sure there were no witnesses.

He laughed. "Not a chance."

I didn't lock my arms around his neck. It was nothing like I pictured a guy sweeping me off my feet would be like. It was very awkward.

Luckily, we were able to make it in the trainer's room without being noticed. He rolled up my pant leg and removed my shoe and sock to get a better look. I asked him, "Do you mind," (deep breath) "filling that basin up," (a sharp intake of air) "with ice and water?"

"Sure."

After the tub was filled, I was working up enough gumption to put my already hurting ankle in that ice cold mixture.

"Are you sure you want to do that? Looks painful to me."

"You got a," (pause) "better solution?"

"Actually I do. Did I ever tell you that my *tunkasila*—my grandpa, was the medicine man for our tribe?" He looked toward the door before he asked, "Will you be okay by yourself a minute?"

I nodded my head.

If I wanted to be able to get my ankle well, I knew I had to get it in that ice. There was no easy way to do it, either. I bit into my arm so I wouldn't scream while I plunged my foot up to mid-calf into the tub. It hurt. It hurt a lot.

"I can't leave you for a minute," he said when he returned and saw my foot in the ice. By this time the prickly pain of the cold was gone. In its place was throbbing numbness. At least I was able to talk in full sentences now even though my teeth were chattering. "Really this works," I told him. "Just ask Jeff Sheppard. Do you know who he is?"

"I think they made me take the UK Wildcat basketball test before I was able to cross the Kentucky state line. Sure, I know who he is."

"Well, he had a bad sprain in the semifinals of the 1998 NCAA tournament. He took the icy plunge over and over before the final game. Not only did he play in the championship game, he was the tournament's Most Valuable Player too."

"I bet the icy plunge hurt Jeff Sheppard too, didn't it?" He kneeled down in front of me and lifted my foot out of the tub. He then gently towel dried it. I'm sure it would've felt great had I been able to feel it. Using both of his hands he began to squeeze and tug on my foot all the way up to my knee. His eyes were closed. Mine were not, they were wide open.

"What are you doing?" I nervously asked.

"I'm asking Wakan Tanka to show me the place of the hurt."

"Why are you asking him? Just ask me. I can tell you where it hurts. My dad will disown me if Chief Wakan Tanka fixes my leg."

"He's not a chief. He's the Great Spirit—the Creator." He opened his eyes and began to rub on one spot of my ankle. He then took out a little plastic container and began to rub the minty, mud-like mixture on the spot. He placed a warm washcloth over the mixture and used plastic wrap to hold it all in place. "Now sit still for a few minutes."

"I wonder if your Great Spirit is the same as my Holy Spirit."

I could tell he was not interested in giving me a theology lesson today. "Why does it matter as long as you're healed? Let me go check on my class, and I'll be right back."

"Be sure and check on Sadie Long while you're at it."

He turned and threw a towel at me as he walked out.

I could feel my ankle getting hot. The substance felt cool and soothing when he first put it on my ankle. Now I was afraid it was going to burn through my leg.

As soon as he stepped into the room, he asked, "Getting a little hot and bothered, yet?"

"I'd say. What in the world did you put on my leg? Hydrochloric acid?"

"Medicine men never tell their secrets."

"Never?" I purposely asked it with as much flirt as I could muster. The anger I'd felt at him earlier was gone. I didn't even care he was a teacher or that he practiced voodoo. I just liked being with him.

"Never. Oh and by the way, *Ms. Long* said to tell you hello."

This time I was the one throwing the towel.

I couldn't contain the smile when I sat down with Kelsey and Beth at lunch.

"What canary did you just eat, Leslie, dear?" Kelsey eyed me with suspicion.

"You wouldn't believe it if I told you."

"So you really did eat a canary?" Beth was completely serious.

Kelsey and I both looked at Beth. There were no words.

Beth said, "Quit looking at me like that. I was just kidding."

In a playful mood, I said, "Thank goodness. I was worried that your blond hair had finally impacted you."

"Leave my blond hair out of this. So what happened?" Beth asked. "By the way, we missed you this weekend."

"I missed you all too. Would you believe me if I told you I fell and sprained my ankle right before first period?" I stood up and hopped on the bad leg.

"You look perfectly fine to me," Kelsey said.

"I'm serious. I ran into Coach Z in the hallway and twisted my ankle. Then Coach Z *carried* me to the training room and put some Indian salve on it. Now I'm just fine."

"No way." Kelsey looked at me like she was expecting me to say I was joking.

"Yes, way. I promise you it happened. I still can't believe it myself."

Beth wasn't as concerned about my miraculous healing as she was about me spending time with my gym teacher. "So he actually cradle carried you where your head rested on his shoulder like this?" She demonstrated.

I didn't answer but my smile did.

"Look at her," Kelsey said. "Bam! She's finally admitting she's got the hots for her teacher."

"Purely scandalous," Beth said.

"Okay, enough about me. Fill me in on what I missed out on *Operation Revenge*."

"The stage is set. *Henry ...*" Using the two fingers on both hands, she made visual quotation marks. "Wants to meet me on Thursday evening when *he* gets back from the game at around nine," Beth explained.

"Is everything ready?" I asked.

"*Almost*," Beth said while she looked to Kelsey for help in explaining the *almost*.

I recognized the look that both of them were giving me. They wanted something from me. Probably money. "Guys, I haven't worked in a couple of weekends. My money is going out faster than it's coming in with my new wardrobe and all."

Kelsey very convincingly played on my natural guilty conscience. "I understand. I just kind of thought you'd want to contribute to our little project. Beth and I worked *all* weekend getting things ready while *you* were away on vacation. But, I guess we'll just have to go work the street corner."

"Okay, okay, how much do you need?"

Beth said, "I have twenty-five dollars, so all we need from you is fifty. Scout's uncle is going to give us a good deal on a trail camera."

I reluctantly gave them the forty dollars I had in my pocket. "I'll bring the other ten tomorrow."

As soon as Beth saw Paige and Sadie, she called out to them.

"Oh, Paige, Sadie, come here. I've got to tell you about my latest text from Henry." Beth had become quite the actress.

Paige's expression didn't give anything away. "What did Henry say now?"

"He's begging me to meet him on Thursday night after he gets back from his game, but I haven't decided for sure if I should go or not. What do you think? Should I play a little harder to get, or should I meet him?"

Sadie hadn't spoken until now. "I think you definitely should go for it."

"I don't know, Beth." I then looked to Paige. "Didn't you say Misty Shane had found the first text? It may be too risky."

"Yes, she did, and I think she wasn't happy." Paige was still playing the game.

Sadie piped up, "Maybe they've broken up."

"No, I don't think they have," Beth explained.

Sadie was all smiles when she said, "Beth, I still think you should at least go and see if there's chemistry between the two of you."

"So, Beth, what are you going to do?" I asked.

"Just like Sadie said. I really need to see if there's any chemistry. I would hate for him to break up with Misty Shane only to find out we're all wrong for each other," Beth rationalized.

I guess Paige heard all she needed. "I'll see if I can find out where Misty Shane's planning to be on Thursday night. That way, you won't have to worry about running into her."

"That would be great if you could get that scoop. I've had one run-in too many with her," Beth explained.

As soon as Paige and Sadie were safely at their corner table, Kelsey made a prediction. "Tomorrow, Paige will tell us Misty Shane has some big plans and will not be in town on Thursday."

CHAPTER 32

Every morning, I would give Laurel a questioning look and every morning, she would continue to give me a thumbs down sign. Though she seemed to be handling things better than I was. She said she just kept hanging onto what God and Brother Mugs told her on Friday night about how everything was going to be okay.

Other than Laurel's situation, Perry pouting on me, Paige and Sadie watching my every move, and Joseph Seeley wanting to kill me, the week up until now had been a good one. Coach Z was what made it good. He sent me at least one or two texts a day checking on my ankle. In one text, he asked me to refer to him from now on as either "Oh Wise One" or "Great Healing Hands." I still argued that his mud didn't do the trick but rather it was the work of the Jeff Sheppard icing. I was pleased and relieved he gave me a Sunday weather forecast.

Since today was D-Day for our *Operation Revenge*, I had a lot on my mind. But, my biggest worry was not about our revenge act, but that tonight was church night. Laurel would have to encounter Joseph Seeley without me being there to protect her. There was no way around it. Whitley promised me she wouldn't leave Laurel's side. If he came around her, then she promised she would immediately go and get either Momma or Dad. Even though Laurel said she wasn't concerned about seeing him, we both knew he had a manipulative way about him. He could mess with Laurel's mind, making her more afraid of the repercussion of not having sex with him than going ahead and doing it. I hadn't understood the extent of his cruel and exploitive ways until he used them on me.

Perry was acting like a little punk. She refused to ride to school with Laurel and me when I drove yesterday. She said, "I don't want to be where I'm not wanted. I know you and your *best friend* have a lot to talk about." She was out of control and needed a good spanking. I was very close to being the one to give it to her.

I tried not to think of the foreboding feeling I had about Perry the other day. Actually as I ponder more about it, I realize I could've misread it. Instead of a warning about Perry, it could've been a warning about Laurel's problem. I didn't want to legitimize this feeling by talking or thinking about it.

My parents seemed to be over the rumor issue. Momma had yet to mention anything about the Nashville fiasco. I don't think she will. She did ask more questions about my need to stay with Beth tonight. I explained that Beth was supposed to meet the Adonis of her dreams in Clarksdell but wanted me and Kelsey there as chaperones. Although what I told her was the truth, I was guilty of the sin of omission. I left out all about our devious plans of revenge. If she knew exactly what we were doing, she would never allow me to be a party to it. Sin or not, I was sticking with my friends on this one. These girls had it coming.

Coach Z, Laurel and I, and Momma and Whitley arrived at the same time and we all walked from the faculty lot together. I could tell Whitley could barely contain her excitement. Then one by one everyone went their separate ways leaving Coach Z and me to walk to the gym together. I didn't bother to stop in the front foyer since neither Kelsey nor Beth was there.

"Aren't you going to greet me properly?" Coach Z asked with a serious scowl once we were alone.

"You'll have to wait a long time before I call you 'Oh Wise One' or 'Great Healing Hands.'"

"Come on. I'm your teacher. You're supposed to respect and honor me. Look at how good you're walking. You at least owe me something."

"Actually, it's Jeff Sheppard I owe."

"Will you get off that icy plunge stuff? Just admit I'm your hero."

I started noticing all the looks people were giving us as we walked boldly down the hallway together. At this point, I didn't care, and he didn't seem to either. "Hey, hope you don't mind using another pole to fish with on Sunday?"

"No way. That's my lucky pole. So does that mean you're not mad anymore?"

"I'm giving you another chance as long as you promise you don't have *another* girlfriend that's going to call me more names."

"I promise."

"My little sister, Perry, will have to come with us on Sunday. My dad said I couldn't fish alone with you anymore."

"Why did you have to tell him?"

Something in my stomach just did a flip-flop. "Well, my dad had a lot of questions after *your girlfriend* told everyone that I was a lesbian and had been fishing with you. Having your parents know all the gossip is one of the disadvantages of having your mom on the school's staff."

"Ex-girlfriend," he corrected me. "I didn't even think about that. I really am sorry."

"I'm over it now, but I really thought about leaving a copperhead in your truck or something."

"Oh that would have been so nice of you. Those mean copperheads are my favorites."

"Actually I really was being nice since I figured you had a better chance of surviving a copperhead bite than a rattler's."

Making a bold move, Coach Z put his arm on my back and patted it lightly. Then his hand rubbed along my back as it traced its way to my waist. Then he said, "Leslie Lewis, you are one of a kind."

Although the physical contact was over, my body's reaction to it wasn't. My knees were threatening to buckle; I could almost see my heart beating through my sweatshirt. When I finally got my bearings, I said, "Maybe I will call you 'Oh Wise One' on special occasions." *Where in the heck did that come from?*

CHAPTER 33

Our plan was pretty much foolproof even if I can't take credit for any of it. We traded Beth's car for her grandmother's truck, explaining we needed something bigger for a few hours. Her grandmother didn't ask any questions and seemed pleased to help us out. Her house was immaculate—so clean I was afraid to touch anything, but it smelled like mothballs. Actually Sister Rose smelled like a combination of mothballs, peppermint, and rosebuds when she hugged me. Today was her beauty parlor day, and her long hair had been piled up high on her head. This used to be the sign of a good Holiness woman—the higher the hair, the closer to God. *Tease us to Jesus* should've been the name of her beauty shop. Also like a good Holiness woman of years ago, she drove a pickup truck. Her house and hair may've been dated, but her pickup truck was a new black dual-wheel Chevy

Silverado. She was proud of her truck and had to show us every detail about it.

Beth explained to her that I would be the one driving it since I was more accustomed to pickup trucks. "Well, good," she stated. "Beth, honey, I've been a little worried since you're only half Holiness that you may struggle with my truck. But now, this little Lewis gal, she's a full-blooded Holiness. She should have no problems with it."

"Grandma, when did you become such a Holiness snob? You know people of all kinds of faith can drive trucks."

Sister Rose didn't comment. She pointed her finger at me, and said, "Take care of her." *I knew she was referring to the truck and not her granddaughter.*

I was the getaway driver, Beth was the timekeeper, and Kelsey was the engineer. Kelsey had us complete a walk-through before we left Sister Rose's house. Everything had to be timed perfectly, or our plan would not be effective. Our first stop was at the Root Beer Drive-In just to get us a bite to eat.

"I wonder if this is how bank robbers feel before they rob the bank," Beth said while drinking her root beer float.

Kelsey added, "If it is, then I may need to rethink my college major."

"I really don't think you'll find a college with Bank Robbery 101 as a course," I explained.

"Quit being a wet blanket. Just because your aspiration is to be living on a reservation somewhere doing rain dances, don't be hating on my Bonnie and Clyde dream," Kelsey joked.

Beth put in her dibs. "Well, I at least want to be Bonnie."

"But I'm not *dyke* enough to pull off the Clyde part," Kelsey protested while getting a dig in at me.

"Ouch." I let her know her dig was effective.

Beth said, "How about Bonnie and Clydette?"

Kelsey interrupted her. In a loud whisper, she said, "Quick, let's get out of here."

"What? Why?" I asked.

"Nine o'clock. Convertible BMW." Kelsey was taking this act of espionage a little too seriously.

"It's Aphrodite!" Beth cupped her hand over her mouth.

Although I was experienced in driving a truck, this one was a lot bigger than mine. There was no whipping in and out of a parking spot. We also had a tray full of glass mugs and garbage hanging onto the window. "We can't leave until the curb girl comes and gets this tray." I rolled my window up as far as it would go with the tray still on it to at least try to conceal our identities.

Beth demanded, "Beep your horn so she'll come and get the tray. We've got to get out of here before Misty sees us. That would ruin everything."

I did as she said, but the horn sounded more like a cruise ship than a truck horn, low and thunderous with a ripple of vibrations that continued after the initial blow. Nothing about it was inconspicuous.

Kelsey demanded, "Stop it! Everyone's looking at us."

"I just did what y'all told me to do. I didn't know it was going to sound like the freaking Titanic."

As soon as we were freed from the curb woman's tray bondage, I slowly pulled the truck out of the spot. I tried hard not to draw anymore unwanted attention to us.

Kelsey's lips were pursed when she smugly said, "Surprise, surprise. I guess Paige's *intel* was a little incorrect since she said Misty Shane would be out of town rehearsing for a beauty pageant tonight. And who was the one that called that?"

I added, "I'm sure both Paige and Sadie think that because we go to ACI that we're dumb hillbillies."

"We're about to show them dumb hillbillies." Beth's chest plumped out with her ACI pride.

I called out to Kelsey in the back seat, "So what next, Maestro?"

Kelsey said, "Drive by the stadium, and let's see if it's empty. According to all the online schedules, no one should be playing a game at the greyhound stadium tonight."

I slowly drove the dually through the stadium's parking lot. There were several cars parked in the lot, but they must've belonged to the traveling players because no one was on the field.

While we sat parked in the lot, we finalized the exact location of where the camera should be mounted. After we decided on the spot, Kelsey donned a red Clarksdell baseball hat as her disguise. Using my dad's battery-operated drill, she mounted the camera underneath the overhang of the concession stand.

"Perfect," Beth said when we synched up the camera to Kelsey's laptop. We could even zoom in and out using the mouse. "Gotta love technology."

It dawned on me that if we had a camera system in the snake room then we could've caught Brother Seeley red-handed. I handed Beth fifty dollars.

"What's that for?" she asked.

"I want to take this camera home to put in our basement." I left out all the details.

She scrunched up her nose. "Don't you all ever get tired of looking at the snakes?"

"If I owe more, let me know cause I'm taking this camera."

Beth was more interested in *Operation Revenge* than hearing about our snake room. She took the money and shrugged non-committedly.

For the next hour and a half, we drove around Clarksdell. "We're at t-minus twenty minutes until sunset," Beth the timekeeper said using NASA speak. "If we drive slowly, then we'll be just a few minutes early."

The online sources were correct; the sun gently dropped down and out of sight behind right field at eight-seventeen, and we were there to watch it.

"T-minus zero. It's time for liftoff, "Beth said while she hopped out of the passenger side door wearing another Clarksdell hat—this one with a big C in the middle of it. Using her cheerleading flyer skills, she easily climbed into the bed of the truck.

Just as we rehearsed, Kelsey exited the truck from my side. Beth timed it so that she handed her the cutout from the bed of the truck, and in one fluid motion, Kelsey took the cardboard image like she was taking the racing baton as part of a relay.

Kelsey placed the cutout in the location we decided upon, and then Beth used the laptop to help her position it for the best camera coverage.

"We have thirty minutes before the scheduled meeting. Do we have to leave? Can't we just stay here and watch it live?" Beth asked.

"No, it's way too risky to be this close," Kelsey explained.

I am enjoying this way too much. I wanted to stay too. "But wouldn't it be fun to hear what they were saying. The camera doesn't have sound. We can stay parked back here."

"I guess it'll be okay," she relented.

Then we waited, and waited, and waited some more. Finally, we heard a car.

"It's her. It's her BMW," Beth explained as the car drove slowly by the curb where the cutout was on display. Then the car stopped with a screech.

Kelsey placed the laptop so we could all see the up-close action. We were counting on Paige to get word to Misty Shane about this setup meeting between Beth Rudder and Henry Noble. She didn't disappoint.

So far it was playing out just as we'd hoped. Kelsey had worked very hard to Photoshop one of Aphrodite's pucker-face pictures onto Marilyn Monroe's red-sequined body. She added some sequined covered devil horns on top of Misty Shane's head as well as a red devil tail coming from behind. The best part was the message and signature at the bottom of the cutout: *I may be gone from Clarksdell, but I still know how to make Henry happy! All my love, Paige.*

We all heard the vibration of Beth's phone, Paige's text said. *Good luck. Hope you have a great chemistry-filled night with Henry!!!* The text message was followed by two emoji—a thumbs up and a heart.

Beth texted back. *I fully intend on having an awesome night.* She used the emoji with the devil's horns.

"Hurry, put your phone down. The show's about to begin," I ordered.

Beth began doing her best play by play even though we were sitting right next to her. "Misty sees it. She's getting out of the car. Oh no. She's reading it. She kicked it. She kicked it again. Oh-em-gee. Now her friends are pulling her back. She kicked it over. Uh oh. Now, she's stomping it!"

I cracked the window more so we could better hear everything being said.

"All my love, Paige—who in the world is Paige?" one of the other goddesses asked.

There was no mistaking the owner of the loud and angry voice I heard next. Misty screamed, "It's got to be Paige Benton! This is so like her to send me an anonymous message to set me up like this."

"I thought Paige was on probation," a calmer and more rational voice stated.

"She's messed with the wrong girl this time. She's gonna pay dearly for this," Misty Shane threatened while taking her anger out on her car door. She drove a hundred yards then she stopped.

"Oh no! Does she see us?" Beth asked.

We could see the red tail lights begin to back slowly toward the curb. One of the girls hopped out and retrieved the cutout. It hung from the back of the car as she sped away.

We waited over thirty minutes to make sure it was safe to leave. When the coast was clear, Kelsey slipped out into the night and retrieved my new snake room camera. As we drove, Kelsey successfully uploaded the video footage to YouTube from an account belonging to some unsuspecting soul living in Portsmouth, New Hampshire.

I turned to Kelsey and said, "Maybe you shouldn't rule out a future in crime." I raised my Styrofoam root beer cup and said, "Well done, Bonnie and Clydette, well done."

CHAPTER 34

The next day was a blur—a good blur. While we were sitting at our normal morning perch in the school's front foyer, Beth texted Sadie's phone. *Paige and Sadie, (A.K.A Henry Noble), let us know the next time you want to play games with us! We had fun.* She added a couple of devil-horned emojis for effect.

We were sitting across from them and watched as they read Beth's message. When they looked over at us, we just waved and smiled. For someone with an injured leg, Sadie sure maneuvered quickly as she and Paige hightailed it down the hallway.

During first period, Sadie sat alone on the bleachers. Every time I looked over her way, her laser-like stare was slicing me to pieces. I let her dice me up. As far as I was concerned, it was over. The score was now even as we redeemed ourselves from the fake texting and her involvement with the Emily fiasco.

Today, we played full-court basketball, and our teacher also played with us. I didn't even care what the other students thought when he guarded me a little too closely. No one could say I went easy on him; I threw a few elbows at his midsection just as I would've anyone else.

The tide had changed in our relationship. Although Coach Z was my teacher and my friend, I wanted more. I hadn't planned on falling for him, but I was hooked. I no longer questioned his motive for a relationship with me. After the game was over, I stopped and talked to him for a few minutes. My hair was matted to my head with sweat, and my t-shirt and sweatpants were equally wet. I looked a mess, but if he noticed, he didn't act repulsed.

It wasn't a coincidence that Sadie fell in line behind me as I left the gym, it was planned. I could hear her uneven gait and smell her loud perfume even before she said, "Y'all think you're so smart, don't you. Just know that you're bound to mess up, and when that happens, we'll be there."

I was in such a good mood that I almost let her by with her threat ... almost. Instead, I came to a sudden stop and wheeled around so I was facing her. "You know, Sadie. You really need to focus on getting that ankle healed up before your behind starts spreading." I knew it was corny as soon as I said it and wished

I could've thought of something with more bite, but that was the best I could do.

"You will slip up," she said as she and her medical walking boot tried to increase the distance between us.

At lunch, Kelsey told Beth and me what she'd heard about our incident last night. Our upload on YouTube had over fifty-five hundred views already. Scout's Clarksdell connection called him and encouraged him *not* to go out with Paige Benton. He said she was psychotic and had messed with the wrong girl last night. He told Scout he wouldn't be surprised if a lynch mob wasn't hot on her trail. Paige would have to move a lot farther than the end of Leslie County to get away from this girl's wrath.

According to a good source—my momma—a sheriff's deputy had been to school today serving papers on a student for violating some kind of court decision. She said the student had been issued a date to appear before the judge next week. I knew she was talking about Paige, but I didn't comment. It could've been my guilty conscience, but I was pretty sure Momma was baiting me to see what I knew. I didn't take her bait. I also made myself a mental note to wait a few days before installing the snake camera.

Although everything on the home front was not perfect, at least church went okay last night for Laurel. According to Whitley, Joseph Seeley stayed away from Laurel the entire evening. He didn't even make eye contact with her. Before church started, he and Jacob played basketball with Perry, but Whitley said she watched them the entire time they played. Hopefully, Joseph had taken heed to my warning. I knew that was wishful thinking, but miracles still happen. *Right?*

CHAPTER 35

Perry acted more like her sweet self than the spoiled brat of the last few days when I asked her to go to work with Dad and me on Saturday. I'm sure she was happiest because we would be alone— Laurel would not be going. Today we had to design a large butterfly in the middle of an outdoor patio. I think this was my favorite project ever. The morning temperature was perfect for working outside, and a nice breeze continued to blow. The butterfly's wings would be a mixture of pinks and greens broken up by dark lines.

After a while, Perry and I were in the groove and so focused we didn't need to talk to communicate. Perry would have the exact tile I was looking for before I asked for it. I let her finish the last of the lower right wing while I ran and picked us up something for lunch.

When I examined her work after returning, something didn't look quite right with the finished product. It took me a minute before I figured what was wrong. Perry had hidden something in the middle of the bottom wing. The dark line separating the pink block from the green one was not a line at all, but rather … a snake. This snake's tail exploded with vibrant shades of pink. The snake was not obvious; the owners probably wouldn't pick up on it unless they studied it very closely.

Perry came and stood by me while Dad finished his sandwich over by the truck. Even without me saying anything, she knew I'd found her hidden artwork. "What do you think?" she asked.

"About the hidden snake?"

"Yeah."

"I'm curious. Why did you do it?"

She looked up at me with her big eyes and started to speak. Her words were not ones of a ten year old. "The way I figure it is that one of these days, somebody is gonna look close enough to notice the snake. At first, they may be a little mad about a snake being inside their beautiful butterfly, but in the end it will make a good story to tell. They will have their guests try to find the snake, and once their guest finds it, they will tell about the preacher's daughters that designed it. It will be our mark."

I didn't say anything at first. I just studied my little sister. "Are you really only ten years old?"

"You know how old I am." She punched my arm slightly before saying, "Well, can we keep the snake?"

"Absolutely. I think we need to put our own 'Easter eggs' in all our work from now on."

"Easter eggs? It's a snake not an Easter egg."

"Next time you're on the internet look up *Easter eggs in art.* That's what hidden objects in art are called." I put my arm around her shoulder, and she put her arm around my waist while we admired our masterpiece.

CHAPTER 36

I had never initiated any text messages to Z, I only replied to his. Until today. I texted him pretty early this morning explaining I wouldn't be able to meet him at the river until after church was over. I had to wait for our chaperone. I encouraged him to feel free to warm the spot up for us.

After my family left for church, I washed the morning dishes, swept the house, cleaned out the barn stalls, turned up rocks to fill a coffee can with worms, and even washed the work truck. The clock was ticking too slowly for me. I took a long shower using some of my sisters' flowery body wash.

Finally, I heard gravels crunching in the driveway. I went to my spot at the end of the sidewalk to meet my family. Perry was the first one out of the van. I rushed her. "Go on and take your good clothes off so we can go fishing."

"What's your hurry, girl? Why didn't you go ahead, and I could've had Dad drop me off as usual?" Coming to a dead stop in the middle of the sidewalk, she asked, "What's that I smell? Do you have on perfume?"

I didn't answer her. I smacked her on the behind and said, "Do you want to fish or what?"

"I'm not sure I like all these changes in you. Who wears perfume to fish in?" Thankfully, her back was to the rest of the family and hopefully sounded like garbled-up noises to them.

I grabbed a couple of the snake boxes out of the van. I made sure the latches were locked before I picked them up. With the Seeleys around, I couldn't be too careful. Whitley carried a couple too. She filled me in as we walked down the stairway.

"Joseph tried to talk to Laurel during Sunday school, but she wouldn't answer him. He followed us down the hallway and asked why she was mad at him. The only thing she said to him was that she wasn't mad at anyone but herself. That was it."

"Thank you, Whit, for taking care of Laurel." I was pretty sure she was pregnant since I continued to get the thumbs down sign every morning, but I wasn't going to give up hope, yet.

Dad brought the rest of the snakes downstairs, and I helped him transfer them into the cages. "How was the service today?"

"Revival seems to perk everyone up. It was a good day. We had a lot of folks at the altar and Ole man Duran handled snakes for the first time in twenty years." Just when I thought he was finished talking, he asked, "Are you going fishing with that teacher?"

"Yeah, as long as it's okay with you and Momma. Perry's going too."

"You like this fellow, don't you? Are you sure you know what you're getting into?"

"Yeah. We're just fishing. It's not a date or anything."

"Has he been a gentleman?"

"Dad, absolutely nothing has happened. Actually, he touched my ankle when I twisted it one morning at school. But that's it. Oh, yeah. He was pretty brutal the other day in class when he guarded me in basketball. I definitely wouldn't use the term gentleman to describe how he plays basketball."

He studied my face.

"Dad, I'm telling you the truth."

"I just don't like it. He's quite a bit older than you. The school would fire him."

"Remember I turn eighteen soon so that only makes him five years older. How much older are you than Mom?"

"Your momma was quite a bit older than you when I met her."

"Just three years older."

He blew out some air and shook his head. "Leslie Esther, what am I going to do with you? You're sure this boy's a Christian."

"No. I'm not sure." I may've danced around the other subjects, but I wasn't about to dance on this one. "He told me his grandmother married a Baptist missionary. He said he was baptized when he was younger, but, Dad, I don't think he practices his Christian faith anymore. Remember this isn't even a date. I'm just going to fish with him and Perry for a few hours. That's it. Besides I feel safe with him. Do you know how long it's been that I felt safe around a guy besides you?" I held my breath waiting for his reply.

He didn't say a word for what seemed like an eternity. "I know you're about to graduate and all, but he still needs a job. You be careful. You're messing with fire, little girl. You know what happens when you play with fire."

Now what did Emily say about playing with fire? "I'll be careful," I told him.

Relieved I walked up the stairs only to find my mom waiting on me. "Les, sit down over here, and let's have a chat."

"I just had a chat with Dad."

"And what did he say?" Mom's arms were defensively crossed in the front.

"He just asked a bunch of questions about Coach Z."

"Honey, your dad and I worry so much about you. I want you to be happy, but Coach Zuzeca scares me."

"Why?"

"He's so much old …"

I stopped her. "Mother, don't go talking double standards. Like I told Dad, I'm not marrying him. I'm only going to the river to fish with him and Perry's going too."

"My mom always told me that I should never go out with a guy unless I could see myself spending my life with him."

"Mom!" I was ready to forget the fishing trip.

"Okay, okay. Just know that he's still in his probationary period at school. If they even suspect he's acting inappropriately with a student, then they will terminate his contract. You're messing with fire, sweetie."

Enough about this fire stuff. Couldn't she have found another analogy?

I felt like I'd been through at least a couple rounds in the boxing ring by the time I made it to the truck. I texted Z and told him we were heading to the river. I hoped that I wasn't about to have my toughest round. "Perry, I hope you don't mind that I invited someone to fish with us."

Her head turned in my direction, and she eyed me suspiciously. "Who's coming fishing with us? Is it your new best friend, Laurel?"

"Are you kidding? Laurel would enjoy fishing about as much as a cat enjoys a bath."

"So who is it? That Native American teacher?"

"How do you know about him?"

She looked at the floorboard as she spoke. "I hear a lot of things around the house. Everyone just thinks because I'm young that I'm deaf too."

I had to laugh at her before I said, "His name is Coach Zuzeca."

She tried to pronounce it. "Zoo-zech-ah. Is that right?"

"Just put it all together, or you can call him Coach Z."

She didn't say much the rest of the ride. I'm sure she was thinking things through.

Coach Z was waiting at our normal parking place. As soon as Perry saw him, I expected her to react over him like all the other girls, but she didn't. She didn't say anything and had a hateful look on her face.

He smiled and reached his hand out to her, "Hi, I'm Z, your sister's friend."

In typical Perry form, she said, "Friend. I thought you were her teacher."

He looked at me for help, but I offered him none. He was going to have to come up with his own explanation. I was interested too.

"I'm only her teacher for a few more weeks, but I will be her friend for a lifetime."

Good answer. I'm not sure if he passed Perry's test, but he passed mine. "Come on, guys, I hear the fish calling our names," I told them as I headed down the path.

"Actually, I think that big ole bass was calling mine," Coach Z said playfully.

"I think you're both crazy. Last time I checked, fish don't talk." Perry was not cutting either of us any slack.

Coach Z challenged her, "Sure they do. Even this blade of grass has a voice. All of nature cries out to its maker."

"Les, are we going to have to listen to this Indian mumbo jumbo all day?"

That was it. I'd had all I was going to take. "Z, go on ahead. We'll catch up to you." I grabbed her by the arm and pulled her next to me. I squatted down so I was looking her straight in the eye. "That's enough. I don't know what your problem is, but Coach Z has never done anything to you. You better straighten up, or I'll never fish with you again."

She turned toward the truck and started walking in that direction. "Fine. Take me home." *Was I just outsmarted by a bratty ten-year old? Was it a coincidence that she said this, or did she know that I couldn't be alone with Coach Z? Only I wasn't born yesterday.*

"Sure. I'll take you home, I'm sure I can convince Laurel to take your place."

"She doesn't even know how to bait a hook. You'd spend all your time baiting her hook and getting her line unstuck."

"So. At least she would be kind to our guest."

She sighed loudly before she said, "Let's get this straight. He is not *my* guest. He's yours. I'll be nice to him, but that doesn't mean I'm happy about it."

"If you're not nice to him, I will take a switch and stripe your hind end."

She started laughing as she took off running. "You'll have to catch me first."

I was at a disadvantage since I had my hands full, but I still caught up with her right before she made it to the fishing hole. We both were laughing when we came into Z's line of vision, which was much different from how he left us.

The good Perry—the one I adored—walked over to Coach Z and extended her hand to him. "Can we start over? Hi, I'm Perry."

"Hello, I'm Z." They shook hands.

We all found our places to fish. I was pleased Z chose to fish close to me.

"I'm not sure I can fish with this pole." He said while baiting Dad's bigger one. "I'm so used to that pink one."

Perry said, "Pink pole? So you two have fished together before?"

"Yes, we have. Dad knows all about it," I explained.

"And you let *him* use *my* pole?"

Coach Z's voice was soft as he tried to diffuse the situation. "I hope you didn't mind. I kind of just showed up one day while she was waiting for you to come. She let me use your pole."

I gave Perry my most stern look. She saw it. She spoke almost sweetly at first. "That's fine about you using my pole. I'm just surprised that *my very best friend* has been keeping things from me. That's all."

We were saved by the fish. Perry's bobber went all the way under. "I've got a big one," she said as she cranked her little arms as fast and hard as she could. It was a nice-sized catfish.

Coach Z asked, "What kind of contest do we want to have today?"

"How about the loser buys the winners milkshakes?"

"But I don't have much money," Perry protested.

Coach Z answered, "Then all the more reason not to lose."

"Bring it on, Mr. Native American. Prepare to buy milkshakes," she confidently stated.

Now that was more like *my* Perry.

"So when do we want to have these milkshakes?"

Perry explained, "Anytime but next Saturday. Les is going to prom."

"I didn't know you were going to prom. Do you have a prom date?"

"No. I'm going stag. I guess me and Ellen Jarvis will keep each other company since she's the only other senior I know who doesn't have a date." Ellen weighs a good two hundred and fifty pounds and doesn't believe in taking showers but once a week.

"Wait till you see Les's dress. It's the most beautiful dress ever. Are you going to prom?" *Now* my sister decided to be a chatterbox.

"I was one of the lucky teachers that got drafted to be a chaperone," he explained.

I could tell the minute the light bulb went off in her head. "I've got a great idea. Why don't you be my sister's date?"

Point me to the closest rock to crawl under.

"Sorry. It's against the rules. Teachers can't be their students' prom dates."

"Coach Z, do you have a girlfriend?" she asked.

"Perry Gail Lewis, don't be asking personal questions."

She was relentless. "Well, do you?"

"Not yet, but I'm working on it." He looked me straight in the eye when he said it.

CHAPTER 37

Perry is *officially* mad at me for several reasons: (1) not telling her about my fishing trysts with Coach Z, (2) spending *her* time with both Laurel and Coach Z, and (3) letting Coach Z use her pink fishing pole. And Laurel, well she's *officially* late. Whitley is the only sister who *officially* isn't causing me a lot of headaches right now. I'm not so worried about Perry's issues; I'm convinced they can be solved with a combination of TLC and a switch. Laurel's issue—on the other hand—is a life-altering one.

Laurel refuses to take a pregnancy test until after the school year is over. I don't really blame her because it falls in the "out-of-sight, out-of-mind" category. In some ways, I can compare her reluctance to find out about her future with the same reluctance I feel about choosing a college. Until I graduate, I can at least pretend that life as I've known it for the past seventeen years will continue. Even if living my life on a farm at the edge of Leslie County has been full of its bumps and bruises, at least I've had my family there to help doctor my ailments. The bumps and bruises of the future … well, that's another story. The future problems may not be as kind or as easy to recover from. So at least our lives will remain to be lived in the status quo until after May 16.

Coach Z lost the Sunday fishing contest, (surprise, surprise), and will be buying me and Perry, if she straightens up, milkshakes next Sunday. He says he lost on purpose, but we both knew better. Even Perry on her worst day is a better fisherman than he is. After Perry warmed up to him, I think she liked him a little.

I've dreaded May 16 for so long, but now that date holds some potential for me. That's the day when just maybe Z can be more than a fishing partner since I will no longer be his student. My graduation date looms ahead as both my tormenter and my hope.

School, although busy, has been tolerable this week. Paige Benton was off the first part of it. Rumor had it that she had some legal issues she had to take care of. When returning, she and Sadie didn't even pretend to like us—they gave us the evil eye anytime we were near.

Coach Z and l were no longer ignoring each other. We talked like friends. When the class ran laps, sometimes he would run them with us, and he always managed to fall in line with me. I could feel my classmates watching and whispering. I didn't care.

All Beth and Kelsey wanted to talk about was prom. They were both wearing me out with it, especially Beth. Since I refused to spend any of my precious time planning for prom, she'd enlisted Laurel and Whitley to do her bidding. They'd been coordinating everything from my wrist corsage (which was to be bought and given to me by my dad since I didn't have a date) to picking out just the right shoes. Since Beth's mother and I wore the same size of shoes, seven and a half, Beth brought a couple of pairs for me to choose from: a pair of black strappy high heels and a pair of dress sandals with a one-inch wedge. That was going to be an easy decision. Les Lewis walking in sexy high heels sounded like an accident waiting to happen.

The junior class was responsible for decorating the gymnasium for the prom's derby theme. The theme was appropriate since it coincided with the one-hundred-forty-first running of the Kentucky Derby. The gym was already unrecognizable. Red and white streamers were hoisted up to the top of the gym's ceiling and then draped and attached to the walls to transform the hollow gym into a festive party. The agriculture team was working overtime to prepare the prom meal since the bulk of it would come from the meat and produce raised on the farm.

Like my graduation, I had mixed feelings about prom too. In some ways, I dreaded it, and in other ways I was looking forward to it. My life seemed to be a roller coaster of emotions. There was hope and dread in everything.

Going without a date to prom was giving me a little angst. In some ways, it would've been nice to have someone to share the evening with, if not for the obligatory kiss at the end of the night. According to my friends, the guy's main objective for the date was to speed the dinner and dance up so they could get to their reward at the end of the date–the kiss. It was not only expected, it was owed to them. I'd made my mind up to do exactly what I set out to do from the minute I agreed to attend prom, and before I turned into a pumpkin or my glass slipper broke or whatever happened to Cinderella, I would say my adieus and leave.

Since Whitley's church group had plans to go eat pizza on Thursday, I was concerned about Laurel being subjected to Joseph by herself. She would be exposed, and I didn't think she would be strong enough to ward him off. Perry would be useless as a deterrent since she couldn't see any of Joseph's flaws. I either needed to go to church with Laurel on Thursday or come up with a good reason to keep her home with me. Then I got the idea. Actually, I owe Emily for the idea. I've thought numerous times about Emily's manicured hands. They were by far her best feature. My hands—they were a calloused mess. Dad's eyebrows raised in concern when I asked if Laurel could go with me to get a manicure. After I let him feel my hands, he agreed we could go as long as I only used a clear polish and not one of those harlot reds. I invited Perry to go with us, but she said she would rather go to church than go get all gussied up. She looked at me with disgust before she disappeared mumbling something about me having crossed over.

Since I had some extra money this week, I treated both Laurel and myself to manicures and pedicures. It was good for Laurel, plus it was a nice experience instead of the torture I'd always envisioned. *Maybe I was crossing over.*

CHAPTER 38

Beth had given Laurel and Whitley a schedule for Saturday's pre-prom activities that even listed a time for me to brush my teeth. I guess she thought it was going to take several hours for me to get prom presentable. Whitley was up to the challenge. She explained, "We're going to make you into a modern-day Cinderella. All those boys are going to wish they'd asked you to prom."

"I really don't want to turn into a pumpkin or anything, so can you make me into someone besides Cinderella?"

From the doorway as she darted in and out the door, Perry asked, "What about making her into Gracie Lou Freebush?"

Since we'd all watched *Miss Congeniality* about a hundred times, we knew exactly who she was talking about. I liked it. I sure didn't want my hair the same way as Laurel's earlier experimentation. I looked more like Medusa than Cinderella. "Gracie Lou, it is. Ladies, can you do it?"

Laurel turned to Whitley and said, "We're going to need the heavy-duty flat iron."

Pleased that her suggestion had been used, Perry gave a little smile before she disappeared once again from the room. Throughout the afternoon, she would silently re-appear to assess the damage and would leave again after she'd seen enough. Since they wouldn't let me see myself, I had to depend on Perry's comments and expressions to gauge how I was looking. When I had the goop all over my face and some kind of vegetables on my eyes, Perry said, "Are you sure that stuff won't permanently cause damage?"

"Oww!" I yelled when they took turns torturing me with the tweezers. They had the picture of the girl from a movie they could use as a pattern for my eyebrows. *Eyebrows? When did eyebrows become important?*

I saw Laurel and Whitley in a different light as they confidently took charge of my beauty regimen. I felt certain Whitley would have a career in the beauty field; even Laurel followed her lead, and when Whitley spoke, she spoke with authority.

Momma would come in the room and help until she started crying. "I can't believe my firstborn is growing up. Can't I just keep you all little?" She brought my baby pictures into the room and told the story of my life as she walked down memory lane.

Since it was grocery day, Mom had to leave for a little while to replenish our fridge and pantry. Perry went to the grocery with her. As soon as she heard the van leave, Laurel whispered to Whitley, "You better hurry before they come back and catch us."

"Catch us? What are you talking about? " I asked suspiciously.

Laurel bent down so her mouth was level with my ear. Even though no one besides me and Whitley were in the house, she whispered, "Beth gave me a little bronzer to use on your face. She also gave me lip gloss, eyeliner, and mascara too."

I started protesting, "No. I don't want to make Dad upset. You know how he talks about Jezebel and her painted eyes." By the time a Holiness girl turned sixteen, she'd heard the story of Jezebel and how the dogs ate her corpse at least twenty or more times.

Whitley explained, "They will never know. The trick to using makeup is to make it look like you don't have any on. We've been practicing, and we think we can do it so it looks natural on you. Please let us try. If you don't like it, you can wash your face. Okay?"

"Who are you, and what did you do with my little sister?"

Whitley just laughed. Her laugh even seemed older.

Mom and Perry returned just in time to help me with my dress. If Momma or Perry noticed I had makeup on, they didn't mention it.

Since the girls refused to let me look in a mirror, I still didn't know what I looked like.

Momma asked me, "Did you ever try the dress on?"

"No. I didn't."

"Lordy, I sure hope it fits," Momma said.

"Me too. Here goes." While holding my breath, I stepped into the puddle of black organza. I exhaled as soon as the zipper closed all the way up to the nape of my neck.

"Perfect." Laurel broke the silence.

Momma put her hand over her mouth. Her reaction confused me. I wasn't sure if she was going to laugh, scream, or cry. Finally she ordered, "Go look."

I went into the bathroom, and I saw a stranger looking back at me—a beautiful stranger. When I realized I was all alone in the room, I looked hard into the mirror. There she was. I saw her—the old version of me. The one that used to care what she looked like. The one who liked purple, wore long skirts, and wanted to marry and have four daughters. She was older and wiser now, but she was still there. Although the dress was modest, it was not layered or frumpy. Laurel said it best. It was perfect.

I leaned into the mirror and closely examined the Les that had lain dormant for so long. I couldn't believe what a difference my perfectly-shaped eyebrows made. My skin was slightly tanned and flawless, thanks to the bronzer. I wasn't sure if it was the eyelash curler or the touch of mascara that made my already long eyelashes almost touch my brows. But, it was my hair that I'd missed the most. My wild dark locks that normally were hidden inside the safe confines of a ponytail had been ironed and tamed into submission with a natural middle part and the ends slightly curled. *Leslie Esther Lewis meet Cinderella Freebush.*

I touched the exposed area of the V neckline. For some reason, I liked seeing the smooth and vulnerable skin. Most girls would wear a necklace to help fill in the bareness, but this was against yet another one of the Holiness rules. Dad says that gold and costly array goes with a proud look; God despises a proud look. I looked into the mirror to see if I saw any haughtiness in my look—I did. I started to cry. Momma came in followed by the rest of my sisters. She said, "Honey, you are one of God's beautiful creations. It's okay to let him shine through you."

No wonder I stayed confused all the time. Where do you draw the line before God despises you or shines through you? He can't do both, can he?

"You're shining so brightly, you're about to put my eyes out." That did it. Leave it to Perry to lighten the tense moment. My tears were mixed with laughter.

"Momma, I want my wedding dress to look just like this?" Whitley commented.

Momma rolled her eyes when she said, "You want a black wedding dress?"

"No, I want a white dress made just like this one only with maybe a chiffon top layer."

Laurel said, "I thought you wanted one with the lace going all the way up to the neck."

"I did last week, but I think I've changed my ..."

Perry interrupted, "Do we have to talk about weddings today; besides this dress hasn't passed the most important test of all."

"Dad's approval test?" I asked.

"No, silly. The Perry Gail Lewis twirl test."

"Oh? The twirl test." And twirl I did. The dress flowed like I was dancing with a cloud.

Laurel brought me back to earth when she brought me the wedge sandals. "Here, you need to go ahead and put these on. The dress is a tad too long."

I put the shoes on. They fit nicely; however, my dress was still dragging the ground.

"I'm afraid your dress will be ruined. Les, you should've tried it on. You'll have to keep it picked up, or maybe I have time to hem it." Momma was trying to come up with a quick remedy.

Whitley had the remedy in her hands—the strappy heals. "Try these shoes on."

Momma's eyes widened. The shoes had the word "sin" written all over them; however, she didn't say a word in protest because other than a fast hem job, she knew the shoes were our only option.

I was able to stand up straight in them. I mentally calculated that if the heels were three inches tall, then that made me 5'11".

Momma said, "Well they did the trick, but can you walk?"

I tried taking a step or two, and although I was by no means ready for the runway I was able to put one foot in front of the other thanks to all my old basketball drills.

"Go walk down the hall. I sure don't want you to break an ankle tonight," Momma ordered me.

As I was practicing my gait like a fancy filly, Dad came home from work and met me in the hallway. "Oh my," was all he managed to get out.

"Dad, do I look okay?"

"You are beautiful." The spigots in his eyes turned on.

I reached out to hug him, but he stopped me. "Honey, don't come close. I've got enough dust on me to fill a graveyard. I'll get you all dirty."

We all went in the yard to take pictures in front of momma's snowball bush that was in full bloom. When it was Laurel's turn to have a picture made with me, she was struggling something fierce. I knew what she was thinking. I whispered, "You will go to your prom. You will have a normal life, no matter what," I told her and meant it.

CHAPTER 39

Both Momma and Dad offered to drive me to prom, but I explained to them, "When I'm ready to come home, I want to be able to leave and not have to wait on anyone."

They didn't argue with me, but Dad insisted I drive his truck. He had even washed it and vacuumed the inside for me.

I was one of the last ones to arrive to the dinner. I'd purposely decided to come late mainly because I didn't want to be a fifth wheel any longer than I had to be. I recognized my mistake as soon as I stepped into the cafeteria. The normal clatter of conversation ceased. The silence unnerved me. I even heard someone say, "Who is she?"

Beth and Kelsey appeared at my side to rescue me. "Wow," I marveled when seeing my friends. "You two look absolutely gorgeous." I took a gander toward their dates still at the table. "Your dates aren't looking too shabby either." Beth and Kelsey's dresses and styles matched their personalities.

Beth's dress was a short, yellow dress. Her blond hair matched the soft color of the material. Anthony's tie (from what I could tell from the distance) matched her dress perfectly. If she had a magic wand, she would've looked a lot like a little fairy as she scurried around.

Kelsey's purple dress had new meaning for me. The old Les used to be obsessed with the color purple; even my room was painted a nice shade of lavender. But the color lost its meaning after Jeb died. I associated the color with my old life. However, Kelsey's dress made me happy just looking at it. It was long and the straps were lined with jewels. It was probably the most expensive dress here. True to her own style, her purple Chuck Taylors protruded slightly out from the bottom of her dress. Scout's tie and his vest matched her dress. My friends seemed to be more interested in checking me out than in my assessment of them. They touched my hair and turned me around. Beth just kept making me turn this way and that way. "Les, you are absolutely breathtaking. My girls, Laurel and Whitley, get an A plus. We'd talked about curling your hair, but I'm so glad they didn't. I like this straighter look much better."

Kelsey said, "Les, is it really you? She touched my hair. I can't believe you've been hiding this mane all this time." Kelsey had never seen my hair down before.

"I remember this mane. I remember this girl," Beth said.

I hugged Beth, *my fairy godmother.* "Thank you so much." I wasn't thanking her for the dress either. It was so much more.

"I love you," she whispered.

I felt his stare before I saw him. I turned around and saw Coach Z looking at me from across the room. Even though he was some distance away, I could tell he wasn't smiling. I wanted to go to him, but I knew that would only be asking for trouble.

All of a sudden, I was surrounded by a bunch of well-dressed guys. I think they all wanted to see me for themselves. *I guess this is what it felt like to be the belle of the ball.*

A guy from our class started talking to me. "Les Lewis, I didn't even recognize you. You are smoking hot. If I knew what you *really* looked like all this time, I would've been beating your door down. I've got a plan though. I'm going to tell Sydney that I'm not feeling good, and I'll take her home early. Then, maybe we can hook up later. You game?"

"Not my game," I said as I dismissed him and walked to find a seat at the table next to my friends.

Paige and Sadie walked by. I didn't want to get too close to them. It was untelling what they were capable of doing to me—especially while I was wearing these stilts.

The meal was everything it was cracked up to be. My filet mignon was perfect as was the rest of the food. Like herding a bunch of hybrid cattle crossbred with Easter bunnies, we were ushered from the cafeteria to the gymnasium shortly after we finished our meal. In order to get into the dance, we had to go through a rose-lined archway made to look like the derby winner's garland. The punch was mint julep without the bourbon. Silver plastic mint julep mugs were one of the party favors. The tablecloths were a mixture of red and white. Cardboard cutout horses standing in various places in the room reminded me of *our* cardboard cutout for Misty Shane. Kudos to the junior class—the decorations were all creative and fun. Even without a date, I was having a good time. I was glad the girls forced me to come.

Z was dressed in a dark suit with a white shirt and a blue tie. The white of the shirt contrasted with his dark skin. Although he kept his hair in a short cut, I could tell he'd visited the barber today. Every strand looked to be in place. My eyes seemed to gravitate to him each time I looked around. He stood out because of his height and his stunning good looks. Kelsey and Beth were just as enamored as I was with him. Kelsey said, "I can't even look in his direction. My heart starts speeding up."

The closest Z and I came to each other was when he was three people back from me in the mint julep line. Even with the mixtures of the individual smells of those around me, I could pick out his scent. It assaulted every one of my senses even from the distance. *Pheromones, maybe?*

When the music first started playing, only a few brave couples were on the floor dancing to the upbeat music. Then more folks began trickling out to the floor. I'd already been asked out four times and had about ten guys ask to dance with me. I wasn't used to this kind of attention, and I didn't know the first thing about dancing. I found a spot in the back to sit as an observer. I actually looked for Ellen Jarvis so I could sit with her, but that wasn't happening because Ms. Ellen was all dressed up and on the dance floor with a guy that was as thin as she was thick. *What a way to be remembered: Leslie Lewis—the only girl without a date at her senior prom.*

I stayed about an hour at the dance until I heard my pumpkin calling me. I told my friends goodbye and made sure I located my frenemies before I left. I didn't want to have a run-in with them on my way out. Dressed this way, I was much too vulnerable for any kind of altercation with them.

Using my dad's remote, I unlocked the door of his truck from a few yards back. I heard the clicking sound the lock made, but I also heard something else. I turned to the sound. Relieved, I said, "Oh, it's just you."

Z said, "You didn't think you could get out of here without at least letting me look at you up close. I've been admiring you from afar. Dang girl, you sure clean up nicely. I've never seen anyone more lovely than you are."

"Will you call me, *Oh Lovely One*, from now on?" My laughter even sounded nervous to me. Then I added, "Probably can't do much fishing looking like this, though."

"Trust me. It's been hard enough going fishing with you in your jeans, my *katila o'waci.*"

This is really happening. I didn't know what to say. An awkward silence stood between us, making the music playing in the distance even clearer. If I had any doubts about his feeling for me, they were now gone.

"Les, have you ever danced with anyone before?"

"I've danced around at church when I was little. Does that count?"

"Nope. That's not the kind of dancing I'm talking about." He walked towards me. "Can I have your first dance?" he asked with his arm extended toward me like I'd seen on a movie. We were all alone in the parking lot.

I stood frozen with inexperience. "I really don't know how to dance."

"Little dancer, I'm sure you know how. You just haven't found *your* dance yet." He took me in his arms, and I went willingly even if it was awkward.

I realized it wasn't the inexperience that had me frozen. It was the thousand tingles that I felt run all up and down my spine. I slowly put my arms around his neck. I tried to mimic how the other girls did it at prom.

"Okay, just listen to the music deep inside," he said. We began swaying —first this way, then that way. I followed his lead. My body was pressed into his even though that was not my intention. He was the one pulling me closer.

I couldn't hear anything because my heart was beating so loudly in my head. Even his breath smelled sweet. It seemed like we danced for an eternity. I didn't ever want the music to end. Even when the slow sound of Tim McGraw's "It's Your Love" was over, we continued swaying to our own music.

He began to speak in a low whisper. "You are the reason I came here. I followed your calling."

Still embraced, I stopped dancing and asked, "What are you talking about? I just got my phone a few weeks ago."

He leaned up against my dad's truck and held me at arm's length— his eyes looking down at mine. He said, "I saw you for the first time four years ago when I was crying for a vision in the wilderness." He paused. "You looked much like you do tonight. Your hair was long and blowing with the wind. You were free, and you were dancing."

"Are you messing with me? Did I have this dress on?"

Even with little light, I could see the disappointment on his face. "Of all people, I thought you'd understand. Don't your church people ever see and hear things that can't be explained."

"Oh. Is that what you're talking about? Yeah, God gives us dreams, feelings, and visions."

"Our gods can't be so different, can they?"

"Could they be the same?"

"I'd like to think so," he answered as he pulled me to him, and we started swaying with the music that had started playing again.

"Tell me more about your vision." He had piqued my interest.

"The first time I saw you, you were dancing, and you were holding snakes as you danced around the campfire."

I stopped swaying. "You've got to be kidding."

"I'm serious. My sisters knows you as *zuzeca o'waci.*"

So I already knew that zuzeca meant snake and o'waci meant dancer in Lakota. "Snake dancer. I get it."

We continued to dance silently. Even our heartbeats were beating in unison. I know because I could feel his heartbeat on my chest and hear mine pounding in my head. I was even maneuvering quite well in my stilts. My newfound height put my head at just the right spot on his chest. "I'm so glad you found me." I was dead serious.

He moved his hands from my waist and put them on my face. I knew what was coming and prepared myself as his mouth slowly came down on mine so gently and sweetly—I couldn't have envisioned his kiss to be more perfect. The taste of his mouth was just as I had imagined. An explosion of feelings surged from somewhere inside and penetrated through every one of my self-imposed barriers. The electricity of the feelings jarred me. I felt so ... so alive. I didn't want the kiss to end, but—it did.

We both heard the giggles at the same time. I knew exactly who the laughter belonged to even before Sadie spoke. "You two are so busted. Just wait until everyone knows." Then they ran away taking with them their phone and a permanent image of our first kiss.

I started to run after them, but Z and my heels stopped me. I told him. "We've got to go after them. They just recorded that ... that ... what we just did ... you know ... on their phone. We've got to get it." I didn't know whether to worry more about his job or about my parents. I guess I was about to see this fire everyone had warned me about playing with.

CHAPTER 40

I turned my cell phone off on my drive home. I didn't want to know about the carnage caused by my first kiss. It would be only a matter of hours before the entire school and my parents knew all about it. This would be the only calm before the storm hit. I figured the video had already been uploaded and was playing on every ACI student's newsfeed by now.

Coach Z would lose his job. I was certain of that. I know he told me he wasn't staying next year, but getting fired from ACI would not look good on his resume. *Why couldn't we have waited? We just had fourteen more days, and we were home free. It was the dress.*

Since I was getting home fairly early, everyone was still up when I arrived. With my shoes in my hand, I stepped through the door looking much like how I imagined Cinderella looked when she arrived home—a mess. Make that a crying mess.

"Les, what's wrong? Are you okay?" My dad was the first one to reach me. "Did someone hurt you? What happened?"

"Clay, let her alone a minute so she can get her breath," Mom ordered.

Perry said, "Look on the bright side, Les. At least you came home with both your shoes. That was better than Cinderella."

Laurel said, "Hush, Perry Gail, and let her tell us what happened."

Laurel grabbed me by the hand and pulled me over to the couch. "Here, sit down." Then she whispered, "Please quit crying before your mascara runs, or we're all in trouble."

I sat on the couch with Laurel on one side of me and Whitley on the other. Perry was sitting in Momma's lap across the room. I tried to regain my composure.

Dad figured it out. "It has to do with the teacher, doesn't it?"

I nodded my head. "I knew I shouldn't go. They saw me. Now everyone will know about … my first dance."

Perry was the first one to comment. Her words were harsh. "Did you dance with Coach Z? How could you? You know you're only supposed to dance for the Lord."

"I know. I know."

Mom asked, "So what happened? Why are you crying?"

"He kissed me."

I heard a collective gasp from the already captive audience. Then silence.

"While we were kissing, a couple of girls saw us, and they videoed us." I was finally able to talk in full sentences.

"Was it Paige Benton and Sadie Long?" Laurel asked.

I nodded my head.

"Momma, Dad, I'm so sorry. I didn't mean for this to happen. I've worn my jeans and ponytail for so long just so it wouldn't have a chance to happen again."

Perry asked, "Again? So you kissed someone before?"

Dad acted as though Perry hadn't said anything. "Les, I tried to warn you about playing with fire, but sometimes you just have to get burned."

"That poor boy will lose his job. You know that, don't you?" Mom said with a scowl on her face.

"Yes. He said he wasn't staying at ACI anyway and that I was the only reason he came here in the first place. He said he had a vision about me a few years ago." I immediately regretted talking about this as soon as it left my mouth.

CHAPTER 41

I finally turned my phone back on early Sunday morning. I had over ten messages. Most of them were from Beth and Kelsey. Z had sent me one message that said, "I'm not sorry, *zuzeca o'waci.*"

My heart swelled with love for him. Just reading his texts somehow made all the wrongs right. I wrote back. *The only thing I'm sorry about ... is that we didn't wait fourteen more days.*

Today was church day, and I decided to go with my family. Not because I needed to repent for my kiss, but because it was time I stopped hiding behind my fear. I wore one of Laurel's dresses and wore my hair down.

The ride to church was a quiet one. Perry usually sat with me, but today she didn't even offer. I felt properly shunned. Perry may have shunned me, but Laurel was thrilled I would be at church with her today. Plus it was another thumbs down day for her.

I could feel the boys at our church ogling me—all except for Joseph. When he looked at me, he gave me the evil eye. When I came out of the bathroom, he was waiting for me in the hallway. "Don't think you're going to be welcomed back into this fold. I know all about you. I even have proof." He raised his phone and hit play. I watched my first kiss unfold over the phone's small screen.

"Get out of my way."

"I'll make a deal with you. You meet me out back in ten minutes, and I'll delete this video."

"I said, get out of my way." I pushed by him. "Keep the video and watch it every day because that's the closest you'll come to another Lewis girl again."

"You so sure about that?"

I didn't even bother to reply. I headed into the sanctuary and found a seat next to Whitley and Laurel on the second row. We sat and listened to Momma quietly play the piano. Dad was on his knees on the pulpit praying for God's divine instructions. Probably praying a little for me too. I checked the time, and we only had a few minutes before church was to begin.

"Where's Perry?"

Whitley said, "She's back there sitting with the boys."

My blood went cold when I turned around to see Perry sitting next to Joseph Seeley. They were laughing. She saw me when I motioned for her to come and sit with us. He did too. He smirked. I almost thought he was going to prevent her from coming to me.

When the music started, Perry finally made her way to our pew. I grabbed her arm and said, "You hear me? You better keep away from the Seeley boys."

"Joseph said you would say that."

"Please, promise me that you won't be alone with him ever. Okay?"

The wheels turning in her head—the spoiled Perry and the sweet Perry were fighting an internal battle. The sweet Perry won. "Okay. Do you think milkshakes will be out of the question for today?"

"Maybe not. The damage has already been done."

Then she whispered, "Please don't ask Laurel and Whitley to go fishing with us."

"Okay, I won't." Then I whispered in her ear, "What were you and Joseph Seeley talking about?"

"Nothing really important but normal things like basketball and fishing."

"Remember that you just promised me you would never be alone with him, right?"

Perry just gave me one of her looks before saying, "I think you have enough to worry about with your own doings. I'm the least of your worries, Miss Kissy Face Dancer. I can take care of myself just fine."

When we saw our dad looking our way, we both stopped talking.

We arrived home to six large milkshakes sitting on our front porch with a small handwritten envelope addressed to Sister Ruth. We must've just missed him; the shakes were still frozen. Mom didn't read the note aloud. She just said, "The milkshakes are from Coach Zuzeca. He says he's sorry."

CHAPTER 42

All four of the Lewis girls wore our hair in a single braid down our backs on Monday in an act of solidarity. Perry's adolescent moods ran hot and cold. This morning she was fine because Laurel decided to ride with Momma. Our morning ride to school was back to normal. I cautioned her again to stay away from Joseph. She assured me she would.

Paige and Sadie made sure I saw them when I entered the front foyer. I heard Sadie mock me. "I'm *sooo* glad you found me." They even waved at me to make sure their cruelty hadn't gone unnoticed. I didn't acknowledge them. Instead, I walked straight to the bathroom where Beth and Kelsey were waiting on me. At first, I wasn't sure if I wanted to see my starring role in the video with over sixty-five hundred views, but I was also a little excited to relive the moment.

Although the footage was pretty dark, it was still light enough to tell who we both were.

Beth said, "I just realized it, but you do look like Sandra Bullock and Coach Z reminds me of the guy on *Miss Congeniality*. What was his name?"

"Benjamin Bratt," I answered.

Kelsey said, "I think Coach Z is better looking than he is and you are prettier than Sandra too."

"You're crazy," I told Kelsey.

Beth said, "Les, just look at yourself in this video. You're gorgeous."

I wasn't very experienced with accepting compliments. "Thank you, but y'all are the pretty ones."

Thankfully, the video only showed us dancing. Then you could hear me say that I was so glad he found me, and of course, then the kiss. The actual kiss seemed like it went on for a couple of minutes when it happened, but on video, it lasted only ten seconds. It could've been so much worse had they heard all about the snake dancer and him crying for a vision or whatever it was he called it.

Kelsey asked, "How did y'all let them sneak up on you. After all he's an Indian."

"I don't know. I've asked myself the same question."

Beth said, "I know what it was. Y'all were so lost in each other that you tuned the world out. This was the undoubtedly the most romantic thing I've ever seen. I'm so happy for you, Les. I bet every girl at ACI has watched it over and over imagining them being the one he kissed."

"Guilty," Kelsey admitted. "Don't get me wrong. I think Scout is awesome and all, but Coach McDreamy is every girl's Prince Charming, especially how he looked Saturday night."

"He's almost as perfect as the Greek God." Beth sighed when she said it.

I teased her, "Almost?"

"Well, let's just say they're *both* works of perfection," Beth said in compromise.

"Scout is *cuteness* perfection." Kelsey defended her beau. "Oh, by the way, he asked me to go out with him."

"What did ya say?" I asked.

"I said, yes!" Kelsey barely got the words out before the group hug began.

Beth had her lip out. "Les has McDreamy. Now you have your McCutie, and I guess I just have my dreams."

My voice was slow and stern when I said, "He will call."

Beth shrugged her shoulders and asked, "Will he?" She didn't even bother with our normal *because I'm adorable* routine. "I don't want to think about him today. I'm just going to celebrate with you two. Then tonight I may jump in the bathtub with my blow dryer."

Kelsey said, "Don't even say that."

"I'm just kidding. Henry Noble will call because I'm adorable, and he can't resist me." Before we could say anything else to her, she asked me, "Are you in a lot of trouble at home?"

"No. I didn't get grounded or anything."

"What about Coach Z? Is he in trouble?" Kelsey asked.

"I'm not sure. The last time he texted, he told he had a meeting scheduled with the superintendent early this morning."

My phone vibrated. *Meet me in the trainer's room. Go behind the bleachers to the door. It's unlocked.*

"I've got to go and talk to Z while I can," I told them as I headed out the door.

It looked like I was going to the dressing room, but instead of entering the door I veered to the left and went behind the bleachers all the way to the end of the row. The back entrance to the trainer's room was directly to the right. I made sure no one followed me.

Coach Z locked the door behind me as soon as I made it in. Without saying a word, he pulled me into an embrace. His lips touched mine and again, an explosion went off inside me. I pulled myself closer to him and kissed him harder with the same urgency a woman kissed her man before he headed off to war. I didn't want it to ever stop.

We reluctantly ended the kiss. With his chin leaning on the top of my head, he explained, "I need to talk to you. We don't have long. I had my meeting this morning."

"So, everything went okay?"

"Yes and no. They fired me. They are allowing me to finish out the school year because they don't want a lot of drama. The superintendent said he was willing to give me a good reference as long as I had *no contact with you* until you graduated. He said that meant during or after school."

"I'm in your class. How can we not have contact?"

"That's just it. You are no longer in my class. You are to report to your mom's class for first period from now on."

"What about fishing?" I asked. "Can't we even sneak up to the waterfall?"

"No. I need a good reference." He could see my disappointment. "Listen, *o'waci*, The Great Spirit brought us together once. He can bring us together again."

He lightly brushed his lips to mine. Then, he went out through one door, and I left through another headed toward my mom's music room.

CHAPTER 43

A turtle treading in peanut butter went faster than the last week and a half of my high school career. I went to church with my family on Thursdays and Sundays. I still had to encounter Joseph's evil stares and words, but Laurel and I went everywhere in pairs.

I went shopping with my stylist for some more up-to-date church clothing. Thankfully, long skirts are in style. Every store shopped had an abundance of stylish dresses and skirts that would work for a Holiness preacher's daughter. Beth put everything together for me, and my wardrobe now met with her approval. I still wore my jeans when I wanted to, but like my ponytail, I wasn't in bondage to either of them anymore. Instead of surrounding myself with safe rituals, I surrounded myself with those who loved me.

While I was out running errands, I bought Laurel a pregnancy test. Just yesterday, Mom had to pull over to let her throw up. She didn't seem to be the least bit suspicious. She just said, "I guess I was driving these curvy roads a bit too fast." I was certain Laurel had confided in Whitley. She seemed just as protective over Laurel as I was. I didn't have to wait until after graduation before I knew the outcome of my college decision. I would not be going away to college. I couldn't leave my sister to face all of this alone. The community college was my best option.

Since I didn't have to go to school today (seniors got out a couple of days early) I drove all three girls to school bunched up in the front seat of the truck.

Perry asked Laurel, "What's wrong with you? You've just about stopped eating. How much weight are you trying to lose?"

"What? You think I've lost weight?" Laurel asked. Both she and Whitley, like Momma, have battled with their weight all their lives.

"I bet you're down ten pounds or more," I chimed in with Perry.

"You really need to start eating or you'll get too skinny," Perry said as she got out of the truck.

Laurel, Whitley, and I watched Perry as she walked all the way down the sidewalk. We were both relieved that she was in a good mood this morning. Before I dropped Laurel and Whitley off at the front entrance, Laurel asked, "You really think I've lost weight?"

"Absolutely."

I saw a little more life in her step as she almost bounced up the stairs.

When I left the parking lot, a medium-sized black snake was stretched out on the side of the road. At first, I drove past it. Then another idea entered my head. I backed up and got out of the truck and barehanded the snake; I even let it wrap around my arm. "Black Betty, I have a job for you," I told her. She wasn't going to be added to our collection in the basement. I had other plans for her. *Now, I need another one.* Since a lot of snakes travel in pairs, I waded around in the weeds in the ditch close to where I found her to see if I could find another one. *Bingo!* "Hello, Bert," I spoke to the smaller snake.

I called Kelsey and told her I needed to make a little visit to the dormitory and needed her help. She was filling in at the school's office to pass the time away. I explained I needed an accomplice to be a lookout and a hacker to manipulate the cameras for about ten minutes. She just laughed and said, "Clydette at your service. You know I've still not ruled out crime as my career." Then someone must've walked within hearing distance because she changed the topic. "Are you sure you don't want to go to UC's orientation with me and Beth tomorrow?"

"Probably not. I've got a lot to do."

I then filled her in on my sinister plan. She loved it. Before she left the office, she pulled the plug on the cameras in the girls' dormitory.

We only had less than ten minutes to get in and out of the building. I was in luck. Thankfully, Paige was like eighty percent of the other girls and didn't lock the door to her private room. Since I found Bert in the water of the ditch, then I concluded he would enjoy my planned destination for him. I'd seen areas that had been hit by a tornado that was neater than Paige's room. Clothes were strewn everywhere. Her bathroom was disgusting. "Bert, you'll feel right at home in this filthy toilet bowl," I told him. He landed with a plop in the water. I watched to make sure he was able to find a comfortable place around the rim before I shut the lid. "Bert, you stay right here for a bit, okay?"

I called Kelsey and said, "One down, one to go." She opened the back door for me as I made my fast escape. I walked through the woods up to where I left the truck parked to retrieve Black Betty. Kelsey wouldn't be able to help me with my plan for Sadie, but Z could.

I texted him and asked him to leave the outside entrance to the gym opened. The only explanation I gave him was that I wanted Sadie to meet my new friend. He didn't ask for more information.

Just as I'd asked, the gym entrance was unlocked. I was able to slip into the dressing room. I recognized Sadie's gym bag. Black Betty curled up in a resting position in the center of the bag as soon as I carefully placed her in it. I zipped the bag shut and left the gym. Part of me wanted to hang around to hear the screams, but I didn't.

Hopefully, they would learn a valuable lesson—mainly not to ever mess with a snake handling preacher's daughter.

Later I received a text from Z that said. *Lots of zuzeca o'wacis at school today!*

CHAPTER 44

Laurel and Whitley came home from school telling me I missed all the excitement.

"What kind of excitement did I miss?" I played along.

Laurel started off by saying, "Sadie Long really sprained her ankle today. They had to take her to the hospital."

"Really? I thought she just did that."

"She did, but this time it was legit. But that's not the exciting part of it."

"Okay, so tell me what was exciting about someone getting hurt?"

Whitley said, "Let me tell her. Les, you're not going to believe it." Whitley's face was very serious like she was telling a scary story. "After Sadie's P.E. class was over, she went to clean out her locker. When she opened her gym bag, this huge snake crawled right out on her. When she was trying to get it off her arm, she fell and hurt her ankle."

"What happened to the snake?" Panic arose within me afraid my act of revenge would be the demise of the harmless snake. "Did they kill it?"

"No. I heard Coach Zuzeca took it to the woods. But, that's not all." Whitley smiled and looked to Laurel.

"Not all?" I was trying to sound nonchalant. "What else happened?"

"Just wait till I tell you what happened to Paige Benton."

Trying hard not to crack a smile, I said, "Tell me, already."

"After lunch, Paige went back to her dorm room to use the bathroom. She was sitting on the pot when she felt something wet touch her leg. She stood up, and when she did, she felt a weight fall into her underwear. She looked down and saw a black snake half in her drawers and half in the toilet."

I was watching this in my mind. I could see it all unfold. I started laughing. Laurel put her hand over mouth as she giggled.

Whitley shushed us. "Hold on. It gets better. Paige ran down the hallway and outside with her britches pulled down to her knees screaming every step of the way. A bunch of the boys were outside, and they all saw her you know, her *coochie*, when they helped her get the snake out of her pants."

By this time, I was laughing so hard I couldn't breathe. "Not her ..." Another laughing fit. "Her cooch ..." My laughter was contagious. I don't think either of us had laughed this hard in our lives.

After we were all laughed out, Whitley said, "Wonder how those two snakes got in both girls' stuff on the very same day. You think God did that as punishment for what they did to you?"

I put my hands on her face and held it there until she looked me in the eyes. "Whitley, in some ways it's good to be naïve, but the sooner you realize we don't live in a perfect world the better. Not everyone you're going to encounter in life is good."

She looked at me like I was talking in a foreign language. "So are you saying that God did punish them?"

"No. Someone else did—someone who knows all about snakes and needed to settle a score once and for all."

Finally, the light bulb went off in her head. "Ooooh. I get it. You mean *someone* had to teach them a lesson, right?"

"Right!" Then we all three laughed again. All I could think about was that Bert must have heard about Paige's nickname. I couldn't have planned it to have worked out any better.

CHAPTER 45

I was helping my dad unload the tiles on Friday when my phone rang. It was Kelsey.

"Hey, Kels. I thought you were at your orientation."

"Can you hear me?" Her voice was low and serious, almost a whisper.

"Barely. What's wrong?"

"Nothing's wrong. Everything is right. Guess who's at the orientation."

"I have no idea."

I could hear the sound of a door opening, and then she started talking normal. "It's Adonis! The Greek God is going to be playing football here at the University of the Cumberlands. And get this— he's not left Beth's side since we got here. He said his mom washed the piece of paper with her phone number on it, and he's been trying to find a way to get her number ever since."

I started squalling so loudly my dad came running outside to make sure I was okay.

CHAPTER 46

My graduation day should've been one of the happiest days of my life, but it was anything but happy for several reasons. Z had already packed up his belongings and would be heading out as soon as the ceremony was over. Just as we planned, Laurel took her pregnancy test this morning. Even though we were expecting it, when that plus sign showed up on the stick it was gut wrenching. We cried together. She planned to tell Momma and Daddy later today.

Perry woke up in one of her moods. She came to my room and said, "Happy graduation day." But her tone was anything but happy. "I guess you're going to jump into your boyfriend's arms and run away with him, aren't you?"

"Perry Gail, I'm only seventeen years old."

"You'll be eighteen next week, Leslie Esther."

"It doesn't matter. I'm nowhere near ready to make that kind of commitment."

"Well, I guess if you're not going to get married, then you're going off to school."

"Yes. I'm tired of you being a spoiled brat, and I'm going to go as far away from you as I can get."

She gave me her meanest look then she whipped around and was out of sight. I had too many things on my mind than having to deal with her attitude today. Hopefully this preadolescent Jekyll/Hyde thing she had going on would stop soon.

The cars in the parking lots had spilled over to the school's lawn. It was going to be one of ACI's largest classes to graduate. Everyone was dressed in their Sunday finest. Even the dormitory parents managed to come and celebrate this day. Kelsey's mom was there looking like a million dollars.

I wore one of my new outfits, and Whitley curled my hair a little. My eyes were a little puffy from crying. Every time I thought I was finished, I would see Laurel and start all over again. Mom and Dad just thought I was extra sensitive because I was graduating and Z was leaving town today.

Beth, on the other hand, was on top of the world. She had a date with Henry Noble tonight. He'd broken up with Misty the day after prom. He said he couldn't stand to be with her one more minute. Kelsey received good news as well—Scout would be going to school at Union College on a basketball scholarship. Union was only a few miles from the University of the Cumberlands.

After all the pomp and circumstance was over, my friends and I met in my mom's room for some private time together. We exchanged cards and gifts and promises. I promised Beth and Kelsey I would visit them often, and we swore on our graves that we would be best friends forever.

Momma, Dad, and the girls drove on home in the van leaving me to ride home with Z after commencement was over. I guess they thought there wasn't much harm since he was leaving town today. Perry was still in her bratty mood when graduation was over. Dad even gave her one of his most stern looks. She settled down a tad after that, but she still wouldn't talk to me. Since I knew I wasn't going away to college, I figured Perry and I would have a lot of time after Z left to makeup and be best friends again.

It made me sad to see Z's truck bed full of all his belongings. He was leaving town with no job and not a lot of money, but he didn't let that spoil the mood. We didn't go straight home. Instead, we made a stop to our fishing hole at the river. He'd packed a real picnic. After we ate, we kissed so much that my lips felt swollen and tender. We had been so close that our smells combined. I couldn't tell his scent from mine.

"Mahala came to me again last night," he explained.

"And what did she say?"

"She said that my time with the snake dancer was not yet but to be patient and Wakan Tanka would put our footsteps together once again."

I wanted to be bratty. It wasn't fair. I finally found someone that made me feel loved and safe and now he was being taken from me. "But I don't want to be patient. I want to be with you, now."

"I haven't told you about my job interview I have scheduled for next week," he casually mentioned.

I kept thinking of some of the nearby towns: McWhorter, Bacon Creek, Clarksdell, Hazard.

"It's in West Virginia," he said like it was the greatest thing ever. It wasn't.

"Why West Virginia?" I asked.

"I thought you'd be happy."

"Happy? West Virginia's a long way from Leslie County."

"But, my *o'waci*, in West Virginia the snakes are plentiful and dancing with them is not a crime. Isn't that right?"

I tried to be brave on the ride home. When we arrived, I tried to talk him into coming inside. He said, "It's not time yet. Your family's not ready." His last words he said to me were, "Be patient." He kissed me again. I watched his truck until I could no longer see it. Then I listened to the sound of his engine until it was a distant echo in my mind. Only then did I go inside.

I dreaded what was to happen next. How do you tell your parents that their sweet, beautiful, innocent fifteen-year-old daughter is pregnant? As I crossed the threshold, the same feeling I had at Perry's school the other day paralyzed me. It came on me so fast and so hard I had to keep my knees from buckling. It was Perry. Something was wrong with her. This time, I had no doubt; I was certain. I ran into the house screaming for her.

Dad saw the panic on my face. "What's wrong?"

"I don't know. I got the feeling a couple of weeks ago, but it wasn't this strong. Where's Perry?"

"I've not seen her in a while," he answered. He immediately rose to his feet.

"We've got to find her! Something's wrong. I know it is."

He went to the basement, and I ran to the barn. No Perry. Then something she said the other day crossed my mind. I ran to the back of the work truck to see if the fishing poles were still there. Dad followed me. "The poles are gone." The words were shaking as much as I was when they exited my mouth.

Without a word said between us, we both started running toward the place of my nightmares—the woods behind our house. This was a run my dad and I'd made together before.

As I ran, I went back in time. I could see everything as vividly as I'd seen it that day over four years ago. I felt the same emotions. I was back to being that innocent girl who was so excited to spend a Saturday afternoon fishing with Jeb Seeley at the pond. My momma and dad thought Jeb Seeley walked on water. I did too. He was so sweet and was so kind to me. He was like a big brother to me, only I had this huge crush on him even though I acted like we were just pals. For the first hour or so, we fished and talked. It was nice. He even brought a picnic for us with peanut butter and jelly sandwiches and apple juice to drink. Only problem was, I didn't like apple juice. Never had.

I saw my first glance of the Mr. Hyde side of Jeb when he got mad because I wouldn't drink the juice. He called me a baby. I couldn't understand why it was such a big deal. I told him that I wished I liked apple juice, but I didn't. I assured him it was okay though. He told me that if I didn't drink the juice that he was taking me back to the house, and he would never fish with me again. More than anything,

I wish I would've headed home then, but I didn't. I wanted to make him happy so that the good Jeb would come back.

The change in him scared me. I'd never been around a lot of anger before. He was so angry that I thought he would explode. I finally told him that if it would make him not be a sourpuss that I would drink it. Then, poof, he turned back to being the nice Jeb that I was accustomed to seeing. I took my first swig, but it tasted even more horrible than I remembered. I would eat a bite of the sandwich then I'd take a drink. Only I wouldn't swallow. When he wasn't looking, I would spit it out in my napkin. The apple juice was almost gone, and I thought I was home free until he caught me spitting my last drink out. He hit me. Not just a little hit. He hit me with an open hand hard across my face. Then he grabbed my long hair and jerked me down on the ground, pulling it tighter and tighter using it like reins to control me. Each time I tried to get away, my hair prevented it.

The next thing I knew he was on top of me. My skirt and thin underwear offered no protection. I cried and screamed for him to get off me, but he wouldn't. The more I cried the more he hurt me. His eyes were closed, but he was smiling. He just kept on and on and on. I didn't think it was ever going to end. I reached all around me with my hand looking for something to use to make him get him off me. Finally, I felt a rock. I picked it up with my right hand, and with a force that didn't belong to me, I hit him as hard as I could in the head. He went limp.

The blood—it began to trickle from him down on my head and even in my mouth. All I could think of was getting him off me. I lost a lot of my hair as I pried his hands out of my tangles. Then I did the only thing I knew to do—I ran. When Dad saw me, I was a mess. I had Jeb's blood all over my face and in my hair and my own blood was running down my leg.

"Leslie? Leslie Esther? Are you okay?" My dad called to me then …, and he was calling to me now, bringing me out of my past. He brought me out of my nightmare only to realize I'd awakened to one that was even worse—one with my little Perry paying for my crime.

Jeb was dead by the time Dad and I made it back to him. Dad tried to resuscitate him while I stood frozen in place … and in time. Jeb's face was whiter than any white I'd ever seen. Blood was pooled all around his body and running down the bank headed toward the water. I don't remember anything else other than that I've lived with that blood on my hands every day of my life since then.

"Dad, this is all my fault. I should've had to pay for killing him. I killed him. Dad, I killed him! Now, Perry is paying for my crime."

"Honey, you paid enough. You did what you had to do. We're almost there." Then he started speaking in tongues as we came closer to the pond.

I began to scream her name, "Perry! Perry Gail!"

I felt her crying before I heard it. "Help me!"

The sight of my sister pinned to the ground with that overgrown ox on top of her was more than I could take. The memories came rushing over me so fast and so strong that I was having a hard time even breathing. I remembered the pain. I remembered the fear. I remember sleeping for days and days without even talking. I remember waiting to see if his seed took … I remembered it all. Then I heard my dad speak. His voice was strong and powerful, "Joseph Seeley, let her be."

It was enough of a distraction to allow Perry to scoot out from under him. She ran and jumped into my arms. I was shaking just as hard as she was. Joseph stood up and challenged my dad. "What are you gonna do about it, Preacher Man?"

"Joseph, I'm going to do something I should've done a long time …"

Joseph interrupted my dad, "You know that no one will believe you. My dad will have you and all your slut daughters run out of town." Then words like venom began to spew out of his mouth as he told one horrible lie after another about Laurel.

I could see Dad's legs shaking with anger. He was trying to hurt Dad in the worst possible way. Then he turned his words onto me. "It's all your fault that my brother's dead. If you hadn't led him on with all your freaky Jezebel games, then he'd still be alive too."

I had to shut my ears from hearing all the filthy lies he was saying about me. I pulled Perry tighter to my chest wishing I could shield her from his words. "You know, Les. You can't cover your ears from the truth. You can't wear enough jeans to keep from the truth. This was all *your* fault. I wouldn't have messed with your little sister if you hadn't threatened me at the revival. So, Perry doodle, you can thank your big sister for our unfinished business today. Rest assured ..."

He stopped talking and turned to the noise to his left. It was Momma. She had our gun pointed in his direction.

"So now Sister Ruth has come here to have her slutty way with me too. I guess I see where they get it from. Like mother, like daughters."

My mother spoke slowly. "You listen here. Your brother almost destroyed one daughter. If that wasn't bad enough, now my precious fifteen year old is pregnant with your child? I will see you in jail before I see you destroy another child of mine."

His laugh was loud and confident. "Don't you know that I won't spend a night in jail? The judge is my cousin, and the commonwealth's attorney is my dad's best friend. No one will believe you bunch of hypocrites. I will ruin your entire family."

Then I heard the loud sound of the gun when Momma pulled the trigger. In slow motion, I watched Joseph's eyes grow large and his mouth form an O shape. The bullet collided with his head. I heard the crunch of bone as it entered his skull and smelled his blood as it exited. He was gone before he hit the ground.

Dad checked his pulse. He shook his head indicating that there was not one. Mom stood paralyzed with the gun still out in front of her. Dad managed to pry it out of her hand. Then he shot it into the pond. The pond rippled all over starting where the bullet entered the surface. At first, I didn't understand why he fired the shot. Then it dawned on me. Now the gun would not only have his fingerprints on it, he would also have residue from the discharge. It wasn't hard to understand what his plan was—he would take the blame for Joseph's death.

Perry was still shaking. I rubbed my hand along her body to try to assess her injuries. To my surprise and delight, I realized she had a pair of jeans on underneath her dress. Only the zipper was partially unzipped. *So that's the unfinished business he was talking about.*

I asked her, "Did he … hurt you in …?"

Her "no" sounded almost like a whimper.

"It's okay, baby. He'll never hurt you again."

CHAPTER 47

The next few weeks were full of deputy sheriffs, lawyers, judges, doctors, psychologists, and victim's advocates. For the first few days after the shooting, Mom couldn't even put two words together. Her beautiful red hair was now white as snow—it turned overnight. She stayed in the hospital for a couple of days. Even though she still spends a lot of her time in bed, she's getting stronger each day. Our roles have been temporarily reversed. Just like she took care of me four years ago, I'm now taking care of her. I know that she too, will make a full recovery because she's made of tough stuff.

When she felt like talking, she and I would snuggle up together in bed and talk. I was able to tell her the full story of what happened that day with Jeb. It was the first time I ever spoke about it to anyone. That was a secret only between my dad and me. Now Mom and I share another secret. She knows I'm not sorry for killing Jeb, and I know she's not sorry for shooting Joseph. We didn't have a choice. Joseph was right; he wouldn't have spent a night in jail. Brother Seeley and Joseph would've managed to lie their way out of it. We also knew that politics played a large part of justice in our neck of the woods. Just because we weren't sorry about our parts in their deaths, we still had many regrets. Only I refused to let my regrets and my past hold me in bondage any longer. I prayed Momma wouldn't either.

My dad, who never lied and always acted honorable and above reproach told an honorable lie that day; actually it really wasn't a lie, but rather—he didn't tell the entire story. He told the deputies that he was the one who pulled the trigger. He did pull the trigger, just not the time when the bullet entered Joseph's head. Some of the deputies were sympathetic with Dad and told him they would've done the same thing or even worse if someone messed with their daughter. Just because they understood didn't mean that Dad wasn't going to have to pay for the crime, though. Brother Seeley made quite a show. He and his other two boys made threat after threat and had to be led away by a deputy when the coroner came to get Joseph's body.

Dad was in jail pending the grand jury indictment. We could've bonded him out, but he wouldn't let us. He said he wanted to make sure we had plenty of money to live on while things got sorted out. Plus, he was doing just what he'd secretly wanted to do—be a soul winner from his jail cell just like his hero, Apostle Paul.

From that respect, he got his wish. We hired the same attorney who represented him when Sister Seeley died. She was the best, and she had confidence she could get him off.

I've always loved my sisters. We bickered a little every now and then, but we have always been close and loving; Mom and Dad wouldn't stand for it any other way. Now, we are bonded by tragedies and secrets that have caused our love for one another to grow even stronger. I sat my sisters down, Perry too, and told them everything about what happened to me the day at the pond. This seemed to help Perry more than any of her counseling sessions because she knew I understood how she was feeling. Thankfully, we got to Perry in time before she was penetrated, but that didn't mean she was unscathed.

Laurel recognized now that she'd been raped even though it was under different circumstances. Whitley actually felt guilty because she was the only one that hadn't been tarnished by the Seeleys. Her counselor was helping her through "not being raped" just as much as she was helping the rest of us through our issues. Our wounds were deep and the recovery would be long. We were just going to take it one day at a time and do it together.

Kelsey moved in with us for a few weeks until we could get everything sorted out. Beth came over every day as well. She entertained us with her stories about Henry Noble. They were pretty much an item now, and Aphrodite wasn't happy about it. Only she was leaving Beth alone. According to Henry, Misty Shane was told that unless she wanted to find a rattlesnake in her bed that she better not mess with Beth. Evidently, she wasn't partial to rattlesnakes.

Z was offered the head basketball coach position in Logan County, West Virginia, and was staying at the same Holiday Inn Express that we stayed in during the revival. His calls and texts were the bright spots of my days. I started to confide in him about what happened to me four years ago, but he stopped me; he said he already knew.

As a family, we made the decision not to tell the attorney about Laurel's condition. We didn't want Brother Seeley or his sons to ever know that Laurel carried their bloodline. We prayed every day for this baby and knew it was a gift and not a curse.

I was downstairs in the snake room when Laurel came slowly walking down the steps wearing a pair of jeans. She had lost a lot of weight and seeing her in the jeans only emphasized it. She looked like she'd seen a ghost. Her face was ashen, but she was starry-eyed. "What's wrong?"

"Brother Mugs just called."

"What did he say?"

"He knew."

"He knew about the shooting?"

"No, he knew about the baby."

I tried to figure out how he could've possibly known because only the six of us in our household knew—not even Kelsey or Beth had been told. Laurel hadn't been to the gynecologist yet either. "What did he say?"

"He said the Lord told him that I was carrying the baby that God had promised him and Sister Paulette years ago. He wants us to come to Jolo, West Virginia, and stay at least until the baby is born. He says he even has a house for us to live in."

I didn't really know what to say. My plan was for Laurel to go to a doctor in another town, and then we would both stay around the farm after she started showing. Then when the baby came everyone would just think it was mine and Z's. After all, they had all the proof they needed right on YouTube. Laurel could have a normal life after the baby was born. But ... this Brother Mugs proposition could be the best thing for all of us. "Laurel, what do you want to do?"

"This baby's not mine. With everything in me, I *know* that this baby is a gift to Brother Mugs and Sister Paulette. I think I knew it when we were at the revival. I think he knew it then too."

Perry came running down the stairs in her jeans. Whitley was following close behind. She was the only one not ready for pants.

"What's wrong?" Whitley immediately became suspicious when she saw our expressions. I didn't blame her. She'd had so many rugs pulled out from underneath her in the last few weeks that it was hard not to be on edge.

"How would you all feel about going and staying with Brother Mugs for a while?"

"Brother Mugs in West Virginia? Let's go right now! Let's go tell Momma!" Perry was jumping up and down. Even Whitley was smiling. When Laurel looked at me, I can't describe the feeling. I just knew that the Holy Spirit was right in the snake room with us, and he had his arms wrapped around us tightly.

Then I remembered who else was in West Virginia. I said to my sisters, "We're going to West Virginia where the snakes are plentiful and dancing with them is not a crime."

EPILOGUE

Four Months Later

The trees in the forest had begun to turn colors; they looked like God had taken an orange, yellow, and red paintbrush to them. A fog covered the pond with a heavy mist; the air had a nip to it. It was a perfect time to snake hunt too early for hibernation but chilly enough to make wrangling easier. Since snakes were nocturnal creatures, during the nights they use the heat from the roads to warm their cold blood. At daybreak, the snakes slither back to the protection of the woods to find a warm rock to sun on or hide underneath.

Brother Seeley knew the pond by the coal bank was a perfect place to find snakes because of all the rocks and hiding places of the terrain. He took the new pastor and his young son to this snake haven even though it was a place of bad memories for him.

"I can't believe the last preacher's family just turned out the snakes like they belonged to them," the young twelve-year-old zealot proclaimed.

"Rest assured, Brother Seeley, we would never do anything like that. We know that these snakes are tools of the Lord and belong to the church even though we will be caring for them," the new pastor explained.

Brother Seeley felt it was his duty to help the young pastor along. "We should've gotten rid of our last preacher a long time back. He always claimed this property as his own even though the deed clearly says my line goes all the way to the big poplar over there. I tried to talk the elders into firing him after my oldest son died, but those cowards wouldn't do it. Brother Clay said it was an accident, but I know my son just got in his way over this land dispute. I thought he'd finally seen the light after I showed him the results from the surveyor. For four years, he didn't even mention it. Then one day, he up and shot my Joseph in cold blood claiming this property was his. He lost his mind is all I can figure and will probably get off with an insanity plea." His lie came out so naturally it almost sounded truthful.

"I'm sure sorry for your loss, Brother Seeley."

"It's been hard for me losing my boys and my wife."

"What happened to your wife?"

"I'm not rightly sure. I think it was her heart," he lied again. "Boy, that wife of yours sure is a good cook. That lemon pie was the best thing I've ever tasted. Plus, she knows how to brew a good cup of coffee too. What kind of dumpling maker is she?"

"She's the best dumpling maker in three states. Brother Seeley. I'll be sure to relay the compliment to her. I'll see if she can make you and your boys a pot of them this coming week."

"I think you and your family are gonna do just fine at Middle Fork Church of God. You'll have to go with me to the next home football game. Leslie County is really struggling without my boy, Joseph, but now my James is coming right along. He's already caused a couple of concussions this year because he hits so hard. Coach says he may be even better than my other two were."

The young son was more interested in snake hunting than talking about dumplings or football. "Dad, how many snakes do you think we need to find today?"

Brother Seeley answered the boy while he sat on a rock to rest his legs, "Well, we need about six or seven good copperheads and a couple of timber rattlers to start with if we can find 'em. Our church had over twenty of the best snakes in the Holiness church circuit. I just can't believe Brother Clay's family got rid of 'em all. Knowing that family, they probably sold 'em."

"That's a shame. I just can't believe a man of God would resort to killing young boys and trying to steal your property. It just doesn't make sense." The pastor was shaking his head in disbelief as he spoke.

"I just had to learn to forgive 'em and go on. That's all I know to do."

"God bless you, Brother Seeley. I'll be praying for you daily and praying that I can be half the Christian that ..."

They heard the sound before they saw it. The sound of a hidden rattlesnake is one of the most terrifying noises one will ever hear— even the hairs on the back of Brother Seeley's neck stood up. He knew it was directly behind him, and he was frozen in terror when he recognized the sound of the rattle.

The boy said, "Look, Dad! It has a red tail."